"One day you'll get into trouble looking at a man so boldly," Mando said.

"I'm already in trouble, Mr. Fierro," Libby answered.

His thumbs caressed the sensitive area beneath her ribs. "I don't think you have any notion of what trouble is, Miss Hawkins."

Libby slid her hands from his shoulders to his chest, applying pressure that did nothing to push him away. "I've been in some kind of trouble all my life. I always find a way to handle it."

Mando released her and brushed the back of one hand down the length of her hair from shoulder to midriff. "That sounds like a challenge."

"A promise," she replied, pleased that her voice carried most of its strength. "Simply a promise. I've always had a way of getting what I want."

He selected a long strand of hair and brushed it against her nose. "Then you will need to carefully govern your desires."

Dear Reader,

April brings us a new title from Lynda Trent, *Rachel*. In this Victorian love story, a young, impetuous woman falls for a mysterious man with more than a few skeletons in his closet.

With her book *The Garden Path*, we welcome Kristie Knight to Harlequin Historicals. When Thalia Freemont marries a handsome sea captain to escape her scheming brother, her new husband turns the tables on her.

A courtship that begins with a poker game soon blossoms into full-blown passion in Pat Tracy's *The Flaming*. A contemporary romance author, Pat's first historical is guaranteed to please.

Be sure not to miss *Dance with the Devil* from Pamela Litton. This sequel to her first book, *Stardust and Whirlwinds,* is the story of eastern-bred Libby Hawkins and Comanchero Mando Fierro.

We hope you enjoy all our titles this month, and we look forward to bringing you more romance and adventure in May.

Sincerely,
The Editors

Dance with the Devil

Pamela Litton

Harlequin Books

TORONTO • NEW YORK • LONDON
AMSTERDAM • PARIS • SYDNEY • HAMBURG
STOCKHOLM • ATHENS • TOKYO • MILAN
MADRID • WARSAW • BUDAPEST • AUCKLAND

Harlequin Historicals first edition April 1992

ISBN 0-373-28722-4

DANCE WITH THE DEVIL

Books by Pamela Litton

Harlequin Historicals

Stardust and Whirlwinds #69
Dance with the Devil #122

PAMELA LITTON

grew up in West Texas, where she spun adventure stories for her and her friends to act out. A voracious reader then—and now—Pamela's love for history, romance and adventure caused her to begin once more making up adventures of her own, this time in the form of novels.

Pamela now lives in San Antonio, Texas, with her two sons and her husband of twenty years, whom she describes as a "hero." She is a self-proclaimed homemaker and a full-time writer.

For John, who makes it all possible.
Thank you, honey.

Chapter One

The Llano Estacado,
July 1874

"Listen, my brothers."

The Comanche brave singled out each of his audience with a sweeping glance, then turned his gaze to the night sky. Resting his elbows on his crossed legs, he leaned forward.

"Do you hear her?"

The campfire hissed and popped in the silence that followed; the wind moaned through hollows carved into the high rocks. All was still but the whispering flames, the wind and a gold locket that dangled from a thin chain around the storyteller's neck. The round, flat disc turned this way and that, catching the fire's glow as the leader of the small band of Comanche raiders began his tale.

"She rides the wind across the plain. Thunder is her friend and lightning her lover."

The young Comanche pulled his attention from the stars. His black eyes filled with anger and something else, perhaps wonder, maybe even fear.

"Because of the Cheyenne's treachery, the Spirit Woman now walks among us."

The other five Indians in his raiding party hissed curses on the Cheyenne who had caused this trouble. Gradually they quieted down to listen. Their hosts, several New Mexican comancheros, drew in closer to the circle of braves seated around the campfire.

Mando Fierro remained in the shadows. He drew upon a long, thin cigar, then slowly exhaled, wishing he had a drink of the potent brew that made troubling nights pass more quickly. Tonight had such a feel to it, a night of whispers on the wind. Yes, passing the jug helped on nights like this, but, unfortunately, his guests tended to overindulge such hospitality to the regret of their hosts. Mando crossed his arms, his legs spread wide, and listened.

The Indian orator rose to his feet. Firelight and shadow painted his face in black and bronze, as if he were about to set out once again on his war against the white-eyes. Pacing back and forth, his every gesture and movement replayed by his shadow thrown against a backdrop of rocky bluff, he continued his tale, speaking in a mixture of Spanish and Comanche. His words echoed through the small valley of the Yellowhouse River as though spoken by the phantom giant behind him.

"The Cheyenne, Kiowa, and Arapaho heard of our medicine man, Eeshatai, and joined us to rid our land of the white-eyes so the buffalo will return to the plains. All night the warriors danced. The medicine of the Kwerhar-rehnuh was strong. Of all the great chiefs, Lone Wolf and Woman's Heart of the Kiowas, Stone Calf and White Shield of the Cheyennes, our own, Quanah was chosen as war chief."

The Indian stopped pacing and fixed on his rapt audience a terrible countenance. "Our numbers were many. When we rode across the plains, Mother Earth trembled with our passing."

Several young raiders shouted agreement. They sat taller and threw their shoulders back. The Mexican comancheros exchanged glances across the fire.

"We came first to the old fort known as Adobe Walls and found many white hunters camped there. We attacked for we had no knowledge the Cheyenne had killed a skunk the day before. Eeshatai's medicine was destroyed."

He picked up a carbine that lay beside him and raised it over his head. "For this reason our guns were no good." He threw the rifle to the ground. "The hunters' long guns had bullets that ran a long time and never grew tired. Many of the People were killed or wounded."

Mando tossed the cigarillo butt to the rocky soil and ground it out beneath his heel. It sounded to him like the great Eeshatai had lived up to his name—Coyote Droppings. He could see that Dos Rios still stood and wasn't finished with his tale. Mando held back a sigh. These stories always rambled until they reached their grand finale, which he hoped would come soon.

"In our great rage the People scattered to the winds to seek out the white-eyes and so too did the Cheyenne, the Arapaho, and the Kiowa. But, the Cheyenne's bad medicine followed us." His hand traced a wide circle to include his fellow Comanches. "We found no cattle for trading and only two whites and they had no horses."

Mando eased a few steps closer to the fire and rested a hip on a large rock. Though the Indians' attempt to rid their land of the white man had been an interesting story, the end was all too plain. The cavalry had been breathing down their necks all year, waiting for the right time to finish off the Comanches. The fools in Washington wouldn't miss their chance.

The young Indian knelt by the fire. His voice barely rose above the moaning of the wind, as it blew through the holes pocking the high bluff's yellowed stone. Lifting up his head, he inspected the night. "That is when we found The Spirit Woman."

Mando shifted to a more comfortable position. A woman. A smile teased at one corner of his mouth. Now that was different. With a woman in the story, who knew what the ending would be?

And this one was a Spirit Woman. What magic could she perform? he wondered. Was she as powerful as the woman who had worked her spell on his foster brother, Ross, ending a story that had begun over twenty years before when his father had traded Ross from the Comanches?

Moonlight and blue eyes had made Ross finally choose to stay in Texas. Mando had seen the gringa weave her magic himself on that night last spring, the last time he had seen or heard from his brother. Ross had almost ridden with him back home, back to spitting in the eye of the Anglos, back to returning a little of the hell the Texans liked to raise on the New Mexicans. But one look at the gringa, and Ross had forgotten the people who had raised him and loved him like their own. Loyalty came cheaply for some.

Dios! He'd give anything for a drink. He clenched his hands into tight fists and forced all thoughts of Ross Tanner and his woman from his mind. After a while, the rough cadence of the Comanche's voice flowed into his troubled thoughts. His long fingers uncurled. He opened his eyes and listened to the story of the Spirit Woman.

"...men screamed their cowardice when we cut off their man parts. The Spirit Woman rose from their wrecked wagon, shrieking like a winter wind. On her head she wore the crow's medicine." The brave leaned forward and placed his hands on each side of his head, his fingers together and pointing backward. "His two wings were thus on her headpiece."

His companions shifted and mumbled their agreement while quickly looking over their shoulders. Mando noted a smile or two lift heavy mustaches among his men at the description of the woman's hat.

The storyteller touched his cloth-wrapped braid. "Her hair was like flames and held the color of the sunset before a storm." He stroked his fingers on each cheek. "On her skin was splattered the paint of the white man's gold."

A low, ominous rumble rose from the seated Comanches. One grabbed his rifle from his crossed knees and shook it over his head.

"Such strong medicine had made the woman *loco*. She jerked our arrows from the sides of the wagon and threw them at us, shouting curses. We did not kill the white men for we did not want their evil spirits to join with the woman against us. She climbed from the wagon and picked up a gun."

Dos Rios grabbed up his own weapon, which lay in the dirt beside him. "We dared not stop her when she ran to the white men who still screamed like women. She shot each one in the head." He stood and aimed his rifle at the ground and pretended to shoot it twice.

"We knew we must leave quickly before the dead men's spirits discovered they must enter the next life without their man parts and returned for their revenge. But the Spirit Woman pointed the rifle at us to make us

stay. When she walked closer to where we stood, I broke
for our horses. I heard the click of her gun and knew it
was empty. Like a fire that burns too hot, her medicine
had not lasted.

"We made our medicine circle around her. She stared
at us with eyes the color of the Navajo stone." He halted
and stared at each of his listeners. Some of the Comanches jerked away from his intense portrayal of the Spirit
Woman's gaze. Mando saw Paco give his young nephew
a reassuring pat on his back.

"Carefully I reached to touch her." The Indian re-
enacted his brave feat, extending his hand, then he
snapped it back. "She pulled an arrow of the evil Little
People from the crow's headpiece and struck at my hand
with it. I was too fast, for all know if pierced by an arrow of the *nenuhpee* I would be dead." He showed his
hand all around. Even the comancheros craned to see his
brush with death.

Mando shook his head. What a redheaded hellion! *Por
Dios,* attacking a Comanche with a hat pin. He leaned
closer, despite himself, wondering what happened, hoping this freckle-faced Spirit Woman had not run out of
medicine after all.

The brave tossed his rifle into his right hand. "I
knocked the crow's medicine from her head." Poking his
chest out, he illustrated how he had done this with the
barrel of his weapon. "This angered the Spirit Woman.
She shouted for the spirits of the dead to join her and
stabbed her evil arrow at us. Her eyes blazed with magic.

"This I could not allow, for the shadow of Mother-
Moon already shared the sky with Father-Sun and the
spirits of the dead would find her soon. I struck her
head." He gave the rifle a swinging motion. "She
slumped to the ground, her medicine gone."

Mando rose to his feet and walked away. Anglos or not, his stomach had turned at the mutilation of those poor devils, but he had hoped the woman had escaped. He didn't want to hear of the redhead's finish.

"At first we thought to kill this troublesome woman since the bluecoats will no longer pay ransom for captives, but with the crow's medicine lost, I wanted to bring her to El Aguila and trade her for a long gun with bullets that do not tire."

The Comanche's words caught Mando before he had taken two steps. El Aguila, the Eagle, was the name his years on the Llano had earned him and he turned to listen how he now played into this drama. That the Eagle traded for captives was well-known among the Indians, and he wasn't surprised Dos Rios would attempt to bring the woman to him. Why then had he shown up with only mules and not the redhead? Of two minds whether he wanted to know, Mando hesitated, then, with a dread that lay in his stomach like rotten meat, he settled on the rock and picked up the rest of the Comanche's story.

"We rode all that day and into the night. We stopped but once the next morning and saw signs of buffalo soldiers following us. We had no time to tame the Spirit Woman as she deserved. She never cried like other white women, but stared at us with her eyes of magic." Again he looked aggressively at each man gathered around him.

"Yesterday we noticed more of her gold paint on her face." He stroked his cheeks. "How could this happen? Her hands were tied. She carried no paint bag." Dos Rios's voice grew grave. "Her medicine was growing strong again."

The Comanches sitting around the fire nodded and grumbled among themselves.

"She began to sing her medicine song. Again I hit her head and once again she slept. I was too late to stop her magic, for already she had summoned the storm clouds. They traveled across the sky like charging buffalo. Rain poured from the angry sky and washed away our war paint, but not hers. She slept no more. She opened her mouth and drank of the rain. She shouted to the sky and laughed when it shouted back to her." He paused here to let that information sink into his listeners. "When the rain slowed, we stopped to make camp where the Mucha Que rises from the plain.

"I pushed the Spirit Woman off her horse and cut her bonds to show her we did not fear her running away for she had no place to run. We waited and watched for signs. No crows flew by. The sky no longer spoke. The Spirit Woman stood before us until she weakened and dropped to the ground. I pulled her to her feet. Now was the time to show her our strength, to destroy her medicine before it grew strong again."

Mando stood without thinking and walked to the edge of the circle. He couldn't take his eyes from the young Indian as he told his story. Mando hardly breathed.

"We tore one dress from her body and found another. The white dress beneath revealed gold paint spotted her skin here and here." He touched his arms and neck. "She fought like a warrior." He brushed a finger over a long scratch across his chest. Several of the other Comanches rubbed at bruised cheeks and scratched faces. One of the comancheros threw down the stick he was whittling and watched the Indian.

"She stood before us straight and proud. She never wept or begged. I thought of keeping her." Staring into the fire, Dos Rios rubbed the locket between his thumb and finger. "Such a woman would make strong sons," he added in a low voice. Dropping the locket and his reverie, he said, "That is when she started her chant."

The poor woman had begun her prayers, Mando surmised. A strange heaviness settled in his chest. He saw this woman's story affected his men, as well. Cinco Cantu had removed his hat. Even Gordito had quit eating. Mando caught Louis Lavant watching him before the Frenchman stood and walked away. Mando crossed his arms. This was one final act he would like to walk out on, too, but he wouldn't. He would stay to the end.

Dos Rios sliced the night air with his hand. *"Silencio,* I told her. She chanted louder. Father-Sun traveled into the clouds and the sky grew dark. I grabbed her and shook her to make her stop, but she wouldn't. I jerked this medicine charm from her neck." He lifted the gold filigreed locket, a knot tied in its broken chain, and held it out so that it twirled and winked in the firelight.

"She screamed as an eagle who had lost her young. Her cry rose to the spirits for that is when they let loose the waters."

The Comanche dropped the locket as if it burned as hot as the fire it reflected. Mando focused on the softly glittering ornament as it swung to and fro on the Indian's dark chest. For a moment he saw the woman with the fiery red hair, a woman who had fought to the last, and knew her locket should not belong to the Indian. Mando fought the powerful urge to yank it from the Indian's neck. He wanted that locket.

"This time the waters did not fall from the sky, but flowed with great anger down a small creek that ran behind the Spirit Woman. The angry waters brought the Spirit Woman the strength of a hundred warriors, for how else could she have pushed me to the ground?" The vainglorious young brave hit his fist against his chest.

The gathering of braves chose to look at the fire or to study the beadwork on their leggings. None would meet Dos Rios's gaze as he looked from face to face. His fist dropped to his side. He sank to his knees and joined his friends in their contemplation of the fire, as if the flames could provide an answer. He finished his tale in a weary voice.

"She shouted her curse upon us, then leaped into the water...we saw the Spirit Woman no more."

Only the wind made comment on the Spirit Woman's demise, that and the fire, which hissed and popped as it filled the air with the sharp scent of burning mesquite. The Indian storyteller gathered the gold locket in his fist and continued to stare into the dancing flames.

His companions took turns gauging the height of the bright full moon and peering into the darkness beyond the fire as if they expected the Spirit Woman to walk from the shadows.

One or two of the comancheros crossed themselves while the others simply remained still and quiet, looking at their boots or perhaps the stars, but never at each other.

Mando's quiet, deep voice broke the fragile spell. "I will trade for the Spirit Woman's medicine charm."

Chapter Two

Comanches and comancheros rose quickly to their feet.

Dos Rios clutched the locket against his chest. "This I cannot do, El Aguila."

Mando recalled the Comanche's name. The way the woman had vanished into the water would have significant medicine for him. And the woman had pushed him down to escape. That didn't help. He'd have to come up with something Dos Rios wanted dearly to make him trade. With a quick mental inventory of the items he had on hand, he searched for something worth more than the Spirit Woman's medicine, more than Dos Rios's pride. Joining the group gathered around the fire, he placed his hand on a rotund Mexican's shoulder. "Gordito, more meat and bring *panoche,* too."

Gordito peered at Mando from beneath heavy brows, his long black mustache twitching. *"Panoche?"* he asked.

Mando nodded.

A huge sigh hefted Gordito's round belly. *"Sí,* El Aguila." Shaking his head, he struggled to his feet, then huffed and puffed over a rocky incline to one of the dugouts gouged out of the terraced embankments under the bluff. Mando had to smile. The old buzzard was already counting his losses from giving the Indians the flat bread they liked so much, instead of making them trade for it. But Mando wanted the Indians in a good mood without giving them liquor, which put them past a good mood into craziness.

After greeting each of the six Comanche warriors, Mando nodded to Cinco, then sat down by the fire. Cinco led two other New Mexicans up the rise toward the dugouts. Before speaking further, Mando noticed Louis melting into the darkness toward the horses. He wished the Frenchman, with his sour looks and frowns, would stay at the rancho, but then, who would he trust on these forays into the plains?

Mando cleared his head of troubling thoughts and directed his attention to Dos Rios. He didn't glance once at the round gold locket on the Indian's chest. The time would come for that. "It brings me great pain to hear of the Cheyenne's treachery."

Mando spoke in Spanish, which Dos Rios knew well. He suspected the Indian had a Mexican mother by the looks of him. Too tall for a Comanche.

The young warrior pulled his gaze from the burning mesquite and looked at Mando; his eyes reflected tiny fires in their black depths. He gripped the locket in a tight fist. "The Spirit Woman's medicine will bring me power that will blow the stench of the Cheyenne to the land of deep snows forever."

Mando nodded, his features fixed in a solemn frown, while inside a spark of irritation lit the short fuse on his patience. "You say this Spirit Woman possessed the medicine of the crow and the *nenuhpee?*"

Dos Rios dropped the pendant from his clasp. He sliced a glance toward the other Comanches, who had begun eating the food Gordito had brought them. They slowed their chewing and studied him.

Mando noted these changes, though his expression remained indifferent. All those years of traveling the plains with his father's *ciboleros* as a boy had taught him more than how to hunt buffalo. From his grandfather's time, the New Mexicans had shared many camps with the Comanches. While trading goods they brought to ensure their welcome, he had learned many of the Comanches' superstitions.

"*Sí*, El Aguila, her power was great," Dos Rios finally answered. "I will need great power to war with the white-eyes and buffalo soldiers." He took a scorched antelope haunch Gordito offered him and bit into it.

Mando waved away any food for himself. "That is true. The white men will be as bees when their honey is stolen. They will swarm out of their hives to search for the thief."

Dos Rios wiped his hand across his greasy mouth. "The buffalo soldiers can ride like angry bees over the plains, but the People will be hidden in the Palo Duro or we will go to the reservations where they will make a great noise but cannot sting."

The Indians laughed at the stupidness of white men who gave them places of refuge where the soldiers could not follow.

Mando joined their laughter, then said, "With the Spirit Woman's charm around your neck you will take her magic to all the hidden places and to the reservation."

The Indians stopped laughing. Dos Rios took on a stubborn petulance about his mouth. "I will have great powers," he repeated, and gave each of his followers a hard glare.

Mando said, "Power can be great like that of Eesha-tai, but it can bring disaster with the killing of a skunk or with the charms of a woman."

Dos Rios grabbed the locket and started to rise. Mando never moved, only looked at the younger man with the intensity that had earned him the sign of the eagle. "Bring the mules. Let's trade," he said softly.

Dos Rios eased back to his seated position and, with a wave of his hand, signaled the Comanches to get the mules. Three stood and ran into the shadows.

Cinco and two other men approached the campfire, their arms laden with blankets, cases of ammunition and bolts of blue and red calico cloth. Mando changed the subject from magic to mules and was soon negotiating for the supplies the Indians needed.

Mando drove a hard bargain for the winded animals. He pushed the growing mutterings to a dissatisfied grumbling, which he gauged carefully. At the right moment, he whispered into Cinco's ear. Cinco hesitated, his heavy lids narrowing over dark eyes.

"Get it," Mando said. He turned his attention to Dos Rios, who had remained quiet while the goods and a small amount of ammunition changed hands. "What do you want for the Spirit Woman's gold charm?"

Dos Rios grew still as did the other Indians. "Nothing. The Spirit Woman's charm must stay with me."

Cinco arrived with a big bundle. He set the brightly colored wool blanket on the ground between Mando and Dos Rios. Then he stepped back, joining Gordito and the other comancheros who gathered behind Mando.

Taking his knife from its leather sheath, Mando cut the twine holding the bundle together, then flipped it open with its sharp point. Silver trinkets of all description took on the gold of the campfire. The Indians inched closer for a better look. Excitement moved through them like wind through fallen leaves.

"All of this, I will give you for the Spirit Woman's charm," Mando said.

A high price, he knew, but if he couldn't trade for the woman, he could at least trade for her locket. Again he wondered why he wanted it so badly, but he couldn't say, except that the woman's struggles to survive had moved him and so little did these days. Whatever the cost, Dos Rios would not ride away with the locket.

The Indian's braids brushed back and forth against his chest as Dos Rios shook his head. "No."

Mando stared at him for a moment, cursing the Indian's stubbornness. He had offered too much already, but he knew he would offer more. "I have whiskey."

The Comanche warriors' heads jerked up almost in unison. They looked at Mando then at Dos Rios.

Dos Rios swallowed down a mouthful of antelope meat. "Bring it. We will talk more."

Mando shook his head. "It is buried far from here. Someone will take you to it tomorrow. But he won't unless I possess the Spirit Woman's charm."

With warnings of the Spirit Woman's bad medicine, Dos Rios's fellow braves urged him to trade. They reminded him of her connection with the crow and the Little People. Dos Rios silenced them with a slice of his hand. "No."

Mando and the Indian eyed each other over the array of silver jewelry. Some kind of powerful medicine was involved here, Mando thought. There had to be something Dos Rios wanted more than the questionably evil power he placed in that locket.

Mando noticed Dos Rios running his fingers over the rifle next to him. He signaled to Cinco, who bent to listen to his whispered order.

"El Aguila, no. It is too much. What of our profits?" Cinco whispered.

Mando sent Cinco a glare that spoke of his displeasure louder than any reprimand. Cinco looked at him as if Mando were a man possessed, and Mando supposed he was. For the first time in years he wanted to shout profits be damned.

Instead he asked, "You would question me?"

Cinco swallowed hard, then turned and ran up a low hill to the dugouts.

No one spoke. Even the wind had stilled. Mando reached over to the mesquite roots piled by the fire and threw several more onto the hot coals. He wanted this *bastardo* to get a good look at his next offer.

Cinco slid down the slope and trotted to the group gathered at the fire. Mando took the requested item from the New Mexican's hands. He heard Dos Rios draw in his breath.

Caressing the long barrel of the Sharps rifle, Mando gauged the Comanche's reaction. Envy and desire burned in the young Indian's eyes as hot as the mesquite fire. Mando balanced the buffalo gun on his knees. He had seen all he needed to see.

"The silver, two cases of ammunition, three barrels of whiskey." Mando paused.

Dos Rios tore his gaze from the Sharps in one quick glance at Mando, darted his tongue over his lips, then stared again at the oiled and spotless rifle on Mando's knees. Mando slowly lifted the rifle. Dos Rios followed the gun's progress like a hungry dog teased with a bone.

Mando opened his hands. The rifle rested in his palms. "And my Sharps."

Dos Rios wrapped his hand around the locket so hard his fist shook. "Take it!" He jerked the chain from his neck.

Mando snatched the twirling pendant then shoved the rifle at the Indian, who took it and stood. The five other Comanches quickly joined him in admiring the fine scrollwork on the barrel and the polished perfection of the wooden stock.

Mando wound the gold chain around his hand and held the locket up to the firelight. An intricate design of flowers and vines circled a smooth center engraved with the letters *L* and *H*. Mando considered the possibilities. Leticia, Lenore, Lavinia. Perhaps Lodona, she changed into a river to escape Pan, but more likely Lorelei, the siren of the Rhine who lures men to destruction.

Cinco squatted down beside Mando. "Open it," he demanded.

Mando arched a dark brow at the other comanchero. "Why not?"

He thumbed the tiny clasp at the locket's side, opening it easily. The portraits of two young women, one more a girl, stared back at them. His eye was caught by the picture of the youngest, which lay in the palm of his hand. He didn't need to see the unruly red hair to tell him this was the Spirit Woman. He saw that in the challenging angle of her chin, the way her mouth tilted upward at the corners, the devilry in her eyes even the small portrait couldn't dim. She wasn't beautiful, not yet, but she would be...or would have been. He gazed at the picture, wondering how old it was, and didn't notice Cinco moving around behind him.

"*Madre de Dios!*" Cinco whispered.

Mando snapped his attention to Cinco, who continued to stare at the locket's opposite portrait. His brows gathered in a frown as he maneuvered the opened charm so that he could see the other picture.

"That is Ross's woman," Cinco stated in a tone just short of amazement.

"Impossible," Mando replied, yet an unexplainable sensation swept through him, as if the wind had suddenly turned chill.

He looked again, turning the locket closer to the fire. There was no mistake. He would never forget the calm beauty of the gringa who had been with Ross the last night he had seen his brother. Ross had looked at the woman beside him, then had refused to return to his friends, his family and his struggle against the Anglos. No, he would never forget this woman.

"It is the woman," Cinco insisted. "A man does not forget a beautiful woman such as that one."

Mando snapped the locket closed. "No, he doesn't." He stood so abruptly, Cinco almost lost his balance. "Get Paco to pack a mule with supplies."

Mando slipped the locket inside his jacket and started up the small hill toward his dugout. He knew what he had to do. From one heartbeat to the next, he knew.

Cinco rushed to catch up with him. "We can't leave tonight."

"*We* aren't. I am."

"But—"

"Tell Paco and do it now. Tell him to pack a shovel." No matter what her connection was to Ross's woman, the Spirit Woman deserved a decent burial.

Mando didn't stop to see if Cinco would obey, but ducked inside his dugout then stepped back outside. "Get

somebody to saddle my gray,'' he shouted to Cinco's retreating back.

A candle gave little light to the cavelike room, but it
was enough to see. He gathered two cartridge belts, extra shells and his black sombrero. Shrugging the bandoliers over his head, he blew out the candle and bent
through the opening once again. He crammed on his
wide-brimmed hat and started down the embankments
toward the area where the horses were hobbled.

Mando nodded to Louis, who had just finished sad-
dling the big gray stallion. He checked the straps and
fastenings on the silver-studded saddle and bridle, then
gave the horse an affectionate rub on his velvety nose. He
heard the pack mule clattering toward him and turned to
receive its lead rope. Mando wasn't surprised to see Cinco
pulling it along. He would want to know what to tell the
men. Mando slapped his mount's reins against his leg. He
would think of something.

Cinco glanced over the mule's pack. "Everything is
here. I checked myself."

Mando made a quick inventory of filled canteens,
sacks of jerky, coffee, a bag of the *panoche* that had been
missed by the hungry Comanches, and various other es-
sentials.

He turned to Cinco. "Show Dos Rios where we buried
the whiskey, then head for the north fork of the Brazos.
Camp at our usual place. I should be there by tomorrow
night."

"But, El Aguila, the two gringos will not like this. The
best trading will be along the Las Linguas."

Mando directed a sharp look at the comanchero, a
slight grimace deepening the grooves slashed on each side
of his mouth. "I say where we go and when. Do you have
a problem with that?"

The short man smiled, revealing his five gold teeth. "No, El Aguila. We will be at the usual place."

Mounting his horse, Mando took the pack mule's rope from Cinco and wrapped it around his saddle horn. He was surprised to see Louis reappear, leading his roan, saddled and ready to go.

Mando held in his restless mount. "Where are you going?"

"I heard something about Ross and this red-haired woman," Louis replied.

Mando's eyes narrowed. The Frenchman knew he never spoke of Ross since his defection, yet he saw no reason to avoid a reply. "There is a picture of the woman I saw last spring with Ross in the locket. She may be the red-headed woman's sister, but you need not come on such an unpleasant journey," he said.

Louis stared back at him, his eyes' blue depths as revealing as an icy pond. "I think perhaps I should. Besides, you will need a good tracker. One better than even El Aguila."

Mando held the Frenchman's gaze with his own, then slowly smiled. *"Vamanos!"* He wheeled his horse around and gave him the spur.

Louis swung into his saddle and rode after him.

"Where are you going, El Aguila?" Cinco shouted after them. "The men will want to know."

Mando shouted back. "Tell them I have gone to the Mucha Que in search of a Spirit Woman."

Chapter Three

Libby Hawkins was flying.

Skimming over the land, her arms outstretched, the wind against her face; she was flying. The earth dropped and the wind lifted her high. In the far distance, water sparkled and glistened like Ali Baba's treasure. With a tilt of her head, she swooped down to glide above the flat, dry plain, the lake growing larger with every quickened heartbeat. She planned exactly how she would plunge into the blue, shimmering depths. She could almost taste the freshness in her dry mouth, feel the coolness on her hot skin.

Suddenly, like a black cloud stealing over the sun, a shadow engulfed her. She peered over her shoulder and her eyes widened in horror. An enormous eagle, his wings spread in wide majesty, his predator's eye trained on her, reached powerful talons for her. A scream lodged in her throat, choking off her breath. She faltered, lost her momentum, and suddenly the earth below reached to grab her. The land drew closer and closer; the eagle's talons stretched toward her....

She bolted up, her eyes wide and staring.

Heat clutched her senses and shook her dizzy. Pain seared every other sensation from her head but thirst. She squeezed her eyes closed and hung on to consciousness. The dark edge, close and inviting, beckoned to her with its dreams of water. Water and terror. She drew in a gasping breath that burned through her lungs and opened her eyes.

Where was she? She darted frantic looks from left to right, searching for... she didn't know. Then she saw it. A long veil of shade lay over the rocky soil to her feet. The slightest bit of coolness touched her arms and face. The shadow.

The earth beneath her dipped and tilted. A roaring rush filled her head. The shadow split into two. Libby clutched at the petticoat beneath her hands and blinked until the dual shadows slid into one. She took another deep breath. The roaring ebbed away into the sound of the wind's sweep over the land. This wasn't a dream, she told herself. Dreams didn't hurt so. Too frightened to look, too confused not to, Libby followed the darkened path to its source.

A tall silhouette of a man, his features lost in an explosive halo of fiery light, cast his long shadow over her. Behind him, the horizon blazed in vivid reds and golds, leaving no trace of blue skies, only a view into what was surely the fires of hell.

The dazzle of light and color hurt her eyes, pounded into her aching head. She brought her forearm to her brow and tried to make out more than an outline. All she could determine were long legs, broad shoulders, black clothing and wicked spurs, their sharp points catching the crimson glare. She pulled her attention from the still and silent figure, her eyes searching her surroundings for an answer to his identity reason would accept. The vast empty plain held more questions still.

The land, barren and cracked, sparkled with heat so intense it rose in shimmering waves that fused the earth to the heavens. Plumes of dust roamed between low thorn-covered bushes and clumps of tall grass that looked more dead than alive. And the wind. Like lost souls chased straight from the inferno, the wind scorched over the plain, its mournful sighs the only sound that broke the deep silence.

Reverend Carmichael would be pleased, she thought. Hell did indeed exist and he had been right about her final destination. She looked up at the dark figure.

"Are..." The word came out a hoarse croak. She began again, managing a raspy whisper. "Are you the... Devil?"

The dark specter laughed softly, a dry, gritty sound that rode well on the harsh wind. Libby frowned. Reverend Carmichael never mentioned the Devil laughed, but the old codger couldn't know everything.

He answered her in a deep voice scored with rolling *r*'s and flowing rhythms. "And you, gringa, are you a fallen angel?"

For one stunned moment, Libby wondered if, indeed, she had died. "I'm not sure... I mean I..."

She passed a hand over her eyes, wondering what the deuce was she saying. If only her head would quit aching so.

"I was on my way to my sister's...Comanches..." she muttered. A slight movement produced a canteen tossed to the dust by her feet. Libby stared at the dented metal container, unable to fathom its purpose. Thinking hurt her head and sent dizzy circles to her empty stomach. She closed her eyes and forced down the sickness.

"Drink," the voice commanded.

She glanced up, an unspoken question knitting her brows, then dropped her attention to the receptacle. Water? Did the Devil offer one water? Was he tormenting her? According to Reverend Carmichael, an unlikely source until this moment to be sure, hell was full of torment. Only one way to find out. Slowly she reached for the canteen, her hand shaking with the effort. She picked it up, but found the cap too difficult to remove.

She was about to admit the good reverend was right about the torment part when a hand gloved in black leather reached for the canteen and pulled it gently from her grasp. Still recalling all those fire-and-brimstone Sunday mornings, a protest gathered in her throat but was never voiced. The long fingers worked the cap loose and offered the water to her.

Libby took hold of the canteen, one hand covering the hard bone and muscle beneath the soft, warm leather, the other clasped tightly to the metal. She brought the spout closer to her mouth. With the water a tantalizing whiff away, she looked up.

Eyes the darkest brown before black peered into hers. Set beneath a strong brow, they held mystery and danger as if she looked through a window into the deepest hour of night. An unsettling sensation came over her. Dare she unlock the door and step into that dark night of unknown peril?

She was too thirsty to examine the odd notion or even to wonder why it had occurred to her. Her gaze locked with his. It was only water. She closed the distance to her lips and filled her mouth.

Her lids fluttered closed. The wetness slid over her tongue, easing the dry ache in her throat, cooling the fire in her head. She drank until the canteen was pulled from her hands. Sliding her tongue over the cracked surface of her bottom lip, she caught every drop of moisture.

"Thank you," she breathed on a deep sigh of relief. Saved. She was saved. "You aren't the Devil."

A firm grasp on her chin opened her eyes. Leaning in close, dark eyes narrowed, the man said, "*El Diablo* lives in all our hearts and I find angels boring." One gloved finger traced upward along her jaw to her ear, then to her temple. "I have never heard of an angel with red hair. You are no angel, I think."

Suddenly unsure whether that was good news or bad, Libby pushed herself backward until thorns from a bush pricked through the thin material of her chemise. She crossed her arms over her bosom. "Who are you?" she whispered.

"Fate, gringa." He reached for her. "That is all you need to know."

"*Dios!*" Mando caught the woman before she fell into the brush. He touched the soft skin at her neck and found a fluttering pulse. Only fainted. So the Spirit Woman lived and he had found her. Now what to do? He had thought a shovel would end this story.

Mando eased her down onto a pillow she had fashioned from what looked like a bustle. A light shading from the petticoat she had draped over the bushes protected her face. Her skin was burned but not blistered, though she had been in the sun long enough to cause her ramblings. If she hadn't had the sense to erect a shelter, flimsy though it was, she truly would have met the Devil. The Llano gave no mercy to the weak or stupid.

Reaching into a jacket pocket, he pulled out a small mirror and angled it so that it caught the last rays of setting sun. An answering signal blinked back at him from a low hill in the distance. He hoped Louis would bring the horses up quickly. One of Fort Concho's patrols could have picked up the rapid blinks, as well.

Mando scanned the land from horizon to horizon. No telltale dust clouds or winks of sunlight on metal. Though the fort was several days of hard riding away, soldiers continually scouted the area.

Mando flicked a glance over the unconscious woman. He recalled her mutterings and knew his guess was right. She was the blue-eyed woman's sister. Fishing the locket from his pocket, he opened it and studied the miniatures. His eyes rested not on the girl, but on the woman. The woman whose lovely eyes revealed all her thoughts, who had sat beside Ross then and looked back at him now. Her thoughts hadn't been as lovely as her eyes that night, especially when either had settled on him.

"Well, lady of the lovely eyes with the not-so-lovely thoughts, I have your sister. What thoughts do you have on that?" He suspected they wouldn't be too pleasing, and the knowledge gave him great pleasure.

Catching the soft footfalls of Louis's moccasined feet, he snapped the locket closed and tucked it back into his jacket. He looked over his shoulder and noted the hard gaze Louis directed at him. The Frenchman had overheard him. Kneeling beside the woman, he expected a remark of some kind, but none came.

"I brought the shovel."

Mando gathered the limp bundle of petticoats and tangled hair into his arms and turned to Louis. "We won't need it. At least not yet," he added.

Her sunken and dark-circled eyes, cracked, bleeding lips and dry skin were obvious signs of dehydration. Catching Louis's raised eyebrow, he explained. "She rambled something about the Devil and fainted."

Ironic, he thought as he set out for the horses, considering the brown-stained and sand-stiffened camisole and petticoats, proof of her time in the flooded creek. She must have swallowed a great deal of water but had probably thrown up most of it.

One day in this heat and that was it. She would have been dead in hours, though given her hard struggles for life, she might have lasted until tomorrow. Perhaps she truly was a Spirit Woman.

He turned his thoughts to more practical matters when Louis caught up with him, and together they strode toward the horses and mule waiting a short distance downwind. Spotting the woman's scraps of material in the Frenchman's hands, he nodded at Louis. They could leave no clues for a curious cavalry patrol.

Balling up the wind-shredded petticoat and dirty bustle, Louis slanted a dubious glance at Mando. "So she thought she had met the Devil. Maybe she did. Women have been calling you a devil since you were fourteen and more than one man would agree, of course for different reasons."

Mando cast a quick smile at the shorter man. "Of course."

"In fact I would guess the whole state of Texas might crown you the Prince of Darkness."

Mando dropped the smile and replaced it with a dark scowl. The Frenchman never let up. Looking straight ahead, he cautioned, "*Silencio,* old man."

"Old, am I? I was your father's friend, hardly his peer."

"You harp like an old man. No. More like an old woman."

A hand slapped on his shoulder twisted him around to face Louis. Mando had never seen him so angry.

"Don Alphonso would—"

"My father is dead," Mando ground out. "Killed by the Anglos. Am I the only one who remembers?"

Louis's hand dropped from Mando's shoulder, but his icy glare remained steady. Long tatters of red hair whipped and curled around their legs as Mando, holding the woman tighter, waited for an answer.

Finally Louis replied, his voice deceptively soft but stinging. "You're the only one devoured by hatred. Let it go before this madness kills you. Ross—"

"Yes, tell me of Ross. My brother forgot easily enough." Mando shouldered past the Frenchman. "Never say his name to me again."

Shrugging off the Frenchman's hand, he closed the distance to the horses. Ross Tanner! *Por Dios*, the name stabbed like a knife in the back.

Reaching his big gray, he adjusted his hold on the girl and jerked the reins up so quickly the horse whinnied and shied. "Calm yourself, *mijo*," he crooned softly.

Holding the reins in one hand, he quieted the horse with soft words of praise. From the corner of his eye, he saw Louis walking slowly toward them, the Frenchman's handsome face clouded with disappointment and regret.

Mando ran a hand over his horse's neck and turned to the side. He hated these arguments that brought up old hurts and created new ones. Louis had been his father's friend, but more important the Frenchman was his friend, as well. The only one he had left. No matter how disapproving, Louis stuck by him.

Though his horse now stood quietly, Mando waited for Louis to arrive before he attempted to mount. He needed the Frenchman to hold the woman. The Spirit Woman.

She didn't look the redheaded hellion now, though her actions with the Comanches left no doubts she was one.

His gaze roamed over the tender, lightly freckled skin of her neck offered to him in unconscious abandon. The young girl in the portrait was a woman now, and the fullness of her breasts beneath the thin cotton of her camisole rose and fell with each shallow breath. Her hip and thigh draped over his arm felt soft and warm. A smile played at the corners of his mouth as he wondered if a dusting of gold covered those, also.

He remembered the unusual blue of her eyes when she had asked who he was. Fate, he had told her. Perhaps she was his fate, as well.

Uncomfortable with the thought, Mando raised his head and noticed Louis watching the woman with intense interest as he stuffed her undergarments into a saddlebag.

"She will ride with me," Mando said quietly.

Louis shrugged and flipped the cover closed. "Whatever, *mon ami,* but I thought you would not want to go into Santa Angela." He took a step toward Mando and accepted the woman into his arms.

Mando mounted his horse in an easy swing. Settling into the big Spanish saddle, he studied the man who knew him so well. By the skeptical look in his eyes, too well. "No one is taking her to Santa Angela. Remember? We are not welcome visitors in Texas."

A smile flashed across the Frenchman's swarthy face but only intensified the ice in his eyes. "I am willing to chance it. Few know me."

Resting his hands on his thighs, Mando looked over Louis's head at the sun dying on the horizon in a bright pool of red. His fingers gripped the reins he held in one hand. "Remember Polonius Ortiz, the boy the cavalry

captured and questioned at Fort Concho? They learned
of all the routes across the Llano from him and even
names of traders in New Mexico. We have yet to see the
end of the damage done. The army could know my name
or even yours. You are not taking her to Santa Angela.''

"Mando, be reasonable. It is unlikely the boy spoke of
me.''

Mando directed his gaze to Louis. "She will only cause
more questions. Questions you might find difficult to
answer. I found her, Louis, and I will decide her fate. She
will return with us to New Mexico. Now give her to me.
We have trading to do. You are wasting time and time has
become very valuable.'' He held in his restless mount,
waiting.

"You have something on your mind and I doubt it is
lost revenues or fear of the army. Tell me, Mando. Tell
me what you are planning for this girl.''

Mando cut a look to the unconscious redhead. "I have
no plan, Louis.'' And he didn't, at least nothing defi-
nite, only a notion that he possessed the Spirit Woman
and he wasn't ready to give her up. "I will do nothing to
harm the woman.'' Saddened that Louis's opinion of him
had come to this, he added, "On my honor.''

Louis's fingers spread, then took a firmer grip on the
woman's thigh and shoulder. He shifted his weight from
one foot to the next, but his eyes never wavered from
Mando's.

Mando's chin raised slightly at Louis's continued hes-
itancy. "On...my...honor,'' he repeated in a voice so
low it barely carried above the wind.

"Take her and, by the good Lord, nothing better happen to her.'' Louis held her up so that Mando could lean
down and slide his arms beneath her.

Lifting easily, Mando fitted his limp passenger onto his lap. A soft moan of complaint drew his attention from the frowning Louis. Maybe she was coming around. Her brows, a dark auburn, gathered in a troubled frown, then relaxed. He glanced at the soft cheek resting against the bandolier crossing his chest, at her hair rippling over his arm, his thigh, nearly to his stirrup.

"Nothing will happen that she won't invite."

The water woke her. Washing down her throat, trickling down her chin and over her chest, pooling between her breasts, its wet relief was welcome wherever it touched. Libby savored each drop, despite the metallic taste, until the container was removed from her lips. She didn't open her eyes, preferring to focus upon the absence of pain in her head, the cooling breeze flowing over her sunburned skin.

Gradually she became aware of a gentle rocking, a warmth that didn't burn and the pungent scent of gunpowder. Gunpowder and leather. She opened her eyes and encountered a row of brass cartridges snugged through leather loops attached to a leather strap. She followed the line of bullets over a black-clothed chest to the face that loomed above her.

Not much could be discerned in the failing light. Especially with the features cast in shadows by the wide brim of a hat. Her eyes searched for clues to the man's identity. While she worked up strength to voice her questions, a long swath of black hair swept forward, wrapping around his neck. Suddenly she possessed no strength at all.

Memories of painted faces and long black hair flowing in the night wind washed through her. She froze, staring as more hair swept forward, gathering blue twi-

light in its thick silkiness. The man must have felt her reaction, for he looked at her. She remembered his eyes. So
dark. Now darker still and filled with midnight secrets,
not the frenzied blood lust of Comanches. Relief eased
through her cramped muscles, her heart resumed its normal beat; yet she didn't relax completely.

The man wasn't a Comanche, that much was certain.
Dark skinned and sharp boned, he was different from
anyone she had ever met or seen. He was a face lifted
from the history books she had studied at Oberlin College. Libby took careful inventory of his features and
tried to place the man, and therefore herself, somewhere
familiar.

A high forehead promised intelligence and fit smoothly
with bladed cheekbones that hinted of ancient pagan an-
cestors. The stamp of the conquistadors showed plainly
in the long, slightly curved nose, the strong jawline and
the tempered aggressiveness molding his lips.

Unable to draw any conclusions from her inspection,
other than she was lying in the arms of a total stranger,
apparently upon a horse with night closing swiftly in
around them, she decided upon the direct approach.

"Who are you?"

Once said, the question rang familiar to her with a
slight twinge of unease, but no memory followed. It elic-
ited only a crooked tug of his mouth to one side, a gesture that might pass for a smile. The man lifted his head
and gazed at the journey ahead, a journey she couldn't
see, a journey over which she had no control.

Strangely, all the possibilities had lost their impor-
tance. The man's hard warmth seeped into her weary
muscles. He smelled of guns and strength and safety. The
approaching night carried no menace and time ceased to
matter.

For the first time in two days Libby relaxed, the fight to survive, a long battle won. Watching his profile darken against the emerging stars, she allowed her exhaustion full rein and it swept her past disturbing dreams into a deep, restorative sleep.

Chapter Four

Mando guided the horse to the top of a rise, the night sky so bright with stars and the full moon he had no trouble picking the path. Reaching the crest, he paused and waited for Louis to join him. Below, a dark blanket of land spread outward in all directions, its rumpled edge meeting the stars on a faraway horizon. A light nestled among the folds, a campfire casting a feeble glow against the vast darkness. Mando counted the small figures moving within the golden light.

"I count six," he said. "How many do you see?"

"Six," Louis answered.

"No special visitors appeared tonight." Mando scanned the area one more time. "The men will be disappointed."

"Not for long."

Mando pulled the blanket tighter around the woman sleeping soundly in his arms. "I expect some excitement in camp. None from you, I hope."

"The time to make my stand was at the Mucha Que, not here, *mon ami*."

Mando nodded and touched his spurs to his horse, leading the way down the rise toward the campsite. The creak of leather and jingling harness sounded behind him as Louis followed, leading the pack mule. He had wished many times that the Frenchman had stayed at the rancho, but tonight he was glad to have him at his back.

He had no idea how the Spirit Woman would affect his men. So far she had proved herself to be quite a troublemaker. Alive when she was supposed to be dead. A beautiful woman when she was supposed to be a gangly girl. A spirit that challenged the Devil himself when she should have been a whimpering, hysterical female. Yes, he had found himself an armload of trouble, but opportunity often disguised itself as trouble.

Opportunity had ridden across the plains to him on more than one occasion, and he never failed to recognize it and use it without hesitation. He had plucked this gringa from the plain and he would use her, as well. Deciding the best course of action had taken some time, but with little diversion over the past hours other than his own thoughts and her warm, soft weight nestled against him, a plan had formed.

In the spring, he would send the woman back to Ross, after he had charmed her into warming his bed all winter. His brother would see that he was not so easily swayed by a woman's will. He would send word that she was safe with him and that he could hardly chance returning her before the Indian trouble was over. Mando smiled, finding it amusing imagining the blue-eyed gringa's reaction to her little sister's unplanned tour of New Mexico.

Anticipation eased his mouth into a wider smile. The Tanners' winter would be very long, indeed, while his would be less lonely than usual. Who knew, the season might be his last and who better to spend it with than— the smile collapsed and a frown knitted his brow—his family.

He shrugged away the somber recollection of Ross's long silence and thought of his brother's woman, and the irony that had delivered her sister to him—a bad memory, an embarrassment from her husband's past, a Mexican comanchero. Fate had crossed this woman's path with his for a purpose, and he would be a fool not to make it his.

A shout from the camp signaled they had been spotted. Working his left hand free of the blanket, he shook the woman's shoulder. "Wake up, gringa."

Her eyes opened slowly, blinking back the sleep that held on to her. For a moment he wondered if her lids might drift closed, then she stiffened, her head lifting from his shoulder as if a shot had been fired. She gulped in air, the shallow rapid breaths warm and moist against his neck. She tilted her face to his and he watched remembrance fill the startled emptiness in her eyes.

More than remembrance filled her eyes. The full moon's silver light played odd tricks in their shadowed depths. They took on the luminance of an inquisitive cat. He found himself staring at her, watching the interplay of blue, then green, then silvery shimmers. Those eyes possessed magic, just as Dos Rios had said. No wonder the Comanche held on so tightly to the woman's token, Mando thought. He wouldn't have traded the locket away. Not even for a Sharps rifle.

Faraway shouts of greeting reached them as they drew closer to the campsite. The woman blinked and turned her attention to the clamor ahead.

"Where are we?" she asked, her voice little more than a whisper.

Mando peered over her head at the men gathering by the fire. "My camp."

Yielding to the small, insistent pressure exerted against his arm, Mando loosened his hold on her. Cool night air rushed between them. She didn't look at him again.

"Where is your camp located?"

"Out on the plains."

"I can see that clearly enough. Where on the plains? Are we close to Santa Angela? That's where I was going when the... the Comanches... attacked my stage."

"You are far from Santa Angela... very far."

The woman gathered the blanket around her, her hands beneath it, snuggled under her chin. She continued to stare at the small pocket of golden light surrounded by the black night, at the inhabitants growing more distinct with each step the horse took.

"Will you be going in the direction of Santa Angela?"

Mando met Louis's scowl with a steady gaze. "No."

Men's rough voices rose from the camp, their speculations spoken in Spanish easily heard through the night air. His men had noticed the woman.

"I... I see," she replied. "Where will you be traveling then?"

"Here and there for a while," Mando replied. Excitement in the camp grew louder and two men trotted out to greet them. The woman leaned back against his chest, her eyes never blinking.

"Perhaps a... another settlement close—"

"Only a Comanche or maybe a Kiowa camp."

Silence followed, her heart pounding against his chest her only reply. Louis cleared his throat. The woman twisted around, peering over her shoulder. Mando stifled a groan. A man could endure a woman's rounded curves pressed against him for only so long. He regarded the Frenchman with a raised brow.

Louis removed his slouched hat and pressed it against his buckskin jacket, and eagle feather brushing his chin. "Louis Lavant, *mademoiselle,* at your service." His dark head bowed slightly.

Mando tilted his head to catch the woman's reaction to this bit of showmanship. He noted her surprise. Louis surprised many when he chose to display Continental manners that should have been long forgotten. This time, however, Mando thought the Frenchman may have overdone the gentleman-in-buckskins performance.

The woman gave a hesitant nod. "How...how do you do, Mr. Lavant. I'm—"

"El Aguila, you found her...the Spirit Woman." Cinco Cantu shouted in Spanish, only a short distance from them. The cook, Gordito, huffed close behind him.

Mando frowned as the woman eased back and stared at the two. Damn Cinco and his timing. She had almost said her name. He would find out later. Watching the heavyset Gordito pumping his short legs and holding down his sombrero gradually pulled his frown into a smile.

"Have you ever seen Gordito move so swiftly?" Mando asked, slipping into Spanish.

Louis chuckled, a welcome sound after all of his frowns and scowls. "Never. I hope he has saved us something to eat."

Cinco reached them first. He fell into step at Mando's stirrup, his eyes never leaving the woman's face. "A miracle she lived."

Gordito stopped where he was, his mouth agape. As they passed him, he whispered, "The Spirit Woman."

The woman lifted her face to him. "What are they saying?"

Mando shrugged. "They are surprised to see a woman."

She hesitated, her brows coming together in a brief frown, then nodded and faced ahead once again.

Entering the firelight's glow, walled in by loaded two-wheeled carts, Mando wrapped his arm tight around the woman and drew no protests or pressed requests to release her. He scanned the area, picking out each of the men who rode with him and finding no others.

Paco Trujillo whispered something to his nephew, Tomas, who stood dumbstruck before the fire. His uncle's rough shove to his shoulder prompted him to move. He closed his mouth and ran forward, meeting them halfway inside the partial enclosure.

"I'll take your horses," he said, his hand reaching for Louis's bridle but waving ineffectually in the air, his gaze fixed on the woman.

Mando tossed his reins in the youth's face. "Extra oats and a rubdown. They've had a long, hard ride."

Tomas fumbled for the reins, grasping them at last, and finally found Louis's. "*Sí*, El Aguila, I will take good care of them. Where did you find the—?"

"Later," Mando said, too tired and hungry to answer questions. "Louis, come take her." He waited while Louis dismounted, ignoring Cinco's obvious disappointment. He wasn't about to hand her down to the old reprobate. She felt too good even though she had grown rigid as a wooden saint. Who could blame her? A look at these renegades would turn Medusa to stone. He would be rid of them soon, then he could concentrate on changing saint to sinner.

Paco joined the group, shaking his shaggy gray head but smiling beneath his full bushy mustache, still black despite his misspent youth.

"Better the eagle found her than the buzzards," he said.

Louis ducked under the gray horse's neck, giving Cinco a hard look until the other man shuffled to the side. His features changing rapidly to a more pleasant demeanor, he raised his arms to receive the woman.

"El Aguila has found himself a tasty morsel."

Surprised at the Frenchman's comment, Mando glanced directly at Louis, then gave him an almost imperceptible nod. From the start, the men must know the red-haired woman was his.

In English, he whispered against the woman's ear, "You will be safe as long as you do as I say and go no place without me."

She turned her head in a sudden move, slanting those cat's eyes at him as if she wanted to say something. She thought better of it and turned away, but he saw the stubborn tilt to her chin. Grasping her face between his fingers and thumb, he made her look at him again. He kept his voice low, keeping in mind the men understood English. "Don't question my authority unless you want them to do the same. Understand?" He relaxed his hold, trailing his thumb along her jaw.

She swallowed hard. "Yes."

Mando felt a slight tremble shiver through her, but her eyes never left his. He sighed. Truly, this woman possessed spirit. He looked forward to the return of her strength.

"Louis, are you ready?"

"No, I'm standing here in praise of the Eagle's prowess. Of course I'm ready. Hand her down."

Mando slipped one hand under her knees and the other clasped around her shoulder. She gave him a worried look as he lowered her into Louis's arms.

"Don't forget," he said, a touch of sarcasm salting his words. "Louis Lavant is at your service."

"Very comforting under the circumstances," she replied, her gaze traveling over the other four comancheros, who continued to stare at her.

"Oh, but it should be, *mademoiselle*." Louis clasped her to him. "Unlike these other ruffians, I have bathed in the last month."

Mando swung down from the saddle and, once again, took the woman in his arms. "But those buckskins haven't been washed in years."

The men, including Louis, broke out in loud guffaws that followed them to the fire. A look at the woman told him she found the roasting meat spitted over the fire more interesting than their humor.

Mando kicked cups and dirty plates out of the way, then deposited her by the fire. Her eyes raised to the blackened carcass dripping grease into the flames, sending smoke and the thick scent of cooking meat into the air. He felt the woman sway before he released her and saw that her eyes had closed, yet she sniffed the air.

He sat next to her and wrapped his arm around her shoulders, fearing if he let her go, she might fall. Searching the camp until he found a rotund figure, he called, "Gordito, my supper is burning. Get over here and fix us something to eat."

The cook quickly complied.

The woman opened her eyes wide, blinking, holding on to consciousness with an effort. She straightened her back and looked at his hand on her shoulder, then at him. "I... I'm fine now. I won't faint. It's just that I'm... very... the smell, you see."

Her eyes met his, a question hidden in their directness. "Please... remove your arm."

Mando sensed her desperation. Almost starved, surrounded by the harshest elements of man and nature, dependent on a stranger, she still looked him in the eye and made her simple request. How could he not grant it? He slid his arm from around her, watching her, making sure she was as strong as she claimed.

Her eyes closed briefly, in relief, he thought, then she straightened her shoulders and turned her face to the fire. She adjusted the blanket so that one arm was free, her shoulder bare except for the bit of lace strap. He would have to find her some kind of clothing.

"You look like you could use this." Paco stood above him, offering a jug.

Mando gave the pottery a quick glance. A jolt of liquid lightning would do his tired bones good. Pushing his sombrero back to hang from his neck, he combed his fingers through his hair and was about to reach for the liquor. Behind Paco, skulking about the carts, the American Cabot and his pock-faced Irish friend Doyle watched them from the shadows.

He waved Paco aside. "Not tonight, Paco."

Paco shrugged and ambled over to a place on the other side of the fire. He sat down and took up a block of wood that was taking the shape of a dove beneath his knife. Gordito offered Mando a plate piled high with sliced meat. He gave a nod toward the woman and Gordito handed her the plate.

She looked at it for a moment then reached out a shaking hand. With a brief lift of her eyes to Gordito, she grasped the plate and set it onto her crossed legs. She rubbed her hand on her blanket-covered knee, then picked up a piece of meat. Biting into it, she closed her eyes and chewed slowly.

Mando had never seen anyone enjoy a piece of charred, stringy meat so much. It made his own meal taste better.

Louis tossed his hat to the ground, accepted a plate and sat down next to Mando. "You see Cabot and that Irishman?"

Mando took a sip of hot coffee. "I saw them." Always from the corner of his eye, he watched the woman. She was eating faster now, casting anxious looks about her between bites.

"They will cause trouble." Louis started on his own greasy fare.

"Nothing I can't handle," Mando said.

"I hope so, my friend. I truly hope so."

Having no reply for the Frenchman, Mando watched the camp carefully. Gordito turned over a bucket and settled his ample posterior on it, then began repairing a harness. Cinco brought his guitar and sat down next to Paco. He grabbed the jug and took a long drink from it. The tall, thin adolescent, Tomas, collapsed next to his uncle and propped his elbows on his knees, an index finger tracing the sparse hairs of a shadowy mustache. They all watched the woman.

"So, Paco," Mando said, then wiped the back of his hand across his mouth, "what has happened while I was gone?"

Mando listened with half an ear to Paco's recital of happenings in the twenty-four hours that had passed since he had left on his search for the Spirit Woman. His interest quickened when he heard of Cinco's return after showing Dos Rios and his band where the whiskey lay buried.

Mando recalled the location was north and farther west from where they would be traveling. That band should

pose no problems. He didn't care to run into that particular Comanche. The Indian might decide his trade wasn't
so good after all if he knew his Spirit Woman still lived.

"See any other sign of Indians?" he asked.

The older man shook his head. "No. We will see no
profits from this trip if we don't. It's getting harder and
harder to make a living, I tell you. The men are com-
plaining, especially the gringos."

Mando flicked a glance at the two men still standing in
the shadows. "Those two always complain," he said.

He swept a quick look over the two-wheeled carts,
noting the oxen had been hobbled close by, then focused
again on the American and his partner. He trusted those
two even less than he did the others.

His riders were mostly small-time bandits who would
steal a blind man's begging cup, but the gringos were another matter. If the mood struck them, they would kill
the blind man and leave the cup. A nod from Mathias
Wright, their boss and, unfortunately, his very necessary
business partner, was a death sentence. One day he would
be finished with Wright and he hoped he had the opportunity to finish them. If the pair gave him any trouble
over the woman, Mathias would be looking for two new
watchdogs.

Done with his dinner, Mando lit a cigar with a twig
from the fire. He noted the woman had left half her portion on the plate. He wasn't surprised. She would need
many small meals before her stomach recovered from the
lack of food she had suffered. He would see that she had
jerky and dried fruit with her on the trail tomorrow.

He looked up in time to see Cabot and Doyle approaching the fire. It hadn't taken long for the two to
come sniffing around. He leaned back on an elbow, the
hand holding the cigar resting on his upraised knee. The

woman slipped her arm beneath the blanket and found the embers more pleasing to look at than the men gathered around her.

Reaching the fire, Cabot squatted down, his arms hanging over his knees. He gestured toward the woman. "Think she's worth your Sharps, Fierro?"

The woman jerked her head up at the statement spoken in English. Mando drew on his cigar, then blew the smoke out slowly. "Do you think she's worth your life...Cabot?"

The American slanted a brief look at the woman, then dismissed her. "The question is, do you? Wright ain't gonna like what you gave that Comanche buck for that damned locket. He's gonna wonder what the woman's gonna cost us."

Mando smiled. A smile that made the other men shift uncomfortably. "She will cost Wright and the rest of you nothing. The price will be mine to pay."

"This ain't the old days when tradin' was legal. We'll all pay if she goes to the army."

"She won't go to the army. She won't go anywhere I do not send her."

The woman suddenly rose to her feet. "You trade guns to those murdering savages."

She glared down at him, shaking with fear, exhaustion or anger. Mando guessed all three with the latter holding her up. He remained as he was, watching her. All eyes had turned to her. She seemed oblivious to everyone present except him.

"Sit, gringa, before you collapse."

"I won't and I won't be sent anywhere by you, either. You're no better than—"

"Sit...down."

She swayed slightly, then steadied herself. "You have no right to—"

Mando brought the cigar toward his mouth, but stopped before it touched his lips. "I bought you, gringa," he said quietly. "I found you. I own you."

He finished the cigar's trip to his lips, its end glowing brightly as he inhaled.

"You *are* the Devil and—" she gave all of them a look that needed no translation "—these are your disciples."

Mando exhaled, watching her through the veil of smoke. "And you, gringa. You sup at my table."

Chapter Five

Finding strength in her indignation, Libby gathered her blanket and whirled away from the leering faces and their leader's dark mocking eyes. She searched frantically for an escape but saw only black night beyond the primitive carts. Comanches waited out there, Comanches with their bloody knives, and days and nights of riding, riding, riding.

At least at the Devil's table she was fed.

Libby sighed, her shoulders drooping, her legs shaking beneath her. He was right, of course. If she didn't sit, she would collapse and that would prove even more humiliating. Libby hitched up her chin and slowly turned to face the truth. The Devil had saved her life and she must dance to his tune—for now.

The man, Fierro, lay at her feet like some pasha, smoking his infernal cigar. Behind him, the Frenchman stood, looking at her with a touch of concern. She ignored the others, preferring not to know how her outburst had affected them. Too late, she remembered Fierro's warning. These were dangerous men and only a more dangerous man could control them. Slowly she sat down, feeling a little like a sheep visiting a pack of wolves.

If she behaved like a sheep, they might devour her. Libby forced her chin a notch higher and looked each man in the eye, beginning with the American. Finding a fellow countryman in the company of these gunrunners was disconcerting enough, but this man would send chills down her back if she had met him in church. He was a big man, muscular, with small eyes that narrowed toward the outer corners. His eyes shifted and wouldn't meet hers.

The cook nodded to her and resumed repairs on the harness in his lap. The man with gold front teeth looked from her to Fierro, then smiled and slowly ran his thumb over the strings of his guitar, the beginnings of a melody floating into the night. The older man twitched his odd black mustache and resumed work on the wooden dove he was carving; the boy blushed and looked down at his feet.

Lavant met her gaze. She followed his to Fierro. Sitting at an angle to the two, she had only to turn her head slightly to face the tall Mexican. He probably expected her to cower and sniffle a bit, but he was mistaken if he thought her some insipid female.

Libby took on a proper posture and entered the wolf's den. "If I heard correctly, I believe you are in possession of something that may belong to me."

Mando lifted his fingers from his knee. "What would that be?"

"My locket."

Fierro placed the cigar between his lips, his eyes narrowing against the curl of smoke, and reached into his jacket. He pulled out the locket and held it before him, the chain tangled in his fingers. Dropping his knee and sitting up, he pulled the cigar from his mouth and looked at the filigreed circle of gold.

"This?"

Libby pulled her gaze from her most valued possession and found his dark eyes looking at her intently. "Yes. I believe that is my locket. My portrait and that of my sister are displayed inside. If you'll open it—"

"I have seen them."

"Then you know it is mine and you will want to return my property."

"It is mine now. As Cabot said, I paid a great deal for this trinket. Why...?" He shrugged his shoulders. "Still, this locket is very valuable. Is it not, *mi compadres?*"

The others, warming to the game, nodded. One of the men, she couldn't tell which, said, "*Sí,* it is very expensive." Another collaborated. "El Aguila paid a fortune."

The leader threw his cigar into the fire. "I am a trader, gringa. What will you give me for this locket?"

Libby grasped for a reply, a glimpse of an answer other than the only one available—herself.

"I have nothing," she stated finally. Ignoring the comments stirred by her answer was easy since she couldn't understand them, but the laughter was harder to take.

Louis placed his hand on his friend's shoulder. "Mando..."

Libby missed the rest of the Frenchman's whispers, but remembered the name he mentioned. Mando Fierro, she thought, putting the two names she had heard together. One should know the name of the man who—what had he said—owned her and now was suggesting the rights of ownership. Why this cruel game with the locket? If he knew the significance of the piece...no, sentimentality would mean nothing to this man.

He nudged Louis away with the back of his hand. "Too bad, gringa. You will tell me when you want to...trade."

"I...I...if..." Libby stopped and drew a big breath. "Trading is out of the question, Mr. Fierro."

Mando snapped up the locket and, tucking it away, turned to Louis, engaging him in a low conversation. She followed his hand, a small ache building around her heart. Her mother's locket in the possession of an outlaw, a gunrunning blackguard who wanted more than she would give to retrieve it. Still, it wasn't lost as she had feared. She would get it back—her way, not his.

All she had to do was come up with a plan. She always had some plan working, and this situation would be no different. Glancing up, she found his eyes examining her, their boldness startling. Perhaps a little different, she thought. Maybe a great deal different.

Cabot rose to his feet, drawing her attention. "Damn locket," he muttered, giving her an ugly look, then strode off toward the far end of the camp.

She noted the man who had stood so silently behind the American for the first time. He stared at her, too, and though she was growing accustomed to such rudeness, his pale, light-colored eyes left her cold.

She welcomed the cook's corpulent body coming between them as he rose and began cleaning up. Her next view of the man was the long tails of his duster and the straggles of yellowish hair hanging limply over his collar from beneath a high-topped hat. Stay clear of those two, she told herself.

Her gaze dropped to the flames dancing among the embers. Louis Lavant seemed the safest of the lot, though he was no gentle soul. Plainly he was his own man, the only one of the band who spoke up to this

Mando Fierro. He even appeared kind at times. A kind gunrunner to the Indians? Oh my, she really was tired. Still, she needed some sort of friend, and his attempts at courtesy elected him.

Libby placed a hand to her stomach and turned her nose away as Gordito removed her plate. She had bitten into the tough, strong-tasting meat with such relish earlier, now she felt as if she were digesting rocks.

She longed to stand and stretch and say her good-nights, but she would sit here all night before she broached that subject. She needed to wash, and needed some privacy, too, but how did one make such a request?

She heaved a sigh. Simply by making it, she supposed. "Mr. Lavant," she said, turning toward him and Fierro. "I...I wonder if there might be a place to wash?"

Louis sent a sidelong look at Mando, who studied her. Libby forced herself to remain quiet and still under his inspection. Antagonizing him further would hardly help her cause. At last he nodded.

Louis stood and smiled. "Certainly, *mademoiselle*. Allow me to escort you."

Giving Fierro a quick glance from beneath her lashes settled any doubts about her choice of escorts. She had no desire to go off in the dark with a man who expressed his possessiveness so clearly with only a look.

Offering his arm, Louis said, "Shall we?"

Libby rose to her feet and took an uncertain step, then availing herself of the proffered arm, accompanied Louis. He guided her into the silvered darkness beyond the carts, past a herd of quiet oxen. Down a shallow incline, a small stream glistened in the moonlight. Walking slowly, they crossed the short distance to the creek, neither speaking a word. Libby welcomed the quiet as

much as the opportunity to splash cold water over her
sunburned skin and a chance to relieve herself.

They reached a small stand of stunted trees next to the
creek. Libby dropped her hand from the Frenchman's
arm and looked about her. A scattering of squat, thinly
leaved bushes dotted the area. And rocks. All shapes and
sizes of rocks caught the bright moonlight.

Louis threw his hands wide. "Your accommodations,
chérie. Perhaps crude, but private. Mando and I will see
to that."

"Thank you." She gestured to a high embankment
downstream. "I'll be just a moment."

"Watch for snakes," Louis cautioned. "They like
these rocky areas."

The two-legged varmints concerned her most, Libby
thought. Nevertheless she turned and examined the
ground with each step. "I'll be careful," she called.

She followed the narrow stretch of sandy bank around
the bend, a shallow crest of land beside her rising as she
walked. Gradually she was hidden from view and
stopped. Opening her arms, she allowed the blanket to
slide to the ground. The evening air caressed her hot skin
like a cooling unguent. The blanket scratched, but she
wasn't about to complain. The rough wool covering was
better than nothing. She didn't want to think about tomorrow, when the sun would scorch everything in sight
and the blanket would be out of the question.

After taking care of her most pressing needs, Libby
picked her way over the rocks and boulders in the wide
creek bed to the trickle of water flowing through its center. Crouching beside the small stream, she cleaned her
hands and face, then drank several handfuls of the cool
spring water. She sat back, the sharp rocks poking her
bottom through her thin petticoat and dried her hands

slowly as she looked up and down the creek bed and along the banks. No one approached.

Louis would be looking for her soon, but she didn't care. She needed these few minutes as much as she had needed food and water. Everything ached. She had never hurt so badly. From her skin to her bones, she felt like one big pain.

Easing off her half boots, she placed her sore feet into the water. Tingles of pleasure raced from her toes to her scalp and back again. With a long sigh, she leaned back on her hands and closed her eyes. Instead of roaring over the landscape, the wind whispered among the leaves on the few scattered trees clinging to the creek bank. The water murmured softly over the rocks. She wanted to stay here forever. That thought opened her eyes. No, she didn't. She wanted to go home.

But where was that? Home. She had sold it. Sold it all. Ohio wasn't home. Two graves weren't home. Her sister's house shared with a stranger wasn't home, either, but at least it was a destination. Santa Angela, Texas. The name sounded foreign and far away, like Fierro had said. Yes, far away.

Somewhere in the distance, a coyote howled. It sounded so lonely, she thought. Lonely and sad. Tears gathered deep in her chest. Lost, she was totally lost in a strange land, with people who frightened her, with a man who claimed to own her. She might never see Amelia again. So much needed to be said between them. There was so much she wanted to tell her sister.

If Libby didn't find her way to Santa Angela, poor Amelia would hear about their parents' death from strangers and wonder forever what had happened to her sister. Amelia wouldn't know about the bank in St. Louis where she had deposited their inheritance. She should

have written to her first, but how could she simply write
a letter and tell a pregnant woman her parents had died?
It had seemed so cold at the time, but now...

The first tears rolled out of her eyes, stinging her sunburned cheeks. She scrubbed the dampness away with the
back of her hand. Thunderation, she would be howling
at the moon next. She was behaving just like some weak,
weepy female, the kind she hated. Glancing about her,
she wiped away the last tears. She couldn't let anyone see
her like this. She had her principles if nothing else.

She didn't have anything to cry about anyway. The
situation could be worse. She could be dead or spending
the evening with those Comanches. Thanks to a flood
and Mando Fierro, she could sit here tonight and feel
sorry for herself, a pastime that was accomplishing little. If she had fought a torrent of cold, wet fury and survived, she could certainly fight one man's will.

For the moment, he appeared satisfied playing a game
of cat and mouse. He would soon learn cats sometimes
went hungry, even sleek, beautiful cats with long black
hair. She would have to be very careful. Nothing domes-
tic characterized this cat. He was wild and determined to
play by his own rules. A frightening prospect to be sure.
She didn't like to play games at all, and now she would
be playing for high stakes indeed. She had no intention
of engaging in trading activities with Mando Fierro.

Uncomfortable with the direction of these thoughts,
she judged her time was up and pulled her feet from the
water, drying them quickly with her petticoat. Something would have to be done about clothes. She supposed she could cut a hole in the center of the blanket and
wear it in a capelike fashion. The young man wore some
kind of similar garment. She pulled on her abused foot-

wear. Her shoes weren't much to look at anymore, but she was glad to have them.

Wincing at the pain shooting through her muscles, Libby rose to her feet and brushed the dirt off her hands. She scanned the ridge along the abutment rising above the bank. She was alone.

The moon shone bright as it had each night she had spent on the plains. The first night with the Comanches had been madness on horseback; last night she had almost drowned. And tonight—she crossed her arms over her bosom—what would the full moon bring tonight?

Bending slowly, Libby picked up the blanket and shook it out, then arranged it around her shoulders. She couldn't quite make herself take that first step. Tonight's prospects didn't bear thinking about. She straightened her shoulders and started for the bend. Cats enjoyed playing with their prey for a long while. She had time. Time to find an escape.

She rounded the curve and searched the area for Louis, but her escort was missing. Shrugging, she started for the camp, then stopped. She sniffed the air. A familiar odor drifted to her like the soft strains of the guitar played in camp. Mando Fierro's cigar. She turned slowly and found him leaning against the twisted trunk of a tree.

"Come here, gringa," he said. "I have something for you."

Chapter Six

Libby clutched the blanket to her throat. He had removed the cartridge belts, his jacket, even his shirt, and wore only a black leather vest over his bare chest. She tried not to look at the mat of dark hair revealed by his state of undress, but the moonlight caught on something shiny nestled there. Though she was too far to see it distinctly, she knew it was her locket.

The bright ember at the end of his cigar arced toward his mouth, burned brighter, then returned to his side. "Gringa, come here."

"I . . . I have a name," she said. She thought of racing back to camp but found no promise of safety there. Better not to turn her back on him.

"Yes?"

Keep him talking, she thought. "Libby. Libby Hawkins."

"Libby," he repeated.

"Yes, Elizabeth Margaret Hawkins from Greenville, Ohio. I was . . . am on my way to Santa Angela to visit my sister."

"Well, Elizabeth Margaret Hawkins, I would say you have taken a slight detour."

"One could say that," she said. "Yes, definitely a detour. I hope to correct it soon."

He laughed then. A low, rumbling laughter that did odd things to her stomach. "Come here . . . now."

Her eyes stole to the locket attached to a long strip of leather lying against his dark chest. He had something for her, most assuredly. She saw no advantage in defying him and she didn't want him to think her a coward.

Taking one hesitant step, then another, she closed the distance between them. Stopping just beyond his reach, her gaze traveled from the gold disk up the strong column of his neck to his eyes. Heavy lidded and impersonal, they were hard to meet. Her mind raced for something to say, something to divert what she feared was coming—another offer to trade.

"I haven't had a chance to express my gratitude," she said quickly.

"I think you expressed yourself by the fire very well."

"I . . . yes, those are my feelings about your activities, but they have little to do with my thanks for saving my life."

"My . . . activities saved your life, gringa. I heard of your capture from the Comanche band that hit your stage. I bought your locket and rode out to bury you."

Libby studied his face, attempting to see past his arrogant perusal, but she found no clues to his thoughts. "Why?"

He didn't move, but continued to regard her with a lazy indifference. Finally he shrugged away from the tree and threw down his cigar. Grinding the butt into the dirt with his boot, he pointed to the ground, not bothering to look at her.

"I brought you some things," he said. "A comb. Something to wear."

Libby gave him a speculative look. He had deliberately avoided her question. Her eyes traveled to the gold trinket, her mother's initials discernible with each breath he took. A curious object, she thought, for a gunrunning renegade to desire so greatly. His reasons might prove more than interesting, perhaps even crucial.

"Thinking of something to trade?"

Libby cast him a withering look and, taking a step toward the tree at his side, she bent and retrieved a small bundle wrapped in a white garment. Standing upright again was another problem. A soft moan accompanied her efforts.

Mando took her arm, steadying her. She grimaced at his touch that rubbed the blanket against her tender skin. "I've got quite a sunburn."

He had little difficulty prying the blanket from her fingers. Carefully he unwound it from her shoulders. Libby clutched the bundle to her chest and tried to appear calm. She knew he had seen her in the chemise and petticoat when he found her, but now she was in possession of all of her senses and they all said standing before a man like Fierro in one's underwear was an embarrassing situation.

"It's bad, but I've seen worse. Gordito knows of a plant that treats burns. I'll have him search some out tomorrow."

Libby nodded but reserved comment. Plants that healed burns sounded unlikely. Probably some evil-smelling nostrum. Perhaps if she didn't complain he would forget to tell this Gordito.

"You look doubtful."

She glanced up at him. His powers of observation surprised her. "It's just I've never heard of plants like you've described."

"You *americanos* don't know everything, gringa—"

"Libby," she said, tired of the word that sounded more an epithet than a form of address. "And I didn't say we did."

"It has been my experience that *americanos* find anything originating from another culture suspicious and inferior."

Feeling guilty at harboring just such thoughts when she prided herself as a modern thinker, she struck back. "Yes, that would be your experience, especially when distributing guns to wild Indians who carve up innocent old men and young soldiers simply doing their jobs. I see your point."

He grabbed her wrists and pulled her close, so close each breath filled her head with the smells of leather, tobacco and him. She curled her hands into fists, her knuckles brushing against the silky hair on his chest, the locket trapped between them.

Tilting her head back, she refused to be daunted by the black fury in his eyes. Her breath came in quick hard gasps, as if she had actually run as far as she wished she could at this moment.

"Don't push me," he said, pronouncing each word slowly. "I'm not a tolerant man."

Libby bit back the retort she would like to give. This man wasn't her papa, who hadn't liked her sassy tongue, or the constable who didn't like her suffragette placards, or the Reverend Carmichael, who didn't like her teaching the young ladies' choir how to smoke.

"You're hurting me." She was proud none of the trembles inside her crept into her voice.

He released her instantly. She stepped back and tried to catch her breath. "I'm very tired," she said. "I'm go-

ing to take these things around the bend there and
change.''

"You'll stay here.'' He took the bundle from her hand
and unrolled it to reveal a white shirt, a pair of moccasins and the promised comb. "Put this on,'' he said,
holding out the shirt.

Libby grabbed the garment and wanted to throw it to
the ground. She curbed that desire with one look at the
unspoken dare in his eyes. Finding the collar, she shook
the shirt out and poked her hand through a sleeve. She
glanced up once and saw him watching her, his eyes directed to somewhere below her neck. Abruptly she turned
her back to him and ground her teeth at that hateful
laugh he enjoyed at her expense.

Jerking the other arm through the remaining sleeve,
she pushed the cuffs back and pulled her hair free. The
realization hit her at once. The shirt was his. It hung to
her knees and had the rich softness of fine muslin. The
musky scent of his tobacco clung to the cool fabric
soothing her skin. She recalled the moonlight splashing
over the carved strength of his arms and chest, and her
thoughts froze along with her fingers on the buttons. A
hand on her shoulder pulled her around to face him.

He brushed her fingers out of the way and began
working on the buttons.

She pushed at his hands. "I can do them.''

"Be still or we'll be out here all night.''

Libby dropped her hands to her sides, too tired to
make an issue of who fastened the buttons. She tried to
think of something else other than the gentle touch of his
fingers skimming down the front of her body. The task
proved impossible. Each button seemed to take longer
than the last. She shouldn't have allowed him this inti-

macy, but her choices were as limited as her strength and she couldn't waste either.

"You can finish the last ones later," he said.

His voice sounded lower, with a roughness she hadn't heard before, definitely dangerous. Libby moved away quickly, turning her shoulder to him. He gave her a long look, one she couldn't decipher, then picked up the moccasins from the ground where he had tossed them. "Try these."

Libby gave the calf-length moccasins a dismissive glance. A tremor of remembrance ran through her. She couldn't wear them, no matter how soft they looked or how badly her feet hurt. "I have shoes."

"Take them off."

"I can't wear those . . . Indian shoes." She crossed her arms. "Please understand."

"You will change your mind after your legs are scratched to ribbons and your feet are a bleeding mess."

Presented with that argument, Libby didn't want to refuse the leather footwear but couldn't accept the moccasins, either. She changed the subject. "I believe you had a comb."

Pulling it from his back pocket, Mando approached her. "I hope you won't refuse to use this. You need it badly."

Libby turned to him and snatched the comb from his hand. "Thank you very much."

He shrugged, the moonlight glittering on the gold ornament hanging from his neck. "My pleasure."

"Yes, I can see that." Vowing to ignore his sarcasms and his twisted attempts at smiling, she turned to leave.

He caught her arm, pulling her around to face him. "Do you remember what I told you when we rode into camp?"

She pulled her arm from his grasp. "Yes. Don't challenge your...authority unless I want the others to do the same."

"Don't forget again."

He didn't wait for a reply, but turned and retrieved the blanket from where it had fallen from her shoulders. Libby followed his movements, wondering how long she could put up with his high-handed commands and veiled threats. Again she had few choices. She looked beyond the moon-splashed stream and saw little to encourage her. Never had she seen such emptiness, yet she knew the land held death in its palm, and until she sensed more danger from this man, she must stay with him. Choices—what a luxury they had been.

With the blanket draped over his arm and the moccasins held in his hand, Mando joined her. "See something?"

Libby shook her head. "Nothing but darkness."

"Morning will come soon enough."

"I hope so," she replied, and, turning away from a land more hostile and savage than the men who traveled it, she faced the camp and started up the incline.

"What a smell!" Louis wrinkled his nose and fanned the heavy black smoke away from him.

Mando gave the shoes another poke with a long stick. "Quiet," he said, his voice a loud whisper. "You'll wake her and then we'll never get any sleep."

"Who can sleep anyway with that smell?" Louis matched Mando's raspy tone.

"From all the snores I would say everyone but you," Mando replied.

Louis adjusted his blanket over his feet and shifted to his other side, turning his back to the fire and away from the offending odor. "Did you have to burn those things tonight?"

Mando threw the stick into the fire and watched the flames crumble Libby's cracked shoes. "Yes, otherwise she would just give me more trouble. Now she will have to wear the other ones."

He stood from his crouch and found his own bedroll laid out beneath the end of one of the carts. Louis had placed his along the cart's side, beside its large single wheel.

"Why should you care what footgear she chooses to wear?" the Frenchman asked.

Mando checked his rifle and repositioned his pistol closer to his side, giving himself time before he answered. He hadn't expected a question like that from Louis and didn't want to put too much into the answer. After giving some thought to his reply, Mando said, "I don't want to hear her complain about her feet for the rest of the trip."

Settling into his blankets, he lay back and crossed his arms beneath his head. The stars were fading and the moon had given up her reign. *Por Dios,* he was tired and most of the night was gone.

"I have never heard one complaint from her," Louis said.

"Have you ever known a woman who didn't complain? Wait until she knows us better." Louis wanted something from him. An admission of some kind. He wasn't going to get it.

"Still—"

"Enough, Louis. Elizabeth Margaret Hawkins is a paragon of strength and beauty," he said in a mocking tone that measured his sincerity. "Now will you go to sleep?"

"Is that her name?"

"She says she is called Libby."

"That couldn't be the *L* on the locket. It must be her mother's."

Mando answered with a vague "Uh-huh."

"Don't you feel badly about keeping the girl's token?"

"No. I think it must be my lucky piece. Didn't it bring me a beautiful redhead? It certainly brought her no luck."

"Armando . . . Mando, my friend, return the locket to the girl and have someone take her to Santa Angela before we all re—"

"Sleep, Louis. If you insist on carrying my burdens, you will need the rest."

A long sigh was Louis's answer. An answer Mando had heard many times before. It had been the white flag Mando and Ross had waited for when they had pestered Louis to join in some escapade, or when they begged him not to tell Don Alphonso when they had broken one of his strict rules. Younger than his father but older than the two of them, Louis had belonged to neither generation, and had tried giving his allegiance to both.

Traveling the middle road was not an easy journey, but it was one Louis Lavant knew well. Louis had never betrayed them to Don Alphonso, and the Frenchman wouldn't turn his back on him now.

Relieved to hear Louis's soft snores join the others, Mando folded his arms across his chest. He listened to the wind but heard her voice; he looked at the stars but saw her eyes. A woman like her, a fighter, a survivor should prove to be . . . a tightness in his gut finished his thought. He brushed a hand over his eyes, blocking out the stars and faraway wishes. Turning to his side, he watched sparks whirl high above the campfire and disappear into the darkness. The woman would prove to be great entertainment. He wanted nothing more.

A small creak from the cart indicated the gringa slept restlessly. He smiled, remembering her expression when Louis had shown her the cart they had prepared for her. A canvas tarp had been thrown over the high railings, and the inside had been emptied of everything but soft buffalo hides covered with blankets. He read on her doubtful face the conclusion she had drawn concerning sleeping arrangements.

No, my pretty gringa. When you sleep with me, your hair will be clean and combed and spread over my pillow. Your lips will be soft and your skin will burn from my touch and not the sun. Getting her to his bed would not be easy, but a challenge only made the rewards that much more pleasurable.

He wondered if there was a husband in the background to contend with, but he hadn't seen a ring or evidence of one on her finger and she hadn't mentioned a husband. He foresaw no problems in that regard to her accepting his bed.

Apparently she had found this bed suitable, for she had fallen asleep almost immediately, leaving her shoes in a corner of the cart where the moccasins now rested. She had asked him to understand and he did. Her experiences with the Comanches had left her hating them. He understood more than she could know. But she must learn to be practical and use the moccasins. Though he hated the *americanos* and what they were doing to his people, he found uses for them. Like Mathias Wright. Like Elizabeth Margaret Hawkins.

Mando turned to his side and closed his eyes, but sleep would not come. Something bothered him inside. Something so deep, he was aware of only the ripples and not the stone that had been thrown into his tranquility. His mind raced through the possibilities, but nothing emerged as the source of his unease. The men had proved themselves to be no more trouble than usual. Cabot and Doyle bore watching, but they always did.

With a sigh of disgust, he turned onto his back. He found the locket and worried the fine etching between his thumb and finger. He saw no answers to his discontent in the dwindling stars, nor in the dark passages of his thoughts. Eventually his lids closed. The memory of Libby's moonlit eyes drifted toward him in sleep. Despair darkened their bright color, filling them with longing. Her voice whispered to him, following him into his dreams, but he couldn't understand her words.

Chapter Seven

Libby threw one moccasin, then the other, out the opening in the back of the cart. On all fours, she stuck her head through the canvas curtain. "I will not wear those . . . things! Where are my shoes?"

"Feeling better this morning, I see."

Libby searched the area for the owner of that deep voice, then looked down. Sitting beneath her, a thin lather of soap covering one jaw, Mando scraped the other with a straightedge razor. She thought of several different uses for the sharp blade and they had nothing to do with good grooming.

"I want my shoes," she said.

"Are you looking for these, *señorita?*"

Libby looked up and discovered two charred lumps stuck on the ends of two sticks, framing the golden smile of one of the comancheros. Her sunburn had little to do with the sudden flush that warmed her skin. "You didn't!"

"I did," Mando answered, and calmly continued his shave.

Libby snapped the canvas closed and sat back. She had wondered last night how long she could tolerate his high-handed treatment. Now she knew. Crossing her arms, she breathed deeply and searched for her lost composure. Instead, she spotted the canteen propped in the corner. Cats don't like to be wet, she recalled. Grabbing the container, she twisted the cap loose and knelt at the end of the cart.

Laughter and rapid-fire Spanish filled the morning outside her small enclosure. She would show them she enjoyed a joke as well as the next person, especially when the joke was on the next person—namely Mando Fierro.

Pushing back the canvas an inch, she saw Mando rinsing the soap from his face. She looked at the canteen, then at Mando, and thrust her arm and head through the opening.

"Let me help you, Mr. Fierro." Turning the canteen completely upside down, she dumped the contents over his head.

Mando leaped to his feet, sputtering much like the big cat Libby compared him to. The deluge had parted his hair down the middle and plastered it to his skull like a black silk hood. Libby tossed the canteen at his feet and glared right back at the watered-down version of his own angry stare. Not a muscle moved but his eyelids, blinking back drips. Libby felt something bubbling inside her like fizz water. She clamped her lips tight to hold it back. Finally he wiped the water from his eyes and shook his hand just like a cat shaking its paws clean.

Libby burst out laughing.

Louis joined in, then one by one the others began laughing, too. Mando's chest rose and fell much the way hers had only minutes before. She knew he was angry, but she didn't care. At last, she had struck back. For the first time in days she felt wonderful. She felt alive. She felt like her old self, before the Comanches, before the flood or the sun or Mando Fierro.

Suddenly Mando threw back his head and laughed with them, a deep, rolling laughter that filled the cool morning air. The sound startled Libby. She found herself watching him. With his hair long and wet against this neck, his broad chest honed to hard-muscled ridges, she imagined a pagan amulet a more appropriate trinket to hang against his dark skin than her delicate locket.

He shook his head, spraying droplets of water against her skin, then combed his hands through his hair, shoving the long strands back from his face. Libby wasn't laughing anymore and neither was Mando.

The camp grew still. Tossing her hair over her shoulder, Libby sat back on her feet, her hands clasped in her lap, one auburn brow cocked in a determined attempt to appear nonchalant. She didn't expect violence, not anymore. Rest, food and her private sleeping arrangement gave her the reassurances she had desperately needed. She held no illusions concerning Mando's character. He sold guns to raiding Indians, but apparently he didn't prey on defenseless women. At least he hadn't yet.

Mando had turned partially away from her, his thumbs hooked in front of his gun belt, and regarded her casually. His nose, with its slight aquiline curve, dominated his profile, while his brow shadowed his eyes. A sharp picture came to her. An eagle. Her brows drew together at the odd experience, then the image vanished into the mists of forgotten dreams. The memory nagged at her for a moment until he stooped and picked up the moccasins.

He brought them to her, holding them in one hand, while the other rested on his hip. "Your shoes were worthless."

He was right, Libby admitted, but she hated accepting the Indian footwear. However, she had gained a small victory here and could afford to give a little. Mustering all the attributes of a gracious winner available to her, she took the pair from his hand.

"They probably won't fit," she said, and ducked behind the canvas.

He whisked it back. "Hope that they do, gringa, because ants, scorpions, thorns and snakes are just waiting out there for a stupid woman's pink toes."

Libby balled her hands into fists. "Thunderation! I'll wear them."

Mando snapped the canvas closed.

With a tight-lipped frown, Libby examined the moccasins. The leather was soft and pliant, yet tough along the soles. Sturdy rawhide stitching pieced the leather together. Libby admired the skillful handwork until she remembered who had done it. Pushing the moccasins aside, she grappled with her unreasonable distaste for them.

This raw hatred for all-things-Indian burned like a fever inside her, distorting everything she had once believed. The Eastern newspapers that had recorded the Indian's plight and had pleaded for understanding from the government had once appealed to her. Now those same stories seemed hopelessly naive.

Her compassion for the noble red man had been butchered by Comanche knives and left on a roadside in Texas. Regaining some semblance of rationality concerning Indians would be difficult if not impossible.

Again, he had given her no choice. She couldn't remain barefoot. Resigning herself to the inevitable, Libby selected one of the moccasins and eased her foot into it. Her hands began to shake; her fingers fumbled with the side lacings.

Unable to continue, she jerked the moccasin off her foot and tossed it to the side. That dreadful man shouldn't have burned her shoes. Staring at her bare feet, the blisters inflamed and painful, she slammed her fists into the soft mound of buffalo robes, then reached for the moccasins once more.

On closer inspection the shoes didn't resemble the Comanches' footwear at all. People on the frontier wore buckskin garments. Louis wore buckskins. She needed to wear these shoes. They weren't Indian shoes. They were frontier shoes.

Libby thrust her foot into the shoe and found it slightly big but much more comfortable than her own shoes had been. Tightening the lacing along the side helped shape it to her foot. She repeated the procedure on the other foot.

Wiggling her toes in the soft leather, she congratulated herself for meeting her fears and conquering them. A cold dousing of honesty quickly washed away her self-satisfaction. Shuffling words was not conquest. She must learn to deal with this overwhelming fear and hatred.

She couldn't let her ordeal with the Indians darken every new experience that carried remote reminders of the Comanche raiders. If that was to be the case, she might as well forget her plans to settle in the west and go back East and marry some boring know-it-all who would be only too happy to manage her inheritance. She could spend her time crocheting doilies for the parlor while she had a baby every year—a future any sensible woman would want, according to her mama and papa and all the other right-thinking people in Greenville, Ohio.

Feeling around for the comb, she found it among the blankets and began working on the snarled ends of her hair. Her parents had never understood her. She needed space, freedom, a chance to explore opportunities. Amelia would understand. Her sister had shocked their parents last year when she had taken off for Texas to join that addle-brained husband of hers.

Libby paused at her task, remembering the hoopla when Amelia's letter had arrived telling her parents she was staying despite Devin's death and taking over the mercantile. Papa was ready to board the train for Texas. She would always wonder what had made Mama finally tell Papa that Amelia was a woman fully grown and should do what she saw fit.

Libby shook her head and again applied the comb to her hair. Secretly she wondered if both Amelia and Mama had been sneaking into her cache of Susan B. Anthony's writings. Certainly neither had ever spoken up against Papa's edicts before, leaving her to carry out all the small rebellions.

The thought brought a smile to her lips until she recalled Amelia had folded up at the last. What had made her ruin everything and marry again, giving her hard-won independence over to a man's control? Still her sister might have some ideas on where to get started.

Maybe she would become a merchant or buy a ranch or discover some opportunity she didn't know existed. The possibilities were as big as the sky and limited only by her own resourcefulness.

A sudden shake to the flimsy walls of her improvised boudoir broke Libby's reverie. "*Andele,* gringa, we have a long journey ahead of us."

Libby jerked the comb through an exceptionally stubborn tangle and scowled in the direction of the softly ringing bootsteps fading into the morning's noisy preparations to leave. One particularly tall and evil-tempered limitation was going to require a great deal of resourcefulness, but she would reach Santa Angela and she would take up what she had started when she bought her train ticket in Ohio—the pursuit of her own destiny.

Giving her hair several more strokes, Libby tossed the comb aside. A thin strip of material torn from her petticoat served as a ribbon to tie back the heavy mass of hair. Coffee had been in the air earlier and she hoped someone had saved her some. Again she poked her head out of the canvas and saw the men busily loading carts or preparing pack mules. Oxen had been hitched to several of the carts, and horses stood saddled and ready for their riders. If she was going down to the creek, she needed to do so quickly.

The back of the cart had no crude railings like the sides, only the long dangling corners of the sheet of canvas that had been thrown over the top. Climbing down carefully, Libby appreciated the calf-hugging leather that prevented an unseemly display of ankle and leg. She immediately found the thought ridiculous. For heavenly days! Here she was traipsing about in her petticoat and a strange man's shirt and she was worried about showing a little leg. Rolling up each sleeve, she shook her head, laughing at herself.

"It is good to see you smile."

Libby recognized the distinctive French accent at once and turned to greet Louis. He held a cup of coffee out to her. "Thank you," she said, and accepted the hot tin mug. She took a sip and found the brew strong and bitter, but she welcomed the aroma and the simple pleasure of starting the day with a cup of coffee. Somehow the morning ritual lent a normalcy to even these unusual circumstances.

Louis presented his elbow to Libby. "Shall we go?"

"I can find the creek, Mr. Lavant."

He gave her a crooked smile full of Gallic charm. "Mademoiselle Hawkins—"

Unable to resist the friendship in that smile, she said, "Please, call me Libby."

"Very well, and I am Louis." At her nod, he continued. "You must let me walk you to the creek or I will be forced into laboring over teams of oxen. I much prefer your company."

"How can I refuse such a sweet compliment?" she replied, smiling broadly to accompany her teasing. "I have always heard how charming you Frenchmen are." Having drunk all the coffee she could tolerate on an empty stomach, Libby gave the cup a flip of her wrist, tossing the contents into the trampled grass. Keeping the cup, she placed her hand on Louis's arm. "Shall we?"

"El Aguila, come quickly," Tomas called. "*Tío* is riding in and it looks like trouble."

Mando jerked the long strap home through the front rigging ring of his saddle and turned to find Tomas pointing toward the horizon. The boy's uncle was riding hard, leaning low over the horse's neck, his sombrero's deep brim folded back against the wind. Mando cursed beneath his breath and walked toward the edge of the camp, Tomas following close behind. A quick look among the carts and milling animals revealed no bright red hair. Louis and the woman were still gone. The Frenchman allowed her too much time away from camp.

Mando stopped by the lead cart and waited for Paco to ride in. Cinco and Cabot soon joined him. "Is everything loaded and ready to go?" he asked.

"Everything except that redhead," Cabot said.

Mando turned a sharp look to the American but didn't give him a reply. "Cinco, check the water kegs. Make sure they're full."

"*Sí*, El Aguila." Cinco gave one more long look at the fast approaching horseman, then trotted off to see to the extra water.

The frantic beat of the horse's galloping hooves trampled the early-morning calm. Gordito ambled over to the small group, munching on a tortilla-wrapped breakfast of chopped meat and mashed beans, and watched the oncoming horse and rider with the others.

"Wonder what's got ol' Paco so riled?" Cabot commented. "That horse is travelin' as if his tail was on fire."

Mando had his suspicions. Sliding a quick glance at Cabot, he drew the corners of his mouth into a tight grimace. Perhaps he could solve one problem and rid himself of another.

Paco pulled his mount to a skidding stop, a cloud of dust rolling over the small group. "Buffalo soldiers," he shouted before the horse had raised itself from its haunches. "About fifteen miles back." Paco paused and dragged in a deep breath. "Riding slow," he managed between breaths, "but they've found our trail." He tossed down a long drink of water from his canteen.

"How many?" Mando asked.

Paco slashed the back of his hand over his mouth. "Eight, including the officer."

Mando calculated they had perhaps half an hour lead over the cavalry patrol. Every minute counted. "Change your mount, Paco. We've got a hard ride ahead of us."

Paco nodded and nudged his spent foam-flecked horse toward the small remuda. Mando turned to Tomas. "Go help Cinco check the water casks and tell him to load them all into the gringa's wagon."

The youth nodded slowly but didn't move, his attention riveted to the horizon as if he expected the army to come chasing after his uncle at any moment.

Mando took hold of his bony shoulders and looked him in the eye. "Tomas," he said firmly, but without censure. The boy swerved his gaze to Mando. Fear clouded the bright eagerness usually seen in his eyes. "These soldiers know little about the plains and we know everything. Many times we have slipped away while they rode in circles, exhausting their horses and running out of water. We will again. *Comprende, chico?*"

A smile teased at the corners of Tomas's mouth. "I understand. The *americanos* will never catch El Aguila."

Mando clapped him on the shoulders. "*Bueno,* now go help Cinco."

This time Tomas gave an enthusiastic nod and ran to do his bidding. Mando watched the youth until he joined Cinco, who quickly put him to work. Paco shouldn't have brought the boy...too young, too much life ahead of him.

"How inspiring." Cabot's sarcasm was as thick as the dust on their boots. "I say let's ambush 'em, scalp 'em. Make it look like the Comanches did it. That way we take no chances with our trade goods."

Mando held back his disgust. The American's suggestion deserved no reply, but he couldn't ignore him. Rattlesnakes tended to strike if disregarded. "Paco probably spotted an advance patrol. Gunfire would bring the rest down our—"

Bright, sparkling laughter entered the camp. Mando spotted Louis and the woman strolling into the area as if they were enjoying a morning walk around the plaza in Santa Fe. The smile she gave Louis hit Mando in the gut. His hands curled into hard fists.

"—throats," he finished.

"That damned woman!" Cabot muttered. "I knew she was gonna bring trouble."

"You sound like the Indians," Mando replied, still watching the pair talk easily to each other. "Don't tell me you believe their nonsense?"

"What she's done to you ain't no nonsense. We'd be clear up on the banks of the Canadian exceptin' for her."

Mando's gaze took in the coppery swath of hair that hung over her shoulder, the curling tendrils reaching a bright yellow sash tied about her waist, a gift from Louis, no doubt.

"You would do well to stay out of my business," Mando said in a deceptively calm voice.

"So long as it stays out of mine, Fierro."

Mando pulled his gaze from Louis and Libby, fixing it on Cabot's sullen face. "Load four of the carts with guns, ammunition, whiskey and anything else you think you'll need, except the water casks. Louis and I will lead the soldiers into dry country and we will need all those. The patrol will turn back by sundown, tomorrow at the latest. Take the northern route through the Quitaque and the Palo Duro. You might find some more trade."

Cabot spat brown tobacco juice in the dirt. "Whatever you say...boss man." Jerking his head at Doyle, the American took off for the carts.

"Gordito, you will come with me. Divide up the provisions quickly. Paco and Cinco will go with the gringos to keep an eye on things. The others will travel with us."

Gordito swallowed quickly. "But our share of the profits, El Aguila. What of that?"

"Go with the others then. If we miss each other in Puerto de Luna, come to me at the rancho with a full accounting."

"I will see that the count is honest," Gordito said.

Mando slapped the fat cook on his back. "I know you will. Just be sure you divide the provisions as honestly."

Gordito laughed. "*Sí*, El Aguila. You will have plenty, I promise."

Mando returned to his horse, mounted and headed him toward the back of the line. No profits would come from this trip, he was certain. Damn those vultures in Santa Fe. They would have to wait for their money this time. He passed Gordito rummaging through the cart loaded with foodstuffs and reminded himself to check their portion of supplies before the others left.

He passed the oxen standing patiently in their harnesses, waiting for the command to take up their burden. He wasn't surprised to see Cinco hurry over to the horses, probably to hear Paco's news firsthand, leaving Tomas to load the kegs.

Louis joined Tomas, helping him stow the keg inside. Mando could almost hear the excitement he saw on the youth's face as he spoke to Louis. Only half-listening, the Frenchman looked up and gave Mando a speculative gaze. Mando frowned at the question he read in his friend's narrowed blue eyes. At the arrival of the woman, her expression shining with expectation, the frown deepened to open displeasure. Mando suspected he was about to ride into more difficulties.

Chapter Eight

Libby's hopes cracked under the heavy frown Mando wore. He wasn't going to allow her to go to the soldiers. She recalled the night before when Cabot had mentioned something about her going to the army and his answer, "She won't go anywhere I don't send her." What arrogance!

She struggled to control her outrage. Calm thinking was needed here. Perhaps if she promised to say little about Mando and his men, even point the soldiers in a different direction, if she took that tack, he could hardly deny her this chance to proceed to Santa Angela. It was a feeble hope, but it was all she had and she clung to it.

Libby waited until Mando drew his horse close enough for her to address him in a normal voice. "I won't say anything about you and the others if you let me leave now. I owe you a debt and I want to repay it with my silence."

"An unacceptable trade, gringa." He turned his attention to Louis. "Ride—"

Libby stepped closer. "I'll tell the soldiers you took another direction. Let me go to them. They won't be able to follow you with me along. They will have to take me to Santa Angela."

Louis joined her. "She might have something there, Mando."

Libby almost winced at the look Mando passed to the Frenchman. Undeterred by Mando's displeasure, Louis placed his hand gently at her elbow. His presence gave her waning courage a little boost, enough to speak again.

"I must go to my sister. I have to tell her about the death of our parents. She's in the family way and the blow will be hard coming from strangers. When she hears I was on that stage, she will think I've been captured by the Indians or killed. Our parents' death will be doubly hard for her. She could lose her baby."

Something had flickered in Mando's dark eyes when she mentioned her sister. She didn't want to beg, but her chance to escape was so close.

"Please, Mr. Fierro. I need to go to her."

Mando gathered up his reins. "Your sister has her problems and you have yours." He turned the horse to leave.

Libby grabbed the bridle. The gray almost reared, his nostrils flaring, his eyes rolling at the unexpected move. Mando cursed and held him in.

Libby stepped back, but not far. "What problems, Mr. Fierro? What problems do I have? Tell me why I can't go to the soldiers. Tell me, damn you. Tell me."

"I told you she would run to the army."

Libby swung around and faced Cabot. Like a faithful dog, Doyle hung at his heels. Of all the comancheros, these two revolted her the most and the look she gave them said so.

Cabot spat a glob of tobacco juice inches from her toes. "She's seen us and likely knows names. The next trip ol' Mackenzie and his soldier boys make into New Mexico will have him knockin' on all our doors."

Libby opened her mouth, ready to promise anything.
"Silencio!"

No translation was needed. Whether the command was directed to her or Cabot mattered little. Mando was so angry, pressing her cause now would do little good.

Mando switched his gaze to Cabot. "You have your instructions. Take the carts you need and move."

Cabot pointed at Libby. "What're you gonna do with her? She's a loose end, Fierro, and Wright don't like loose ends."

Libby held her breath. She had her answer, but she didn't like it. Surely she could convince Mando she wouldn't say anything. She had to try.

Mando didn't take his eyes from Cabot. "Put her in the cart, Louis."

Libby started to protest, but Louis took her arm in a hard grip and pulled her toward the end cart. She tried to jerk free. Now more than ever she wanted to go to the soldiers. The Frenchman held her fast.

"Louis, let me—"

"Sh-sh-sh, Libby. Going to the soldiers is impossible."

Libby wrenched free and faced Louis. "But, you said—"

"I was wrong. You would never make it to Santa Angela."

Her brows shot together in a worried frown. "Mando—"

"No, but the others, Libby. . . the others."

Libby turned her head and found the truth in Louis's statement. They all stared at her, no longer with curiosity or harmless interest. She saw it in their narrowed eyes, the hard edge that had suddenly appeared on the faces that had looked, if not friendly, at least unconcerned.

The three Mexican men had grouped together, talking softly. The Irishman fixed a downright malevolent glare on her. Evidently they saw her as a threat, not only to themselves, but if what Cabot had said was true, a threat to their homes, as well.

She meant them no harm. She just wanted to see her sister, make some plans for the future, but she saw in their faces they had little interest in her future beyond the next breath she drew.

Her gaze traveled to Mando, who spoke to Cabot in a low earnest voice that didn't reach her ears. The American's face had gone brick red, his hand rested on the pistol at his hip, but his fingers remained lax. He looked as if he were choking on his restraint.

At Louis's urging, she reluctantly climbed in among the water kegs. Her last view of the confrontation between the two men was Cabot's eyes as he turned away. His gaze had rested on her for only a moment, but she felt the impact of his rage as if it were a blow.

Shaking, Libby found a small space between some kegs and lowered herself to the hard, splintery boards. She folded her legs close to her chest and hugged them, resting her forehead on her knees. Shouts and the sounds of horses moving about filtered through the canvas. Libby hardly noticed. Misery stole past her best defense, the one she had used all her life. Not even anger stopped the flow of tears.

How long she sat, swamped with fears and frustration, she didn't know. The silence pulled her head from her knees. For one explosive heartbeat she thought the comancheros had left her for the army to find, until she remembered the water kegs. They would never leave those. A shrill whistle and the first lurching movement of the cart proved her right. What had she expected? Decency? Kindness? Mando Fierro didn't know the meaning of either word.

The back canvas was suddenly flipped to the side. Libby quickly scrubbed the tears from her face. Mando leaned from his saddle and peered beneath the make-shift canopy.

"Gordito found something for your sunburn." He tossed a bundle of pulpy, gray-green plant spears at her feet. "Squeeze out the juice and smear it on your face and shoulders."

Unhooking a canteen's long strap from his saddle horn, he held the tin water bottle out to her. Libby had to push the strange-looking plants aside and stretch to reach it. "You'll get no more water for two days," Mando said. "There's food in that burlap sack." He dropped the canvas and galloped somewhere ahead of the lumbering oxen.

"Thank you," Libby whispered to the flapping piece of material. Stunned and confused, she set the full canteen on a keg at her elbow and looked about her small conveyance for the sack of food. She found it pressed into a corner. Inside, she discovered a generous supply of dried meat, dried apples and other fruits and a small stack of a round flat bread. She shook her head, wondering what kind of man Mando Fierro truly was. One minute she wanted to curse him with every blasphemy she had learned on the stage journey across Texas, the next she found herself saying thank you.

Bracing herself against the hard jolts of the rapidly moving cart, she bit into one of the wrinkled apples and puckered her mouth at the tart burst of flavor. Curious about this wondrous plant, she picked up a large, blade-shaped stalk and gave the wide end a slight squeeze, then a harder one. A clear thin liquid appeared along the edge where the stalk had been cut from the plant. Another squeeze to the long, thick leaf produced more liquid. She shrugged and set it to the side. Breakfast came first. Whatever the future held, she wanted the strength to meet it.

Libby finished off the apple, a stick of the dried, spicy meat and, mindful of how scarce water could be, a few swallows of water. She supposed the kegs were for the animals. With a shove here and a yank there, she managed to enlarge her cramped quarters and tried to make herself comfortable.

Her stomach full, shielded from the sun, surrounded by sloshing water, Libby remembered where she had been yesterday. Lost, without food, shelter or water and with the sun using her head for an anvil.

Surely she would have been dead by now if Mr. Fierro hadn't found her. And what of that flood water coming to her rescue when she had been held by the Comanches? Hope might look like death or the Devil himself, but as long as she drew another breath, she would watch for some opportunity to get out of this mess.

That opportunity could very well be Louis Lavant. She recalled the time spent by the creek that morning. With his quick smile and gallant attempts to cheer her, he had lifted her spirits considerably. Such an amiable, charming man. How had he ever linked up with these renegades? Mando Fierro, of course. Their friendship was obvious, which added to her puzzlement.

Libby took up one of the smooth-skinned, fibrous leaves and pressed some of the liquid onto her fingertips. Sniffing at it, she wrinkled her nose, then gingerly dabbed it to her cheeks. Squeezing and dabbing, she eventually covered all of her face and found the effect sticky but soothing. Mando had been right about the plant. His concern for her painful sunburn added another piece to a puzzle that grew by the hour.

She unbuttoned the shirt he had given her, another act of consideration, and pulled it off her shoulders, leaving the soft material to spill around her elbows. She applied the healing plant juice to her shoulders and chest, the absence of her locket evoking images she would like to forget—water trailing over Mando's broad bare shoulders and wide expanse of lightly furred chest, the thick cords of his neck thrown back in laughter, and the laughter itself. Had she met him under any other circumstances she would have found him attractive, unorthodox, someone she would want to know.

The thought startled her. Slowly she pulled the shirt over her shoulders and began to fasten the buttons. Mando Fierro was a handsome devil. She smiled at the term she had chosen. Never had it been more appropriate. Who else could control the brigands that rode with him? Yet she doubted any woman would pass him by without a second look. A man of great contrasts, she thought. Whatever could his plans be for her? Cabot had mentioned New Mexico.

Edging toward the rear, she tossed back the canvas sheeting and noted the sunrise behind them. They were headed west. Recalling maps she had seen along her journey to Texas, she knew that direction would take them to New Mexico. Why all the way to New Mexico? Libby grew uneasy thinking of all the possibilities. From what she knew, New Mexico was a lawless place, not even a state, a United States territory for barely twenty years. One could easily disappear in a place like that.

A teeth-jarring bump forced her to grab hold of a corner post and let go of her disturbing thoughts of the future. Another jerked her toward the hard ground.

Wrapping her arm around the thick post, she pulled herself safely inside. Leaning back, she breathed a sigh of relief, but cut it short with a small gasp.

Peering out the back, she discovered no one following them, just the long trail of wheel tracks narrowing to a sharp V far behind them. If Tomas had been right, and from the hurried leave-taking she was certain he had spoken the truth, the cavalry was following those tracks. She could walk right to them.

She gauged the distance to the ground, the speed they were traveling and estimated the impact of a jump. The landing would be rough, but hardly bone breaking. Her thoughts traveled down those parallel lines in the dust until they disappeared into the sunrise. This might be her only chance. She had to take it.

Louis hadn't made an appearance since they had left and Mando had ignored her. Maneuvering to the front of the cart, Libby peered out between the canvas curtains. She saw only one other cart ahead of her. Tomas led the first oxen team from his horse. A rope attached her team to that cart.

She searched for the others and just made out Mando riding his big gray horse far ahead of the small caravan. The rest of the comancheros had apparently gone another direction. She didn't see Louis anywhere. He must have gone with the other men. Good. Her decision made, she was glad to have one less pair of eyes watching her.

Libby adjusted the canvas so Tomas couldn't see inside her cart and crawled back to the end. Already the day's heat rolled in with the dust. She braced herself against the corner post once again and examined the harsh terrain. Broken hills and dry ravines broke the rock-strewn surface of the land. Tall grasses quivered before the wind, their color faded by the sun. Hardly an inviting landscape, but weighing the risks, she chose to take her chances with the land.

She had water and food to last two days, but considering Tomas's statements, she would reach the soldiers before nightfall. She could be on her way to Santa Angela by morning.

Backing away from the edge, Libby located the canteen and slung it over her shoulder, then tied the burlap bag through the sash wound around her waist. She peeked out the front one more time and saw that Mando was farther up the trail than before. Scooting to the back, she sat on the edge and readied herself to drop.

With one more look to each side, she placed her now-damp hands against the rough boards. She looked out once more at the hard, lonely wilderness and hesitated.

Comanches roamed this area and the sun was a killer. She might miss the cavalry patrol. They could have turned back or followed the other comancheros. Yes, and they might be just beyond sight, riding toward her into the desert. Libby closed her eyes and pushed.

The ground hit her quick and hard, knocking the breath from her lungs. She lay stunned, gasping for air. Wetness seeped beneath her back. Libby pulled in a huge breath and sat up. Her hand went to her back, then she brought it before her, expecting to see blood. Her palm was merely damp.

Jerking the canteen up, her eyes widened in horror. A sharp stone had punctured the metal in the fall. Water flowed freely from a half-inch hole. Immediately she tilted it to stop the water's escape, but she had already lost half the contents.

She bowed her head and mourned the loss of those few cups of water as if she had lost her dearest friend. Now what of her plan? She turned and looked at the disap-

pearing cart and thought of running after it, but fought
down the urge. If she didn't find the soldiers before she
ran out of water, likely she would never have found them
anyway. What difference would a few more hours make?
Libby knew that answer. It could mean the difference
between life and death.

She shrugged. The water loss couldn't be helped now.
Best to keep going. The sooner she got started, the faster
she would find safety. Struggling to her feet, she was relieved to feel only a few minor additions to the aches and
pains she already suffered. She held the canteen as
though it were a newborn and started down the trail.

Looking over her shoulder, she saw the cart continuing on its hurried way, the horse and rider so far ahead,
she could no longer make them out. She picked up her
pace. If she could see them, she could be seen. Every
other second she peered over her shoulder and the cart
grew smaller, but not small enough.

She imagined Mando Fierro riding back and checking
on her, finding the cart empty and seeing her, a spot of
blinding white in all these shades of brown. She looked
back again. Had the cart stopped? She drew to a halt and
turned completely around. No. She breathed again, but
panic dragged each breath through her dry, burning
throat until she managed to quiet her pounding heart.

She needed someplace to hide until the carts had traveled completely out of sight. Should Fierro discover her
missing, he would look around and see nothing. Searching her out would consume too much time.

She turned a slow circle, scanning the open country for
a deep ravine with a gradual grade she could walk down
easily. She didn't want to chance spilling another drop of
water.

Just ahead and to her right, she found exactly what she needed. With one last glance at the disappearing carts, she crossed the wheel tracks and descended the shallow side of an arroyo. Once at the bottom, she followed the sandy bed until the sides rose steeply above her.

The buckskin moccasins felt wonderful. A few blisters still plagued her, but she didn't want to think how they would feel if she still wore her stiff leather shoes. She had to smile at the irony of it all. She could never have walked back to the cavalry patrol in her own shoes, but because Mando had insisted, she now wore shoes that made it possible.

She fully intended to make the soldiers take her to Santa Angela, even if it meant playing the frail female.

Libby settled herself on the shady side of the ravine, carefully placing the canteen close by. She glanced up and down the narrow defile and found little movement other than the swirls of sand that flowed with the wind along the bottom. The rocky areas received special attention, but she saw nothing she supposed looked like a rattlesnake. Relaxing back against the dirt wall, she closed her eyes and tried to rest.

The morning had already grown hot. She didn't want to think about the long walk ahead of her, but memories of the day before crowded past her anticipation of finding the soldiers. She reached for the canteen but only rested her hand on it. Gradually her thoughts quieted to the sound of the wind blowing over the ravine and the whisper of sand following each blustering gust.

Neither the wind nor the sand touched her. Nothing touched her here in this safe place, not the sun, not Mando Fierro's eyes.

Libby dozed, her ears still tuned to the land, but her mind was far away in time and place, to Ohio and her mother's soft laughter and her father's boisterous voice greeting customers. Then she traveled forward to Amelia's surprised and happy face at seeing her again once she reached Santa Angela.

A low, distant rumbling trembled through the earth along her spine, sending shock waves through her imaginings. She opened her eyes wide. A horse? A rider?

Mando Fierro!

Chapter Nine

Deep within the ground, the hard-pounding hooves of the galloping horse grew stronger, their clattering thunder rolling toward her. Libby's heartbeat joined with both until, for several seconds, she didn't realize the horse had slowed and the drumming in her ears and chest was the pounding of her heart. Libby waited motionless, willing the horse and rider to pick up speed once again and pass by the ravine.

The horse's pace dwindled to a quick trot and finally a walk. Libby drew her hand from the damaged canteen and raked it through her hair. He had seen where the water had leaked. A wild urge to run brought her to her feet. She spotted the trail of footsteps pressed into the soft sand covering the bottom of the ravine and sank back down. Mando would see them, too.

Crouched in the dust, her heart racing as if she had run for miles, Libby felt like a rabbit run to ground. She refused to allow Mando to find her shivering in some hole, waiting for that final pounce. Cradling the canteen in the crook of one arm, Libby grasped a dangling root growing from the earthen wall behind her and pulled herself to her feet. She leaned against the rough embankment,

her legs barely able to hold her weight. This idea had not
been one of her best.

The horse halted. Creaking leather and a jingling bridle were the only sounds that Libby heard other than the
wind and her own ragged breathing. Her gaze rested on
the footsteps in the sand. She imagined Mando examining the damp earth where she had fallen, finding her trail.
Still her legs would not move. Mando would be angry,
but she had never feared thunderstorms or fireworks,
being fully capable of her own displays.

Fear, she reminded herself, was a Comanche raider
tearing at her clothes, black water dragging her to perdition and vultures greeting her when she arrived. She
wasn't afraid of Mando Fierro. She simply hated giving
up and facing that arrogant man with her failure. Calmer
now, she debated what to do.

Confronting him down here would be the worst possible culmination of this debacle. Libby pushed away
from the wall and slowly retraced her steps until she could
see above the edge of the ravine. A quick glance over her
shoulder located Mando immediately. Almost even with
her, he swung out of the saddle in a swift, graceful
movement. Long, determined strides carried him toward her. He looked like a man who had reached his
limit.

Having had a great deal of experience with this reaction in others, Libby increased her pace up the gentle incline, composing a likely story as she stepped. He met her
at the brim.

"I'm surprised you rode all the way back for me." She
spoke before he had a chance, a good tactic under these
circumstances she had learned. She spared a glance for
his horse, blowing hard and shaking his handsome head.
Mando said nothing.

"I tried to catch up after I had fallen out of the cart, but I was stunned for a moment or two and the carts had pulled too far—"

"How much water did you lose?"

"I…" She looked again at the horse. "About half. The canteen hit a rock or something … when I fell."

"Give the canteen to me before you lose the rest of it."

Feeling much like a small child who had lost her pennies, Libby handed the tin container to Mando.

"I suppose you were holding on to the canteen when you happened to bounce out and I suppose you had tied the food bag to your waist as a precaution … just in case you fell."

Libby didn't lie often, and being caught in such a poor one gave her an excuse to turn away from the winded horse and give her shoulder to Mando.

"Why didn't you just leave me?" she said. "The others wouldn't have known."

A firm hand on her arm spun her around. She found the crossed cartridge belts more amiable than the dark fury in his eyes.

"You impulsive little fool," he said, his tone low, a strong measure of control underlying each word. "The soldiers are miles behind us and low on water. They may have already turned back. If not, they will regret it and maybe with their lives. Comanches, Kiowa and Cheyenne are spread over the Llano looking for trouble. Chances are you would never have made it to Santa Angela."

"It was a chance I had to take." She raised her gaze to meet his. "My only chance. The others—"

"Only I will decide what to do with you and when. But I promise you this. You will return to your sister."

Surprised he had admitted this much, Libby pressed for more information. "When?"

"When it pleases me." He spun on his heel and walked briskly to where the gray had wandered and was now cropping at tufts of tall grass. Running a hand down the horse's long neck, Mando ruffled his mane.

A moment of guilt at the animal's hard use stabbed at Libby. Mando should have saved his mount and left her to her own devices. Though thirsty, she couldn't begrudge the water Mando poured from the damaged canteen into his cupped hand, offering it to the horse. He had called her a fool, but she wondered which of them had earned the title more.

Mando tossed the canteen to the ground and remounted. He sat the horse straight and tall in his black clothes and wide sombrero and carried the crossed cartridge belts as if they were a duke's royal sash. What had brought this proud man to such a low occupation? Libby dismissed the thought as soon as it entered her mind. She neither cared nor wanted to know. Yet the question lingered despite her attempts to ignore it.

Giving the horse a gentle touch of his spur, Mando urged him toward her. Libby hadn't moved from the edge of the ravine. Hot wind burned her already tender skin and pressed the petticoat against her legs. She drew her free hand against her brow, shading her eyes from a morning sun that promised another day that could whip the life out of the unwary.

Stopping the horse several feet from her, he pulled his boot from the stirrup and extended his hand. "I have no time for stupid women, gringa. I'll give you a canteen and you can follow the tracks straight to hell or come with me."

Libby wanted nothing more than to turn around and start walking, but found the prospect less appealing now. Both choices had terrible risks, but she had learned one thing from her travels in Texas. Death waited behind every hill, and deliverance sometimes rode a bolt of lightning.

Libby grasped the leather-clad hand and placed her foot in the empty stirrup. A strong pull helped her swing up behind Mando, finding a seat on the saddle's skirt.

"Hang on," he cautioned. "If you fall...again, I won't stop."

Libby wrapped her arms around his waist as the horse sprang forward. She didn't hesitate to hang on tightly, her legs gripping the sweat-slick barrel of the horse, her arms clinging to Mando's firm torso. Again the smell of leather and gunpowder assailed her senses, reminding her of the long ride the night before when she had lain across his lap.

A sinking sensation tickled inside her, surprising her with its unfamiliarity, disturbing her with its strange effect. Light-headed and a little weak, she thought she might have had too much sun.

They rode in a ground-covering canter, neither saying a word. Libby looked over her shoulder and saw nothing of the soldiers, not even a telltale cloud of dust on the horizon. She must stop operating on desperation and use her head. Next time she would wait for a better opportunity to find her way to Santa Angela.

Facing forward, she raised her chin and peered over Mando's shoulder. Her cart's billowing canvas sheeting flapped in the wind far ahead of them, but she saw they were closing in fast.

Relieved, Libby settled back and concentrated on keeping her seat. She turned her head one way, then the other, but the fluttering ends of a red kerchief tied beneath Fierro's hat beat her cheeks and eyes like an angry butterfly. Libby hazarded releasing her hold with one arm and tucked the ends into his collar. Her fingers touched the strip of thin leather lying against his warm skin. Her locket. Her property. He wore it to taunt her, to claim her, to remind her of his power. She was tempted to snatch it from his neck. She wouldn't leave it again.

The creak and rattle of the carts drew her attention. She peeked over his shoulder once more and found they had almost caught up with Tomas. Mando whistled shrilly, a signal, she supposed, for the boy to stop the carts, because gradually he slowed the horse to a walk that passed the lead team. The oxen's heads hung low and she could see they had been driven hard.

Mando called a greeting in Spanish to the young Mexican, who climbed down from his mount. Mando swung a leg over his horse's neck and slid out of the saddle. He turned to her and placed a hand on her knee while gesturing to her with the other to hurry. Libby met his gaze and raised an eyebrow at his proprietary actions. She didn't care for his attitude. He said nothing, but she saw impatience glitter in his dark eyes.

Making the best of a bad situation wasn't a skill she had practiced often, but she was learning. Libby crossed her leg over the saddle, tucking her petticoat here and there at appropriate moments, then placed her hands on his shoulders. His hands clasped her waist and he lifted her from the saddle. Trapped between the horse and Mando's unmoving body, Libby forced herself to look him in the eye.

"One day you will get into trouble looking at a man so boldly," he said.

"I'm already in trouble, Mr. Fierro."

His thumbs caressed the sensitive area beneath her ribs. "I don't think you have any notion of what trouble is, Miss Hawkins."

Libby slid her hands from his shoulders to his chest, applying pressure that did nothing to push him away. "I've been in some kind of trouble all my life. I always find a way to handle it."

Mando released her and brushed the back of one hand down the length of her hair from shoulder to midriff. "That sounds like a challenge."

Libby struggled not to reveal the sudden drop her stomach had taken at his touch. "A promise, Mr. Fierro," she replied, pleased that her voice carried most of its strength. "Simply a promise. I've always had a way of getting what I want."

He selected a long strand of hair and brushed it against her nose. "Then you will need to carefully govern your desires."

Libby jerked her hair from his hand. "Desire and necessity are essentially different issues."

Mando's gaze leapt to hers from where it had strayed along her throat. "Truly? I have not found that to be my experience. The coming days will be..." his eyelids grew heavy, his voice lower "...interesting." He turned on his heel and walked away, his spurs ringing out each step.

Libby turned and watched him disappear behind one of the carts where Tomas had conveniently stayed busy. Just once she would like to be given a chance to have the last word.

Slowly she walked to a rock several yards away and sat on its rough white surface. Peering over her shoulder, she searched the horizon for signs of riders, the hope of rescue not dead despite Mando's apparent nonchalant behavior. Only sand and brush and misshapen hills filled the wide vista of land and sky.

Poor Amelia. She must have been told of the Indian attack on the coach by now. Her sister's grief and worry burdened her heart, but she could think of nothing to do but survive. If only there was some way of letting her sister know she was alive and well.

Propping her elbows on her knees, her chin resting in the palms of her hands, Libby stared at the ground, dejected and frustrated with her efforts so far. She wasn't trying hard enough or she would come up with a way. Other than taking flight...

A flash of herself skimming over the plains, riding the wind, came to her. It was the same odd sensation she had experienced recalling the eagle. She tried to piece the two fragments together, but came up with nothing significant. She shook off the distant memories and concentrated on her present problem. The comanchero leader worried her, but her sister concerned her more. She could at least try to reason with Mando, but she could do nothing to ease her sister's pain. If she hadn't rushed off to Texas... that did little good now. She had to do something.

Her eye caught the fluttering remains of a ribboned bow that had been sewn along the bottom seam of her petticoat. Her mama would have been proud to know her stitches had held through all this turmoil. Libby's eyes misted at the thought, remembering how her mother had attached a little bow above the monogram on their undergarments to make sorting laundry easier for the three females in the family. The block letters *EMH* were still visible in the stained and dusty material.

Libby straightened, an idea coming to her. Perhaps, this once, she could have the last word after all.

She saw that Mando and Tomas were loading the kegs back into the cart and that two new mounts had been saddled. Swishing his tail, a straw feeding bag attached to his bridle, the gray didn't look too much worse for wear. Libby was relieved the horse had fared well after the forced ride to find her and carrying double on the way back. She walked to her cart, a new purpose to her step.

Mando met her at the rear and caught her arm before she climbed inside. "Here."

She slowly turned and faced him, not able to hide her surprise. He held out his canteen. Libby looked up at him, searching for answers to this enigmatic man, and found only dark secrets behind the slow simmer in his eyes. Again she was struck by a consuming curiosity about the man, a desire to discover his secrets.

Remember who he is, she told herself, remember the guns the Comanches used, remember the old driver and the young soldier screaming for death. Yes, remember when supping with the Devil, take only what your body needs and leave your soul well hidden.

She accepted the offered water, drinking only a small amount. "Thank you," she said, her voice subdued.

"Hopefully the water will last longer than the cavalry patrol." He took a quick drink himself, then attached the cap. "Take care you don't fall out again, gringa. The third time I find you won't be a charm, I promise."

"I made my choice...this time," she replied, and immediately experienced a crack in her bravado, recalling she had made two choices concerning Mando this day, though only one was known to him. It was enough she knew the other and she didn't want any qualifications attached to that one.

Mando laughed. "Ah, gringa, you may be worth all my trouble. As I have said, angels bore me."

Not liking being referred to as an amusement, especially with her last thoughts about him still fresh in her mind, Libby turned her back and stiffened at his soft laughter. Grasping one of the posts, she pulled herself onto the rough-hewn boards and jerked the canvas closed. The unmistakable ring of his spurs signaled his leave-taking and she breathed easier. She always breathed easier when he wasn't around.

She had just settled herself when the cart's wheels creaked into motion. Judging from the bumps and agitation, she guessed they had slowed somewhat from their earlier rush across the plain. However, by evening, she would probably wear more bruises from the ride than from the fall.

Libby counted to three thousand, then decided the time had come to put her next plan into action. The plan wasn't much, but even tiny pebbles made ripples that reached the shore. She took hold of the hem of her petticoat and tore out a patch, about three inches square. Her initials centered the scrap. A careful look out the back showed no sign of Mando. She wasn't surprised. Someone had to scout ahead. Again she wondered where Louis had gone, then shrugged off the thought.

Giving the material a kiss for luck, she released it and watched it fly behind them, coming to rest at last on a bush. If the cavalry followed them this far, one of the soldiers would surely see it. Some kind of report could be made to Amelia. Found along the cart's trail, her sister might guess her circumstances, but perhaps she would at least find some peace in knowing she wasn't with the Indians or dead.

Libby watched the fluttering piece of white until she could no longer see it. At least she had had the final

word. The next few days could indeed be interesting, Mr.
Fierro.

Louis put the spyglass to his eye and examined the
small group of cavalry. The horses looked in bad shape
and the men looked worse: chins dropped to their chests,
their black faces appeared white with dust and their uniforms had no color at all. The negro soldiers had been in
the field for several days of hard riding, probably since
the stage had been hit. He remembered Dos Rios had
mentioned signs of the buffalo soldiers following them.
This could be the same bunch.

He moved his glass to the beginning of the strung-out
line. A young man, this officer. An older, wiser man
would have turned back by now. Louis snapped the glass
closed. Save the world from rash young men.

His shoulders raised in a heavy sigh and he opened the
glass once more, inspecting the country in front of the
patrol. Mando had moved on out of sight. His plan was
working. The soldiers would never catch them, and surely
by nightfall the officer would consider his men and horses
more important than his next promotion.

Louis swept the glass back over the route Mando's
carts had taken, the wheel tracks plain to see through the
small magnification provided by the spyglass. Luckily the
patrol had no Tonkawa scouts with them. They wouldn't
have been so easily tricked by the dusted-out tracks of the
north-bound carts, though Louis admitted he was pretty
good at it.

Something whizzed by the small circle of his view of
prairie grass and scrub. Louis maneuvered the glass to
retrace his viewing area. He saw nothing unusual and
took the brass telescope from his eye. These past days of
chasing across the country saving damsels in distress, and

eluding the army were exacting a toll. He was starting to
see things.

He snapped the glass closed again and began to scoot
on his belly down the small hill he had used as his observation post. Before he had gone six inches, he stopped.
He was not that tired. He knew better than to leave anything to guesses, even spots before his eyes. Using his elbows, he pulled himself back to the crest, staying low
behind a bush, not depending for concealment on the
long distance between himself and the patrol he had been
watching since midmorning.

Opening the glass one more time, he slowly moved the
circle of magnification over the double tracks. Far ahead
of the patrol, he spotted the item that had caught his attention earlier. Something white. He couldn't make out
what it was, but something was definitely there. He
gauged the distance between the patrol and the mysterious object and wondered if the distance between them
was far enough. He needed to see what that bit of white
might be. Too late in the summer for anything to bloom
out here. Whatever it was, it shouldn't be there. Best to
make sure it was gone when the patrol passed it.

Louis shimmied down the hill and mounted his horse.
Taking a wide curve that kept the trail to his left and
skirting a line of broken hills, he stayed out of the patrol's sight. An oddly shaped butte marked the spot
where he needed to turn and cross the trail. The bit of
white lay in a direct line from the butte.

Riding at an easy gallop, he quickly came to the land-
mark and slowed his horse, rounding the base at a trot.
Before actually showing himself, he dismounted and,
with the glass to his eye, scouted the trail. The cavalrymen kept to their dogged pace far behind. Still it would
be close and they couldn't miss his trail crossing the

tracks. Louis shrugged his wide shoulders. Even if they should chase him, how far could their exhausted mounts take them? He could even hasten their turning back. Shifting the glass to the reason for this risky operation, Louis saw that it was a tattered bit of material hung up on a bush.

His suspicions alerted, he remounted and rode from behind the concealing hill, swiftly crossing the twenty yards or so to the trail and snatching up the white cloth. Clutching it in his hand, he dug his heels into his horse's flanks and made for more high ground, where he had the advantage of a wide view of the area. He decided on a pile of large boulders and rocks that lay ahead of the tracks, but at a safe distance from the trail.

With a sharp eye for anyone following him, he arrived at his destination without seeing any sign of pursuit. He found he was relieved. A more rigorous game of hide-and-seek didn't appeal to him after all. Perhaps he was getting old, as Mando had accused.

Too old for these contretemps. He wished the young hothead would stop this trading and find another way to finance his interests in Santa Fe. But Mando would listen to no one, not him, not even his cousin Ramon, a man of learning, a lawyer... his lawyer.

Louis shook his head. No, this business would be the end of the Fierro line. Mando knew this also, yet he refused to search for other means to fight his title disputes, preferring to exact some kind of revenge on the Anglos. Now this girl had entered his schemes.

Louis swung down from the saddle and sat on a rock. He smoothed the square over his thigh, his fingers encountering the stitched initials before his eyes picked them out. Holding the tattered patch up to the sunlight, he read "EMH." Elizabeth Margaret Hawkins.

Merde, the minx had come close. Another few miles and the soldiers would have found this. No doubt they knew of the missing woman from the stage and they knew they followed a band of comancheros now. The connection to the wheel tracks would not be missed.

Louis sat forward, holding the flimsy scrap of hope between two fingers, resting his elbows on his knees. Many different chains of events occurred to him had the soldiers found the message Libby had left them. All of them ended badly for Mando but good for the girl.

She was very smart, that one. And pretty, too. Not soft cream and muted pinks in the way of most women. All reds and golds and bright blue green, she was like a ray of sunlight breaking through the clouds at sunset or a rainbow after a storm. He liked this girl, even . . .

No, only heartbreak for all lay in that direction. He was her friend and he would be satisfied with that.

He looked at the bit of muslin fluttering in the wind between his fingers. It would be easy to let it go and allow fate to take its course, but he could not do that. Either he would leave the message where he had found it or destroy it.

"So, Aramis," he addressed his horse. "Should I pretend I never saw this and let Mando pay his piper?" The horse merely turned his head, looking at his master with sad brown eyes.

"You don't know either, I see. Ah, well." He sighed and stuffed the scrap of petticoat into his saddlebag. "That damned piper is waiting with his hand out to all of us."

Chapter Ten

❦

The moon was no more than a dim opalescence tucked among the folds of the black gossamer sky, and the stars not seen at all. Thick veils of clouds had gathered on the horizon at sunset, spilling across the sky, prompting Mando to camp below a high bluff. Libby had overheard something about caves located nearby in case shelter was needed.

For now, they sat in the open by the carts, and Libby hoped they stayed there. Dark, earthy enclosures held a special terror for her. She didn't remember falling down a well as a child, but somewhere inside her the terror lay hidden. After she had grown too big to carry, she had refused to follow the family down the stairs into the cellar on stormy nights.

The wind frisked about them, carrying the scent of faraway places and rain and a whiff of tobacco. Brief flashes of sheet lightning gave faces to the two figures sitting across from her, one lounging on his side, the other huddled beneath the split blanket he wore.

Occasionally the bright glowing end of a cigar cast its faint illumination against Mando's stark features, but Libby did her best to avoid viewing those disturbing images. They fit too perfectly with her own unsettling musings of the morning.

The day had been long and hot, with nothing to do but brace herself against the worst bumps and fret about Mando's plans, Mando's moods, Mando's beautiful dangerous eyes. Like the storm clouds, their languorous heat had swept into her thoughts, bringing dark stirrings and a promise of dangerous power. Tonight, she sought shelter in silence.

A fire had not been laid, and dinner had been more of what she had eaten all day—jerky, dried fruits and the flat bread she had learned was called *panoche*. They had each drunk a cup of water. Libby couldn't help but wonder how their supply had been shortened by the loss of her canteen, yet neither Tomas nor Mando had mentioned the smaller ration. She almost wished they had. She could use a bolstering of her defenses, and there was nothing like snarls, curses and accusations to do the job.

"Do you think the soldiers have turned back?" Tomas asked, his voice cracking a little toward the last.

The boy had tried to peer through the layers of pitch black surrounding them more times than she, and her neck had a crick in it from craning. She listened carefully to Mando's answer.

"Louis would have ridden in if they had," Mando replied.

Startled to hear of the Frenchman, Libby asked, "Louis will be out in this storm alone?"

A shimmer of lightning illuminated Mando's considering gaze. A roll of thunder passed before he answered. "Such concern, gringa, for a what? A disciple of the Devil, I believe was the phrase."

Called out on the very contradictions that preyed on her peace of mind, she wished she had kept her mouth closed, but she hadn't, so she might as well continue. "Louis has been kind to me. Certainly I'm concerned about him."

The cigar glowed brightly against his face, his lazy perusal of her disappearing in a cloud of smoke, then darkness. "Ah, some disciples are not as damned as others?"

Libby slipped a look at Tomas, who shifted uncomfortably, combing his hand through his longish hair in a gesture that mimicked Mando's. His smooth features remained hidden in the darkness, but she knew he must be disturbed by all this talk of devils and disciples. She certainly was.

She sought a change of subject, to spare the boy, of course, but she was reluctant to try again. If only Mando wouldn't stare at her so. Everything had been quiet until she had mentioned Louis.

"The Comanches will expect the Spirit Woman to walk on a night like this," Tomas said.

Libby wasn't sure what Tomas was talking about, but she was relieved he had taken the conversation on a different course. They could talk about something safe.

"A Spirit Woman? That sounds like an interesting story," she commented, doing her part to distract Mando from unpleasant subjects.

"I thought so, too," Mando replied.

"Then tell me about her."

Tomas broke into laughter. "Gringa, you are the Spirit Woman."

"Please, Tomas, address me as Libby," she said, weary of being referred to as someone without a name. "Now what were you saying?"

"Tomas said you are the Spirit Woman," Mando explained. "You left quite an impression on that band of Comanches."

Libby hugged her knees. "They left one on me as well."

"They have given you magical powers." Mando drew on his cigar, allowing the smoke to drift from his mouth. "Even evil powers."

Libby straightened. "Evil powers? Me?"

"Oh, yes," Mando continued. "You wore the sign of the crow—"

"My raven's-wing hat."

"And you stabbed them with the deadly arrow of the *nenuhpee*."

"My hat pin? I was so frightened, I don't really remember everything. What kind of arrow, from who?"

"The *nenuhpee*, the Little People. Very evil spirits."

"I see." But she didn't. She had been wild with fright and anger. Never had she lost control so completely.

"I suppose it depends on which side of the hat pin a person finds oneself when judging the evil of others."

This conversation had taken a sudden twist that left her feeling a little off balance. She paused to regain her bearings. If he was trying to imply his activities might be acceptable to some while abhorrent to others, he was wasting his breath. No one could excuse selling guns to wild Indians. She refused to hear more about it.

"I'll be turning in now." She rose to her feet with the help of the gnarled hub of the wheel behind her.

"Bring your blankets out here," Mando said.

Libby froze. "I would really rather not. With the inclement weather—"

"That scrap of canvas will do little good in a blowup like this. Tomas, cut the ropes—"

"I'm sure the canvas will do fine. I'll be out of the mud and if it leaks a little—"

"You don't understand...Libby. You won't be sleeping in the cart anymore. I don't trust you."

She turned and faced him, relieved the darkness hid her surprise. "From one night to the next?"

"From one fall to the next."

"But I said that—"

"You said you had made your choice...this time. How do I know when you will choose to do something even more foolish, endangering not only yourself, but all of us?"

"I'm not a child, Mr. Fierro. Until this morning I had no idea what your plans were for me except that you refused to take me to Santa Angela, then I hear that I'm a loose end in your nefarious enterprises. I did nothing you yourself wouldn't have done, given the same circumstances."

"Exactly." Mando rose to his feet and walked toward her. A flash of lightning revealed he was smiling. A big smile that only needed a cutlass between his teeth to complete the look of a pirate. With that red scarf brandished around his head and his chest only partially covered with the black leather vest and a belt of cartridges, he could have sailed into New Orleans with Jean Lafitte...not a comforting thought. Libby backed against the wheel in spite of her determination to hold steady against his domineering tactics.

He came to stand practically on her toes. "Only I would have done more." Propping a hand on the wheel rim next to her shoulder, he leaned closer. "I will have to keep a closer watch on you."

Libby braced her hands against the soft leather of his vest and pushed with all the renewed determination she could muster, slipping from between him and the wheel. "Not that closely, Mr. Fierro."

"As close as you make me," he replied.

A long roll of thunder slid along the heavens toward them. He raised his head and listened, then gave her a glance as he turned. "Get your blankets, Libby." Striding toward the horses, he called out instructions to Tomas in rapid Spanish.

Libby carried her reluctance bravely to the end of the cart, his use of her name making the burden slightly lighter. She had made progress of some sort anyway. Leaning inside, she explored the rough boards until her hands contacted the tightly rolled bundle of wool blankets.

She heard the ropes securing the canvas cut in quick thumps, then the covering slipped from the top with the freshened breeze that cooled her flushed cheeks. Thunder clapped, no longer muttering, and lightning zigzagged its brilliance across the sky. They were in for a storm. She supposed shelter of some kind could be found under the carts.

Holding the blankets close to her, Libby proceeded around the cart and, in the short flashes of lightning, she saw Mando tying the four horses to a picket line strung under a deep overhang located along a curve of the bluff. Tomas was tying hobbles to the oxen. Libby looked about her for something to do, but she had no idea what needed attention.

Useless, dependent and controlled, she found herself trapped in the very fate she had come west to escape, only the conditions were worse and the man in charge was more autocratic than her father ever had been, or any husband she could imagine herself marrying. It occurred to her that life was nothing more than a drawn-out joke, only she wasn't laughing.

What a terrible mess her bid for independence had turned out to be. She had been forced to kill two men, fought off Indians, almost drowned, baked under the sun and . . .

The words to describe her present situation failed her. She hadn't been abducted; she had been rescued, but she couldn't go to her sister until it pleased *him*.

She glared at Mando's broad muscular back as he gathered some articles from the other cart, placing them in the gunnysack she had used earlier. She didn't care to speculate on what might pass between now and whenever his pleasure dictated she return to Santa Angela.

Why couldn't anything turn out as well for her as it always did for Amelia? She didn't begrudge her sister, but just once she wished her plans enjoyed the successes Amelia's did.

She shrugged off the old hurt with a lift of her shoulders and a tilt of her chin. The Comanches, the flood and the sun had not bested her, and neither would Mando Fierro.

Dancing to his tune wasn't easy, but she would watch for her chance, and one day she would whirl away to her own music.

"Tomas," Mando called to the boy who was trotting toward him. "Take the lids off those empty kegs."

The young Mexican nodded and veered toward the second cart. Mando glanced skyward and shook his head. They probably wouldn't need the extra water now. Every arroyo and buffalo wallow on the Llano would be filled with water and the creek beds would run high. The soldiers would now have plenty of water to follow them if they could pick up their tracks again. *Por Dios,* why did it have to rain?

Surveying the carts and thinking of what else could be done, his gaze fell upon Libby, and the coming storm faded to splashes of light and grumbling skies. She stood with feet firmly planted, her shoulders squared and head held high, her hair a blaze of color in the black-and-white night. A woman like that could take on a storm and win.

She had done so before, he reminded himself. Her eyes settled on him, appearing more green tonight, and he saw defiance flash in them as quick and intense as the lightning. He wondered at the jolt of pleasure that shot through him. He needed more trouble like he needed tonight's rain.

Thunder crashed overhead and the heavens split in a blinding crack that raced across the sky. Mando slung the heavy gunnysack over his shoulder. Time to go to the caves. He covered the distance between the two carts quickly and tugged on Tomas's pants leg until the boy looked down at him.

"Go," he shouted, and pointed his thumb toward the bluffs.

Tomas jerked a nod and jumped down from the cart. He gave a passing glance to the woman before racing toward the high ground, stopping only to grab up saddle-bags and their two sombreros. Mando watched his progress up the rocks until he disappeared into one of the dark chasms scattered over the rocky embankment, then turned to Libby.

"We have to go." With a wave of his free hand, he gestured for her to follow him. She didn't move. "This is no time for your stubbornness. I can hear the rain. *Andele.*" Again he hooked his hand in her direction.

Staring at the rocks behind him, she shook her head slowly. Cursing under his breath, he stalked toward her. She didn't bother to look at him.

He gave her arm a shake. "Did you hear me? We have to go. This storm is about to crash down on our heads."

Her gaze flew to his. He saw something in her eyes he had never seen before. Fear. Of what? Not the storm. She hadn't looked frightened at all a few moments earlier.

"Please . . ." she said, the bluff drawing her attention again. "I . . . I could get under one of the carts, or—"

Mando pulled the sack from his shoulder and, grasping it in his fist, swept her up into his arms. "You are being ridiculous," he said, walking briskly toward the sheltering caves.

He had no time to calm her fears or argue with her. Once in the cave and safety, she could do her worst. The prospect might prove entertaining.

"Let go," she railed. "Put me down. Storms don't frighten me. I want to stay out here. You have no right to force me into one—"

"*Madre de Dios,* you are a troublesome woman," he muttered, cutting off her rantings. "This storm has hail in it. I can smell it. We'll be lucky if it's only hail. Now be quiet."

He halted at the base of the bluff and set her on her feet. Pointing to a gaping hole in the wall above them and to the right, he said. "That's where we're headed. Now move."

She shook her head. "I can't. I'm going back to the carts."

He grabbed her arm before she took one step. "You can't? I'll be right behind you. You won't fall."

"You don't understand. I can't, I tell you. I can't."

He heard the panic in her voice now. High and breathless, she sounded as if she were about to lose control. He didn't understand what was happening to her, but he didn't need to. Bending slightly, Mando wrapped an arm around her thighs and hefted her to his shoulder. He climbed from boulder to boulder, her cries of "I can't, I can't" trailing behind them.

At the mouth of the cave, he threw the sack of supplies inside the opening and lowered her to her feet, this time keeping both hands on her shoulders. She still clung to the roll of blankets, her eyes round and frantic. Big, single drops of rain whacked against the rocks and dirt, splattering against his face and hers. She didn't seem to notice. He pushed her toward the entrance, but she dug in her heels, resisting with all the strength she possessed.

He lowered his face to hers. "What's wrong with you? It's starting to rain."

Her eyes rolled toward the black recess in the rocks. "I don't care." She shook her head. "I don't," she repeated, her voice fading. "I don't," she whispered.

A sudden protectiveness welled inside him at her distress. He wasn't certain what to do. Obviously the cave frightened her past reasoning, but he had to try.

"We have to go inside, Libby," he said gently. "I've seen hailstones the size of oranges fall from storms like this. You could be killed. There are no wild animals. Tomas and I checked them out before dark. We'll be safe, I promise."

She looked up at him, tears trailing down her cheeks mixing with the random drops of rain. "Please..."

Mando heard a plea for help in the single word and pulled her to him, pressing her head against his chest. His hand brushed over her eyes. "Close your eyes, Libby," he said in a quiet voice. "Trust me."

Her lashes tickled against his palm as her eyes closed, yet her breathing remained rapid and shallow. Taking her up in his arms again, he gave her a moment, then slowly entered the cave, thankful he didn't have to duck very low. Inside, bursts of lightning lit the walls, giving bright though brief views of the interior. The floor consisted of sand and pebbles while the walls were stone and hard-packed earth that tapered high above him to a narrow crevasse. Indian paintings trailed along one wall.

Mando picked a place to settle under the primitive art, not wanting Libby to see the faint drawings upon opening her eyes. At this point, he didn't know what might put her over the edge. Dropping to his knees, he placed her next to the wall.

She folded her legs to her chest, her hands gripped into tight fists upon her knees, her eyes squeezed shut. He watched her in the infrequent light, wondering what he could do for her, hoping the hard, fast breathing would slow. Softly he touched her shoulder. "Libby, we're safe and dry."

Her eyes flew open and darted about the small cavern. "I can't breathe," she said between breaths. "I... can't...breathe."

Mando swiftly moved to her other side, allowing the eddies of air that swirled in from the entrance to flow over her. He circled his arm around her shoulders.

"Yes, you can," he said, his tone firm and unyielding. "You can breathe."

She shook her head from side to side, each breath jerking from her throat. Mando slid his arm beneath her knees, ready to lift her once more. Suddenly a curtain of rain dropped from the sky, canceling his plan to take her outside. Icy shards of pea-sized hail tumbled down with the rain. He could not take her from the cave, but he had to do something.

On the edge of desperation, Mando took her face in his hand, grasping her jaw tightly. "Libby," he shouted above the din. "Libby."

At last he received a response. Her eyes blinked and she focused on him. He dropped his hand from her jaw to her shoulder. "Libby, feel the air against your face. Now take a deep breath."

Her eyes rolled to the entrance, then back to him. He shook her. "Breathe!" he shouted.

She took a gulping, hesitant breath.

"Breathe with me." He pulled in a deep breath, then let it out, repeating the procedure over and over until his head felt light and Libby gauged her breathing to his.

"Now turn your face toward the rain." He deliberately avoided using the word *entrance*. "Feel that fine, clean air. Doesn't it smell good?"

She closed her eyes, taking the deep breaths he had coaxed from her. Mando collapsed beside her, resting his arms over his bent knees. Never had he been more aware of the push and shove it took to move air in and out of his body. With a tired sigh, he tugged the scarf from his head, then lifted the bandolier from his shoulder, tossing both to the side. He quickly dispensed with his spurs, adding them to his other possessions.

A glance at Libby assured him she had relaxed her hands and leaned against the rough wall, her breathing calmer, her eyes remaining closed, her troubled brow the only reminder of her struggle against panic.

He looked beyond her tense features to the opening, hoping this would be a short stay. The rain fell in a solid gray curtain, briefly charged by lightning into a swaying, shimmering gauze. The hail had stopped, but experience told him more could be hurled from the clouds at any moment. They would have to stay here all night.

His gaze fell once more on Libby. He found her eyes open, watching him, desperation a shadow below the blue-green depths. A true *valiente,* he thought, in the face of terrible dangers that threatened her very life. He pushed strands of hair from her face. But she was terrorized by this small cave that gave her nothing but shelter.

Fears were secrets all carried within them, unexplainable and private. He had joined her on that dark path through her nightmares, and he felt as though he had shared something more intimate than making love to her, an intimacy that left him uneasy.

"Feeling better?" he asked, only to make her talk, to vocalize, to take one more step from the black void.

Her gaze had fastened on him. "Maybe."

He saw a shiver run through her. "How about a blanket?"

She paused as if processing his words, then nodded slightly. "Yes."

Mando leaned to his left and grabbed up the blankets he had thrown inside earlier. He shook one out and spread it over her, tucking it in around her shoulders. Her eyes followed his face, and he realized she had focused on him rather than think of her surroundings.

His uneasiness grew into hesitation. He wanted to wrap her in his arms and provide her a safe haven for the night, but that need in her eyes stopped him cold. Entanglements and complications did not fit in with his plans for this *americano.* In those magical, bewitching eyes he saw a future he was determined to avoid.

"Damn the future," he murmured, his voice unheard above the rain, and gathered her into his arms. No resistance met his touch. He hadn't expected any, so fragile she seemed. Turning slightly toward the rain, he made certain she faced the cool air that drifted through the entrance, then settled her against his chest.

"Sleep, Libby," he said against her ear. "Your dreams are safe with me."

For tonight.

Chapter Eleven

Libby closed her eyes as bidden, Mando's promise of safe dreams whispering to her through the frenzy of her thoughts, until only his soothing voice was heard. Tension seeped from her muscles and she relaxed against the warm strength Mando offered, his embrace a shield against the crushing effect of the cave's walls.

From deep inside, a quiet, insistent voice told her trusting him was folly, but she ignored it, too grateful to be free of the stark terror that had seized her. Instead, she matched her breathing to the steady trickle of his breath against her scalp, her heart slowing to the strong beat of his against her back.

Mando's warmth, his scent, his strength surrounded her, holding the smothering walls at bay. An occasional flurry of mist cooled her face, a reassuring reminder of the open country beyond the cave. The steady drumming of the rain lulled her toward sleep, but her inner voice refused to remain silent, telling her to beware, her dreams would never be safe with Mando.

She stirred restlessly, fighting the languor spreading through her limbs like warm honey. Mando spoke into her ear, the deep resonance of his voice overpowering the fervent whispers of her doubts. He told of mountains that captured the sunset, valleys filled with pine and quiet pastures where sheep grazed peacefully. Home. His home. A wondrous place of warm days and celebrations that lasted all night. Gradually the drumming of the downpour and the rumble of thunder faded into a sleep filled with the rush of wind against her face and dreams of an eagle.

Libby woke with a start, a sudden sense of loss her first sensation. Disoriented, she sat up and frantically searched the darkness until she saw the dark silhouette standing just inside the cave, looking out into the rainy night. A small sigh escaped her lips, then a frown pulled at her brow. Finding herself alone in a cave with Mando should hardly bring her comfort, yet she couldn't deny that brief moment of relief when she first saw him.

What was happening to her? A calmness she hardly expected silenced her lifelong fear of close, earthy enclosures. Mando had been forced to push her to the limit and stayed to hold her when she fell. She couldn't forget that—not ever. Something had happened between them, something too personal to examine.

Libby remained very still, watching him watch the rain. Softer now, the earlier deluge had tamed to a gentle shower. His hair, dampened by swirls of mist, clung to his forehead and shoulders. He should have looked unkempt and raffish with such long hair, but he didn't. The long, silken black mane gave him an unfettered appeal, that of a man free from society's restrictions.

Libby drew her hair over her shoulder, her fingers running through its heavy mass. She had wanted to bob her waist-length tresses, and now she was glad Papa hadn't forbidden her; for she knew she would have cut it if he had. She remembered Mando's fingers touching her hair, her breast beneath it, and dropped her hand to her lap.

Mando Fierro had been nothing like she had expected from the first moment she had seen him. A devil, a life-saver; a taunter, a provider; a seducer, a savior. He had been all of those. She had asked him once who he was. She wanted to know—needed to know.

Caution held her back for a moment, but its bonds had never been strong. She cleared her throat. His only response was a hand combing through his hair. Something was on his mind. Libby rose to her feet, shaking the sand out of her petticoat. Taking one hesitant step then another, she took a position on the opposite side of the entrance and stared at the rain, her fingers worrying the ends of her sash.

He remained silent.

She thought of saying thank you, but shied away from bringing up the experience they had shared. Too many new feelings and sensations were attached to their earlier hours in the cave. She wanted to ask about Louis, but his reaction to her interest in the Frenchman's welfare earlier that evening hadn't exactly been favorable. She hoped to strike a relaxed mood, one in which Mando might prove informative. She recalled the scenes he had described so beautifully as she had fallen asleep.

"Your home sounds like a lovely place."

Mando leaned his shoulder against the wall, his gaze still lost in the rain. "I was thinking of it just now."

"You must miss your... your family." Libby began unraveling threads from her sash and picturing a dark-eyed beauty with a stair-stepped brood, all of whom possessed their father's good looks.

"I do, but there is no one left to miss me."

The family portrait vanished, leaving a suspicious residue of relief. Libby brushed it away with the sadness of her own recent loss.

"I'm sorry," she said. "I . . . I just lost my parents in an accident, though I still have my sister."

"I had a brother—not of my parents' blood, but still we were raised together and very close. He was a brother and a friend."

Libby wondered at the edge entering Mando's voice. She supposed this brother's loss was very painful. "My sister and I were never friends, really. We had our problems. Still, to lose her, too . . . I'm very sorry your brother di—"

"He didn't die, Libby. He took up with a woman in Texas who hates my guts, so he is dead to me."

Libby turned to face the anger and bitterness so evident in his statement. He had helped her through a bad time, perhaps she could help him. "Sometimes family disagreements can be worked out," she began. "I imagine she disapproves of your trading with the Indians. If you gave up this gunrun—"

"Enough!" Mando turned to her and his voice grew as quiet and menacing as a whip lashing through the air. "He made his choice and I have made mine." He turned his shoulder to her.

Libby rolled the sash into a tight roll. "I didn't mean to pry. I just . . ." Her words trailed off into the soft hiss of the rain. Finding the long silence that followed uncomfortable, Libby settled on the banal for conversation. Anything to break this tension.

"Now we'll have plenty of water," she remarked, gazing out at the steady rain.

Mando folded his arms. "Yes, and so will they."

She glanced at him. "The soldiers, you mean."

He nodded. "We'll have to leave the carts here and let the oxen go free. Can you ride bareback?"

Libby dropped the sash and smoothed it down the long shirttail. "I learned quickly several nights ago."

Mando turned her way, resting his back against the wall. "So you did. We'll do the best we can to make you more comfortable than the Comanches did."

Libby studied his shadowed features, his change of moods a constant surprise. "I don't understand you, Mando. You've been, well, kind to me...rude, almost belligerent at times, but considerate, too."

Libby caught the lift of his chin.

"What did you expect?" he asked. "Rape?"

The candid question caught her off guard. "Well... I..." Oh, stop behaving like a silly schoolgirl. "Yes, I did," she answered as bluntly as he had asked. "Once I knew who you were...what you do," she went on to explain.

"And now?"

Libby turned and regarded the night. Uncomfortable with the subject, she hesitated to answer. Then she grew impatient with herself. She had started this discussion, and she would continue it through to the end.

Choosing her words carefully, she said, "If you had wanted to commit some type of violence upon my person, you would have done so by now."

"You sound very sure of yourself."

"Perhaps I am becoming more sure of you."

"Ah, Libby, you are such an *inocente*."

"I don't think so, Mando. You're different from the others."

"You mean I am no longer the Devil?"

She faced him, wishing she could see that crooked smile of his so she might judge his frame of mind. "I don't know what you are anymore. You've the manners of a gentleman when you choose to use them, and I'll wager you've an education, too.''

Hesitating only a moment, she plunged ahead. ''Why do you trade with those murdering savages?''

''Because, my sweet, I am no different than they. When fighting to keep your land, to preserve your very way of life, savagery comes easily.''

Detecting the intended insult to her own people's pioneering spirit, Libby struck back. ''I suppose you and your men ride under profit's noble banner.''

Libby stiffened as Mando stepped toward her, closing the gap between them. She tried to slide away, but he took hold of her hair and pulled her closer, her head tilting back so that her lips trembled just beneath his. ''Your mouth is as bold as your eyes ... gringa.'' He emphasized the last word. ''I know of one way to shut it, a very pleasant way. If your face was not so dirty, I would show you.'' Abruptly he released her.

She sagged against the wall, one hand braced behind her, the other going to her face. Sand crumbled beneath her fingers from the roughened film of caked plant juice. Embarrassment warred with outrage. Coherent words refused to form. Her mouth opened then closed, and she discovered, for the first time in her life, she couldn't think of a thing to say.

She fumbled for words in earnest as he whipped off his vest and threw it inside the cave. ''Wh ... wh ... what?'' was all she managed.

''What am I doing?'' Mando finished for her. He sat down and tugged off his boots, then stood and began unbuttoning his pants. ''You will discover that soon enough.''

Libby couldn't believe this was happening. After he had been so gentle, so helpful. She had thought... That was foolishness, but this was frightening.

"Don't touch me," she declared.

"Why would I want to, gringa? You should join me outside," Mando added. "The cleaning would do you good."

Libby sidestepped back inside the cave, presenting her back to Mando. Never had she been so humiliated, but she should be relieved. Oh, she didn't know how she should feel anymore.

His implications were plain enough. She smelled and she had no doubts he was correct. But she absolutely refused to cavort in the rain naked. She heard the slide of his pants over his legs and soon they, too, joined his clothes inside the cave.

Naked. Mando Fierro was completely naked.

She remembered that morning when water had trailed over his muscled torso. Now he stood out in the elements as naked as Adam. Well, she was no Eve.

Libby found her place on the blankets, carefully keeping her back to the entrance. The interior of the cave was dark and damp smelling, the rear closed off less than four feet from her. If she was forced to remain seated in such a way that she couldn't see the entrance, she might invite a return of the panic she had suffered earlier.

For her own health, she really must turn around. She would keep her eyes closed, of course. The air hitting her face would suffice in keeping back that awful smothered feeling.

Slowly she rotated in her seated position, keeping her eyes tightly closed. She listened carefully for movements of any kind, but heard nothing other than the rain and a drip in the back of the cave. He might have fallen, or he might be sneaking up on her at this very moment.

Libby opened her eyes and beheld a sight she knew she would never forget. Mando stood just outside on the narrow ledge in front of the cave, with his face turned upward, receiving the rain like a benediction from above.

The dim light gave him a shadowed effect, but his outline was plain through the rain that hung about him like a shimmering diaphanous curtain. Libby told herself to look away, but she didn't listen. She couldn't. He was beautiful and perfect. His legs, long and stalwart, were spread, his buttocks rounded, his waist narrow but banded with muscle. Her gaze traveled up to his shoulders, to his long hair slicked in a dark wedge to his shoulder blades, and she wished she had the guts to shuck her clothes and join him.

She felt so sticky and dirty and, yes, smelly. She would give almost anything to be clean. Anything but to stand outside buck naked with Mando Fierro. At last, she looked away, too envious of his lack of inhibitions, too terrified of where her thoughts were taking her. This man had made her a coward where wild Comanches bent on murder could not, where a rampaging river had failed.

She lowered her head to her bent knees, her arms wrapped around her legs. She listened to the soft melody of the rain and imagined how it would feel to have the drops pelt her body with their gentle touch.

How must it feel to him?

Mando stood with his feet planted in the oozing mud, his face lifted to the downpour, every pore and nerve in his body reveling in the soft lashing of tiny droplets. *Dios mio,* what a night!

The gentle stimulation of the rain washed away the dirt, sweat and weariness of days on the trail, but it did little to ease the tension inside him. He had faced down a posse of drunken *tejanos* and not had his guts twisted like this. And all because of a small, sunburned, red-haired woman.

Last spring, he had seen what the beautiful, entreating eyes of a woman could do to a man, but he wasn't Ross. No woman would make him forget his duty to hold his land, no matter how magical her eyes, how bright her beauty, how bold her spirit.

Mando raised his arms to the heavens, the rain pouring over his body, blocking all sensation but the cool shower on his skin, surrounding him in its quiet rush. Reaching deep inside himself, he gathered all the injustices done to his people, all the years given to fighting the Anglo advance, all the loved ones lost to the battle, all the years ahead that would be stolen from him. Stone by stone he repaired his defenses the gringa had somehow managed to breach. He returned to the pleasures of the moment, the only pleasures available to him.

He shook his head, his hair fanning water in all directions. Had anything ever felt this good but a strong, willing woman beneath him?

"Gringa, you don't know what you are missing." He shook his head from side to side, rubbing his hands over his wet chest, laughing aloud at his private joke.

"If you haven't the courtesy to use my name, don't address me at all," came her voice through the rain.

His arms dropped and he whirled around to face the interior. "Courtesy! What do you know of the word? Perhaps you refer to *americano* courtesy. The kind that says it is permissible to dine at my table, then insult me," he shouted back.

"El Aguila," Tomas called, leaning out of his own small shelter in the rocks. "I heard shouting. Do you need help?"

Mando rubbed his hands over his face and through his hair. He was beginning to think he might, but he reassured Tomas. "No, go back inside."

He decided he would do the same. The gringa had grown much too bold and difficult to handle. He must correct her misconceptions of him right now, before more trouble developed. He must show her where she belonged within the scheme of things.

Entering the cave, he found Libby huddled on the floor, her face hidden in her arms that were folded upon her drawn-up knees. She had looked just this way only a few hours earlier, frightened and dependent on him. He had only himself to blame for her asking questions, issuing insults and making demands. He had learned his lesson and so would she.

Grabbing up a blanket, he gave himself a vigorous drying. The woman remained so still and quiet she could have been a rock. "You should have joined me in the rain."

She refused to answer.

He wondered if the panic had taken her again. "Are you feeling—"

"I'm feeling fine, Mr. Fierro, thanks to your help, but I will feel better when you put on your clothes," she replied, her voice muffled. "I have something I want to tell you."

He was supposed to be telling her how much trouble she had caused him, how much she had cost him, where her place was to be. Pulling on his trousers and fastening the buttons, he considered leaving her at Fort Union once they reached New Mexico. He was beginning to wonder how entertaining the winter would be with such a woman. Another woman might do, but she wouldn't be the Spirit Woman and she wouldn't be sister to that blue-eyed beauty who had anchored Ross to Texas.

Anger gripped him as it always did whenever his thoughts strayed to Ross. He used it. He stoked it with memories of the good life his father had given Ross, of his father's murder by Anglo hunters bent on killing Mexicans, as well as buffalo, of Ross's new family among the damned Texans, where prosperity flowed unhampered except when the Comanches siphoned a little his way.

He gloried in the bitter anger, in the release it gave him to ride the plains, free to plunder and use whatever he found, for that was the only way he could keep the woman.

He touched her hair and smiled when she stiffened. The time would come when she would welcome his touch. What pleased him most was he had touched her and the only emotion to stir him was lust. He thought of taking her now but he found he had no desire for a frightened, unwilling woman. Hardly a partner for El Aguila.

"I am . . ." he smiled again at the English word he was about to use ". . . decent now."

She looked up at him. "I owe you an apology."

Feeling a stone or two of his defenses loosening, he deliberately gave his tone an abruptness. "What? Another surprise for me tonight?"

She paused a moment, then said, "Obviously we have vastly different views on your...occupation. But you are right. You have saved my life, given me food and shelter, and helped me through this terrible time tonight. I was ungracious. I will keep my opinions to myself."

Mando turned away from her. "Somehow, Libby, I don't think you will, but I will accept your apology on one condition."

"What's that?"

"Do not try to understand me. I neither need nor desire understanding." He turned to face her then, squatting down beside her. He pulled his shirt and jacket from the gunnysack. "You do not want to know me."

She studied him a moment before answering. "And if I do?"

She was curious about him, and for his purposes, that was all he wanted. A curious woman was a woman almost won. "You will learn to accept what is given."

"As you do?" she asked.

"No, Libby, I take what I want and that is the last warning I will give you."

He stood and walked to the entrance, finding his boots nearby. Pouring sand from one, he pulled it on and began the process with the other.

"Warning taken," she answered, her voice but a whisper above the dwindling rain.

"Bueno." He jerked the other boot on. "Now come over here. I have something to show you."

She hesitated and he understood why. "Don't misunderstand what I said before. I take my pleasures where I find them, but I would find little pleasure in forcing a woman, especially a woman in need of a bath."

"How very gentlemanly of you."

Mando smiled at the renewed verve in her voice. "Now that you are satisfied your virtue is safe, come here."

She took her time about it, testing his patience to the limit, but finally stood beside him.

"The rain is slowing. I think I can see a bit of dawn showing beneath the clouds," Libby said.

"I told you before we would have to leave the carts. They will be too slow now that the cavalry patrol will have plenty of water to follow us all the way to New Mexico if they choose."

He looked down at her. "Don't get your hopes up. Louis will tell me where they are at all times. Once in New Mexico we will simply melt away."

"I still don't understand—"

"It may be hard to believe, but you'll be safer with me. There are those who—"

"Yes, I remember Cabot and his belief that I'll turn you all in, but I see no resolution for that problem."

He didn't either at the moment, but something would occur to him. While at the rancho, she would be perfectly safe. It was a fortress, and later in the spring, who knew what might develop? Cabot and Doyle could be silenced one way or another and Mathias Wright could be reasoned with as long as she never discovered Wright was his business partner. He saw no reason she should learn of their arrangement.

"Let's concentrate on one problem at a time. Now that you will be riding, I will have Tomas give you a pair of pants. You will need a hat, perhaps his *serape*. If we run into more Indians, you will remain silent."

"More Indians?"

He heard the tremble in her voice. "Fortunately for you, New Mexicans have no quarrel with the Comanches. The others." He shrugged. "I am known among most of the tribes."

"Yes, I'm sure you are. How lucky for me to have run into a man who . . ." A long sigh followed. "When do we leave?"

Mando looked down at her, admiring her pretty, turned-up nose lifted so resolutely by her high ideals and low estimation of him. His eyes traveled over the rest of her, imagining her cleaned up, recovered from her ordeal, in a saucy red skirt twirling around her ankles. Abruptly his musings came to a halt, his eyes narrowing suspiciously on her torn hem. "What happened to your petticoat?"

Chapter Twelve

Libby glanced at Tomas, riding at her side and very watchful. Any other attempts to leave signs of her presence on the plains would be impossible and perhaps unneeded. Louis had not been seen all day.

She wasn't protesting much about anything that day. Not the fast pace, the lack of stops, the noon meal eaten in the saddle. The search for the missing piece of petticoat had taken quite some time and a lot of fast talking on her part. She wasn't sure how convincing her story of snagging her hem and saving the scrap to use as a washcloth had been. Mando was still suspicious.

Luckily the storm had tossed around everything left in the camp, giving her story some veracity. The possibility the cavalry patrol could be closing behind them forced Mando to finally give up searching for it, and they had broken camp.

Libby switched her reins to her left hand and edged her right hand beneath the too-large hat. She dug her fingers through her damp pile of hair jammed beneath it. My, but the sun was hot and she would love to lift the hat for just a moment and let the wind blow through her hair.

She didn't dare do it, not after Mando had explained how valued red hair was on the end of a scalp pole. He had been very explicit in his explanations, closing with a parting shot about her particular shade of red being visible for a twenty-mile radius.

An exaggeration, surely, even in this flat country. However, he had made his point, one she was familiar with. The inappropriate color of her hair.

All her life comments had been made about its unlikely color, how it was more suited to a woman of questionable employment. She remembered one particularly opinionated biddy at church who had suggested to her mother that she find some way to tone it down. Her mother had hustled her away but afterward had taken to making her wear awful, dull hats instead of perky bows like Amelia wore in her more acceptable chestnut hair.

Here she was, wearing another hat to cover her hair, but, on this occasion, she was happy to have it. Still, as soon as they reached someplace safe, she would leave it down for days, just to show him . . . show him . . . oh, she didn't know what she would show him, but he better not make any more comments about her hair . . . or touch it either for that matter.

Libby searched the area for something else to think about, something of interest to note for a journal she planned to write about her experiences in the West. There was nothing around them but miles of waving yellow grass and unending blue sky. After they had ridden up an embankment Tomas called the *ceja*, or eyebrow, they had left behind the rough country.

Up here, there were no hills, trees or clouds to break the monotonous landscape, yet Libby found a grandeur in its limitless stretches, even a beauty. This land spoke to her of unbounded freedom, a message she had longed to hear.

Too bad the place was filled with savages searching for other people's hair to wave about on poles. Despite the gruesome thought, a smile worked into the corners of Libby's mouth. At last she had come across a people who appreciated the color of her hair.

Her exploration of the land finally ended on the owner of the hat. She envied the coolness promised by the billowing white shirt Mando wore. She found his jacket as hot and uncomfortably large as his hat, but Tomas's *serape* had been a little too ripe for her tastes. Surprisingly the boy's pants had fit fairly well and were, since he'd saved them for special occasions, rather clean.

Surprised to see Mando stop, Libby traveled the distance he had kept between them and reined in her horse beside his. He had pulled out a brass telescope and was examining the horizon behind them. Open to the waist, his white shirt whipped about his broad chest, and the ends of the scarf flew about his shoulders. Her locket dangled by its leather string from his neck. With the scope to his eye and the bandoliers crossed over his chest, he looked more the pirate than ever.

A curious excitement settled inside her as she watched him. Memories of last night in the cave came to her unbidden. His arms around her. His voice, husky and calming, against her ear. Mando standing naked in the rain.

Foolish woman, he has warned you. She wished he hadn't said that. Now more than ever she wanted to know about him. She twisted around to see what he might be looking at. Anything to keep her mind off Mando Fierro.

The way they had come appeared just like the way they were heading. Empty. She stuffed tendrils of escaping hair beneath the hat.

"See any Indians?" she asked.

He lowered the lens and gave her a frowning glance. Snapping the scope closed, he touched his spur to his horse.

"I guess he's still in a huff." Libby gave her horse a kick of her heels and started after him.

Tomas followed right behind her. "This huff, gringa, what is that?"

"Tomas, I have asked you to call me Libby. Please do. Even Mando uses my name."

"Your name is too hard to pronounce. I will simply call you *señorita*. Now what is this huff?"

Libby searched for a translation. "He is still angry with me."

"You should not have lost that scrap of cloth. Should the soldiers find it . . ." He shrugged at such a calamity.

"Yes, yes, but that can't be helped now. I'm sure it is lost in the mud someplace." And probably it was, she thought.

"He is also worried about the Frenchman," the boy added. "They have been friends for many years."

"Last night he said Louis wouldn't come in until the soldiers had turned back. I guess they are still on our trail." She hoped anyway.

"Storms are dangerous and shelter hard to come by. We were lucky to find the caves."

"Yes, weren't we." She thought of the tentative bond begun between herself and Mando, their argument, his warning. She renewed her vow not to think of him and chose a safer subject. Escape.

But that topic only circled her thoughts back to her captor. Unless the cavalry patrol caught up with them, he was her only safe escort through Indian country. If the soldiers had turned back and Louis was . . . if he was detained for some other reason, then she wanted to look forward to reaching safety in New Mexico, but only more uncertainty waited for her there.

Again her gaze wandered to the dark rider on the gray horse. She was beginning to fear she had more than the patrol's whereabouts to worry about, more than attacking Indians, more than Mando's intentions. He had warned her of guarding her desires. She began to understand what he meant, yet the more he warned her about himself, the more she was intrigued.

She hoped the patrol caught up with them soon. If they didn't, she hoped New Mexico wasn't too far away. Some kind of civilization could be found there and perhaps her freedom, too. Freedom from Mando, before it was too late.

Earlier she had tried to garner some information from Tomas, but he had proved to be closedmouthed about anything relating to their destination. Most likely those were his instructions. She would have to try prying something out of Mando.

Libby quickened her horse's pace, clamping her thighs hard around his middle, thankful for the folded blankets beneath her. Clinging to a galloping mule for two days had a way of making any other riding, even bareback riding, pleasant.

She caught up with Mando and matched her horse's gait with his mount. Tomas had pulled in beside her, leading the extra packhorse. Mando didn't acknowledge either of them, but faced the front, his expression troubled. Libby knew she would have to be careful. He was in an ugly mood, but she wanted some answers. Then she could form a plan.

She was worried about Louis and decided to begin their conversation through a mutual concern. "I hope Louis fared well in last night's storm."

Only the soft whisper of their horses passing through the tall grass replied. Libby swallowed hard and fiddled with her reins. She was *very* relieved he hadn't caught her tossing that piece of petticoat out the back of the cart. If suspicion could put him in such a black temper, what would sure knowledge do?

At least if the cavalry ever showed up waving the darned thing, she would have the United Stated Army to protect her. She should have drawn some relief from that realization, but she didn't. Instead she racked her brain for something to make him talk to her, some round-about question from which she could gain some information.

Absently she reached up and scratched her hot, itchy scalp and an idea came to her. "How long must I wear this hat? It's so hot."

"*Señorita,* you should always wear a hat in this country," Tomas said. "You can wear mine. It is made of straw and cooler."

"No, thank you, Tomas," Libby assured him quickly, wishing he would keep his mouth closed. "This one is fine."

She caught the glance Mando cut her way, a small smile hooking one corner of his mouth. She wasn't about to put Tomas's questionably clean hat on her head and he knew it.

Her gaze was drawn to his mouth, so expressive and...he had almost kissed her. She recalled his comment about her dirty face, her need of a bath. Unable to take the kegs of rainwater with them, she had used the contents of two to rinse her hair and one to get as clean as a scrap of cloth and an audience allowed.

How had Mando interpreted her actions? Libby heaved a sigh and turned her attention to the rippling grass. It was happening again. Distracted by him from her intended purpose...which was...she thought a minute. Oh, yes, discovering information about their journey and possible places to seek help once they reached New Mexico.

She had to think of something better than last time, something subtle. Nothing occurred to her. Her mind didn't work in subtleties. She would simply ask her questions. She had a right to know where she was going and when she would arrive.

"When will we reach civilization, other people, a town?" she asked.

Mando regarded her a moment, then said, "Maybe a week."

"Oh. A week," she repeated. Actually that told her nothing, but he seemed more receptive to conversation.

"What's the name of the first town? Will there be a telegraph, or at least a place I can send word to my sister?"

"No."

"Well, then how—"

"Your sister will be informed. Leave it at that."

She still didn't know anything. "You'll take me to a stage station, I suppose."

"No. I'm surprised you would want to get on a stage again."

"I have to get to Santa Angela somehow. You said I could go to my sister."

Mando looked beyond her to Tomas, who had remained silent. "If you remember, I said you will return when it pleases me. Enough questions."

"I hardly think so," she said, pushed past caring what Tomas heard or thought. "I deserve to know where I'm going, what's to happen to me."

"A woman who travels about the country alone deserves whatever fate she receives."

"I've had enough of your arrogance!" She pushed the hat back to see him better. "And from a man who trades with those bloodthirsty Comanches."

"*Por Dios*, woman, you go too far. The people of New Mexico have had a treaty with the Comanches since 1786, one neither people has broken. The Comanches have kept their side of the bargain well, keeping out the *americanos*.

Libby was tired of his constant attack on Americans. "Since we are quoting history, you might recall the Guadalupe Hildago treaty that made New Mexico a United States territory. Have you forgotten the people of New Mexico are Americans now?"

"The people of New Mexico do not forget their treaties as easily as your people. The ink had not dried on the Medicine Lodge treaty before the buffalo hunters swarmed onto the lands promised to the Indians, killing off the buffalo and their way of life... ours, too."

Despite her own misgivings regarding the breaking of treaties, Libby felt compelled to defend her country. "We bring settlement and progress to all the new territories."

"Progress? All I have seen is greed, larceny and prejudice."

Libby doubled a fist and hit her thigh. "I won't be lectured to by a man who trades with thieves and murderers for their bloody booty."

She cut a glance at the hiss from Tomas. He looked as worried as she should feel, but her temper had taken her too far to care.

"You know little of this country... gringa. You will find it far more healthy to keep your opinions to yourself as you promised last night."

With a reminder like that, Libby fell silent, realizing there was no victory or gain to be made from continuing their argument. She was back to being called gringa. They saw the world through different eyes. Black in her world was white in his and vice versa. Whatever this fascination she held for him was, it must stop. She must find a way to get away from Mando as soon as it was safe.

From under the wide brim of her hat, Libby stole a glance at Tomas. If she didn't learn to leash her temper and her tongue, Mando could become the least of her worries. No doubt, Tomas would tell his uncle of their conversation, of Mando's promise to let her go to her sister. The other comancheros had made their intentions all too clear. She was a threat to their safety from the law.

She may have done herself real damage here, and why? She didn't think before she opened her mouth. She was beginning to understand her mother's complaint that she couldn't learn any other way but the hard way.

Libby kept to herself, following the gray horse ahead of her, trying not to think of her aching backside or the trouble she was riding into in New Mexico. Whenever she began to feel really low, she found consolation by reminding herself she could be with the Comanches or dead, but as time separated her from those horrible days and nights, the future took more of her thoughts.

As the afternoon progressed, Mando began riding out to every high roll of prairie, raising his spyglass to search for Louis or any sign of the soldiers. Apparently from the deep frown he wore when he rode on ahead of them, he found neither.

Worried about Louis herself, Libby occupied her mind by trying to form plans with the information she had, but she had so little, nothing really came together. To reach someone she could trust, she would simply have to be ready to plunge down any avenue that appeared. Finally her chin dropped to her chest and she dozed.

The smell woke her. She lifted her head, her nose wrinkling at the faint sourness that came to her on every gust of wind. Looking far ahead, she made out black dots slowly circling in the blue sky. Something or someone was dead. Dread twisted inside her until she thought she might be sick.

Mando galloped ahead. Libby held her horse back, not wanting to see what the buzzards had found.

"*Vamanos, señorita,*" Tomas shouted, and gave her horse a flick of his reins across its rump.

The sorrel leaped ahead. Libby grabbed a handful of mane, managing to keep her seat. "You little scamp," she shouted after the boy, but he was already far ahead.

Not wanting to be left alone, Libby leaned over the horse's neck and followed. Feeling her hat slip, she gave it a hard smack on the top, then hung on for dear life. The air rushing toward her grew foul with the odor of dead flesh, until finally she knew she would be sick.

Mando and Tomas pulled in their restless mounts. Libby reined in beside them, not believing what she saw. She curled her arm around her face, covering her nose, but still the smell overpowered her. Hundreds of skinned buffalo carcasses lay rotting in the sun where they had fallen. She leaned from her horse and retched.

"Fill your nose with the stench of progress, gringa." Mando handed her a canteen.

Libby took it, rinsed her mouth, then sat up, slashing a sleeve over her mouth. "What do you mean?"

"This feast for buzzards could have fed every family in my valley for a whole winter. The hides now on their way back East would have provided warmth, leather for shoes and many other needed items. We and the Indians have hunted these herds for over a hundred years. Now, within only a few short years of hunting by the Anglos, they are almost gone.''

Libby sat silently, taking in the terrible scene. The low droning of millions of flies filled the air. Buzzards sat on humped, hideless animals—their great heads still intact—and tore at the poor beasts. Tears welled in Libby's eyes at the sight of such waste.

''In my father's day, he rode with only a lance and a brave horse, riding down the buffalo, making the hunt a true contest of man and beast. Now the *americano* hunters use rifles on the stupid animals who stand and let their numbers be slaughtered. This is the progress you speak of.''

Libby blinked back her tears. ''Change can be a very sad process, but perhaps if your people relied on cattle.''

''We have done just that. Right, Tomas?''

''*Sí*, El Aguila, Texas cattle.''

''But, this looks like good grazing land. You could—''

''It is the best. The *tejanos* like your sister will have the plains filled with their herds by the end of the decade. Nothing will be left for us, or...'' he looked up abruptly, giving a nod to the other side of the slaughter ''...them.''

Libby followed his gaze to the opposite side of the shallow basin. One by one, horsemen drew up along the edge of the kill until a long line formed. Feathers danced on horses and lances.

''Oh, my God,'' she whispered. ''Indians.''

Chapter Thirteen

"Don't say a word and keep your head down."

Mando didn't look at her but straight at the band of Indians now circling the death-filled hollow and riding toward them.

Libby barely heard his instructions over the wild beating of her heart. She couldn't tear her gaze away from the Indians, their ponies snaking their way toward her. The feathers, the shields, the lances, the painted faces—a nightmare come to life. Fascinated, she watched the leader, waiting for him to raise his lance, fill the stillness with his howl of attack and charge down upon them. One couldn't escape destiny and this was hers.

"For once, *for once*, do as you are told," Mando warned.

Libby jerked her head down and busied her hands with braiding the horse's mane to hide her shaking fingers. Mando dealt with these savages. He would know what to do.

"Did you hear what I said?" Mando asked.

"Yes," she replied, her fear controlled to a dull roaring in her ears. "I wasn't saying a word."

He let out a long, drawn-out sigh, then he said, "Tomas, you do the same. No talking."

"*Sí*, El Aguila. They look like Cheyenne."

"That's my guess. Let's hope they know we are traders."

Libby agreed wholeheartedly, while she made a tangle of the horse's mane. She heard their horses and fought to stay calm, hoping no long red strands of her hair had escaped the hat. She didn't dare draw attention to herself by poking at her hair.

The Indians brought their mounts to a stop a short distance from where they waited. Libby took quick peeks from under her hat, despite Mando's words. The brim was so large she knew her face must still be in deep shadow. One of the Indians separated himself and rode his paint pony toward them.

Keeping her head down, she glanced at Mando, who gave the Indian a hand signal. The Indian returned it. So far so good, she thought, and pulled a finger free that had gotten enmeshed in the long, coarse hair. She listened to a few starts in differing languages and was surprised when English was finally agreed upon. She supposed the missionaries had done part of their jobs well.

"I am called El Aguila," Mando began. "I trade here on the Llano."

"I am Tall Bear of the Cheyenne. We have heard of El Aguila in our travels among the Comanches. You carry the magic of the Spirit Woman."

"Yes."

"I see you wear her charm. You do not fear her powers?"

"No, for she has cursed only the red man."

A pause followed, and despite her fear or perhaps because of it, Libby sneaked another look and saw the older man nodding.

"Look before us," he said, and swept his arm toward the buffalo kill. "Our women and children will go hungry this winter. We find only dead buffalo. Our raids bring us nothing. The Comanche's medicine failed at Adobe Walls and they have loosed this evil Spirit Woman on us."

At another mention of the Spirit Woman, Libby quickly dropped her gaze to her hands.

"There is no trade," Mando said. "My nephews and I go home."

A long pause followed in which she supposed both men commiserated with each other. She didn't dare look up now and busily mangled the mane.

"What is wrong with this one?"

Libby's fingers stilled. She knew the Indian pointed at her, then her fingers flew through the long horsehair, her braiding becoming a mass of knots.

"The poor boy carries much Indian blood and he saw the Spirit Woman walking through the storm last night. Now he is a little *loco.*"

Libby thought Mando was stretching the Spirit Woman thing a bit too far. She was behaving quite rationally. Surely the Indian would question such a statement.

"We must hurry back to our camps in the north," he said.

Libby barely heard the words of farewell spoken before the Indian rode back to his war party. She knew Mando was only protecting her, but she wished he hadn't said she was crazy.

The Indians galloped past them, waving lances, rifles and bows. She waited until they were well out of earshot before launching her attack.

"Why did you tell them I was crazy?"

"You acted strange, that's why, and they don't like to be around people not right in the head. Now let's get away from here." Mando urged his horse to a canter.

Libby had no choice but to follow, her hand clamped tightly to her hat. He made perfect sense in coming up with that story. She didn't know why it upset her so much, but it did. The sentiment had been expressed too often in her past and her reaction was automatic. After she caught a look at the mangled mess her horse's mane had become, she had to laugh.

Carried on a flood of relief, her laughter veered toward the hysterical. She couldn't stop. It came wrenching up from her belly, taking her strength until the reins grew lax in her hands and the horse slowed then stopped. She didn't care. She laughed until tears blurred the blue of the sky and the anger in Mando's face.

"What's wrong with you?" he demanded.

Laughing still, Libby rubbed the tears from her eyes and tried to gain some control. She saw Tomas had finally given her some distance and she found this hysterically funny, too.

"Tomas thinks I'm crazy," she managed. "You think I'm crazy. And you're right. I am crazy. Crazy to sell off a safe, wonderful home to chase some silly notion of freedom across the country. And look at me."

Laughing or crying, she didn't know which was filling her eyes with tears. "Look at me," she said, her voice becoming high-pitched and strained. "I'll never be free, I'll never be free of—"

Mando's large hands grabbed her about the waist and she was dragged off the horse. He pushed the hat back from her face and she saw either impatience or concern crowd his black brows. She searched his dark eyes for the answer and, as always, found none. There were no answers.

You, she finished, but the word remained a thought, a slight movement of her lips. ''I am crazy in the worst way,'' she said.

The irony of it all crashed over her once more and the laughter returned. Harder, louder, until she was drunk with it, until she could hear nothing else but echoes of laughter.

Fierro's hands clamped on her shoulders and shook her. ''Stop it. Stop it, now.''

Libby pushed at him. He was always crowding her, telling her what to do. ''Beware of the Spirit Woman, Mando. I might put my curse on you.''

''I fear you already have,'' he whispered, and pulled her into his arms.

He kissed her, his lips demanding, almost angry in his taking of hers. Libby welcomed the fierce surge of pleasure that swept through her like the clean, hot winds of the plains. Fears, doubts, recriminations flew to the far corners of her mind, leaving only the rough caress of his lips, and the undeniable knowledge that she wanted more.

He released her, pushing her from him. His breathing was as hard and labored as her own. He looked angry, disbelieving, then his eyes took on their usual hooded expression. She envied his swift recovery, for his kiss still lingered on her lips, his possession still racing through her blood.

''A kiss from the Devil, gringa.'' His mouth twisted in his mocking smile. ''I knew you were no angel.''

Libby dragged her sleeve across her mouth, only to smell the faint scent of his cigars. ''You are contemptible.''

The long crease framing his mouth deepened. "Of course." Suddenly he was serious. "Now get on your horse and no more trouble. At least for today."

"Is it too much trouble to ask for a boost?" She hated asking, but she needed his help to mount.

Without further comment, Mando lifted her to the sorrel's back. "No more delaying tactics," he said, then turned and stalked away.

"I wasn't..."

Oh, what was the use? He wouldn't believe her. His mistaken conclusion was better than the truth anyway. She would much rather he think she had acted like a fool on purpose. Maybe he would think her response to his kiss was used to slow them up, too. She hoped so. Otherwise... She didn't care to finish the thought.

Libby nudged her heels against her horse, and once more they continued their journey west. The late-afternoon sun shone directly in her eyes. Keeping the brim of her hat low, she began to untangle the horse's mane, trying to untangle her thoughts, as well.

Fortunately, the rotting buffalo were downwind. The smell no longer clung to her nose, but their image remained strong in her mind. Mando had told her not to try to understand him, but after seeing the waste, the total disregard shown by the hunters and the business interests profiting from the slaughter, she could understand his outrage. But she could never understand or condone his response to that anger, his trading. Perhaps that's what he meant.

What of understanding herself? How could she have enjoyed his kiss, and yes, wanted more? Dancing with the Devil was a dangerous business. When would the music stop?

* * *

Mando measured the distance between the sun and the horizon. Only three, maybe four, hours left until dark. Where was Louis? He should have caught up with them hours ago, even if the soldiers hadn't turned back.

The Frenchman would have checked in by now. He would need supplies. He knew where they climbed the *ceja* and which watering places they would use on the Llano.

That damned storm last night, and so many unfamiliar tribes scattered over the plains, all looking for trouble, for vengeance. He hoped one of the war parties came across the buffalo hunters and killed every man. Maybe one of them would be the man who had murdered his father. And the others, they deserved no better.

A thought came to him. One that made him regret his hasty wish. Louis in his buckskins could easily be mistaken for one of the hunters. To lose his old friend in such a way would be too much. He had no one else.

He twisted around in the saddle, his gaze falling on the small figure under the big hat, his redheaded reward for seeing no future for a wife and family. Reward or curse? Discovering which would be diverting if her response to his kiss was any indication. And what of his response? A knot of desire still burned in his belly, a reminder of the need that had hit him like a jolt of *aguardiente*. Like the potent liquor, allowing himself to want too much of her would give her control over him. Enjoy the gringa's charms but never fall under their spell—that was the challenge. Ross had failed, but he would not.

Mando lifted his gaze past Libby and Tomas and scanned the horizon, but saw only grass and sky. He would try the mirror.

All day he had debated using the mirror, not only a signal for Louis, but a sure signal for any patrols following them. He had assumed Louis would not use one either, but now he saw little choice. If Louis were within miles of them, and he should be, he would see the mirror flash. No returning flash would mean only one thing. Louis was in trouble or dead.

Mando reined in his horse and found the mirror in his saddlebag. He shined it on his sleeve.

"El Aguila, no!" Tomas spurred his horse and circled it around Mando. "The soldiers will see. Don't forget what happened to Polonius Ortiz when he was caught."

Mando calmly began positioning the mirror to catch the sun's light. "The Ortiz boy was caught with those *idiotas* who would not wait for the Indians to bring them cattle and had tried to steal it themselves. I will not let that happen to you. You will see your *madre* again."

Tomas pulled in beside him. "So did Ortiz, El Aguila, but not until after the soldiers forced him to tell how to travel the secret trails across the Llano. He told them everything. Mackenzie and his soldiers came to my own village looking for comancheros, though we told them nothing."

Mando understood the boy's fears and shared many of them himself. But he must know what had happened to Louis. "Louis would not be out here but for his friendship to me," he said. "A man is loyal to his friends, Tomas."

Mando caught the look Tomas passed to the woman, who had just ridden up, then the boy looked at him. He knew what Tomas was thinking, though he would never question him as Cabot had done.

He had always known taking the woman to New Mexico could be trouble, but only for himself. She could report nothing that would bring the law on the others because by the time he sent her away, the trading business would be finished. The capture of the Ortiz boy and his cooperation with the army had seen to that. The hunters and the army were a formidable combination, even for the Comanches. A man couldn't fight if he couldn't eat.

Spring should just about finish it. Without the income he made from the stolen cattle, the rancho would be finished, too. Yes, spring would finish it all—if not before.

"Do you see anything?" Libby asked.

"No," Mando replied. "I see nothing." He continued to signal in different directions and search for an answering flash.

"Try the spyglass," she urged.

Mando glanced at her and saw the genuine concern on her face as she too searched the far distances. He wanted to be surprised, but he wasn't. This *americano* was not like the others that had come down the Santa Fe Trail with their frowning disapproval of what they found. Only his trading drew her fire, but that was enough—enough to free him from the charms of the Spirit Woman.

"Take this." He handed her the mirror. "Keep signaling." Finding his telescope, he pulled it open and slowly scanned the flat plain. Rippling grass and empty sky met his intense scrutiny. Louis, damn you, where are you?

The sun beat down on his back, burning the question into his head until it ached with the emptiness he saw. A terrible certainty replaced the hopeful doubts he had entertained all day. Louis was gone.

Mando clenched his teeth against the pain that ripped through him. It was like losing his father once more, only this time he could only blame himself. Two days ago he had been relieved to have Louis along on this trip to watch his back. He had sent him to do just that yesterday morning. Had he sent him to his death?

He lowered the glass slowly. "He's not out there."

"Let me look."

Mando turned to the woman. "What do you expect to see? I saw nothing. No soldiers. Nothing."

She pushed her hat back. "You've been looking at the sun all afternoon. I . . . I've been . . ." She threaded her fingers through the horse's mane. "I've been doing some untangling here, and haven't faced the sun. Let me look. What can it hurt?"

"I wonder," Mando replied, then, after a moment's hesitation, offered her the brass scope.

She exchanged the mirror for the telescope and brought it to her eye. She looked a bit ridiculous with his hat fitting over her ears, the jacket hanging past her hands. What small delicate hands she had, with their faint sprinkles of gold. He still wondered if the freckles covered—

"What's that?" she asked.

"What?" Mando snapped his attention back to Louis, cursing under his breath at how easily she distracted him, even from this, the loss of his friend.

"Over there." She held the scope to her eye and pointed to a spot slightly to his left. "Take a look."

Mando accepted the glass and placed it to his eye, looking in the general direction she had pointed. "Where?"

"There." She leaned close, her arm pointing the way. "Something whitish trailing into the sky just above the horizon."

Mando lowered the scope and rubbed his eye, then looked again. He saw what she had described. A vaporous thread he had dismissed. Disappointment sharpened his tone.

"That's a cloud." He didn't lower the glass.

"Are you sure? It could be . . . I don't know. It's the only spot of anything in the sky . . . the only thing different."

She had raised his doubts again and his spirits. It could be something, but was it a trick? "You look, Tomas."

Tomas looked through the scope. "It could be smoke."

Had the woman put thoughts into the boy's head? She had everything to gain by turning back to investigate. "What do you think, Tomas?" Mando asked. "Should we ride back and see if it is Louis? I won't ask you to, but know this. If it is smoke, it could be from the soldier's fires, or more likely the Anglo buffalo hunters who would kill us on sight, or it could be Indians who might shoot before they parley."

"The Frenchman helped our family many times after my father was killed by the *tejanos* looking for their cattle. I want to help him if we can. A man is loyal to his friends."

"I am proud of you, Tomas. You are becoming a man." And your mother was a pretty widow, he thought, but Louis helped many families and not all the widows were pretty or accommodating.

Mando turned to Libby. "What do you say?"

"You're asking?"

"The odds are not with you, gringa. Three to one that we find your soldiers. And, of course, we could be chasing nothing but our hopes."

Libby gathered her reins in her hands. "I've rather a lot of practice at that. I say, let's ride."

Mando reached over and tightened his hat's strap beneath her chin. "Hang on tight. It's going to be a rough ride and I don't want to lose you."

Chapter Fourteen

Desperation had held her to the bony mule's back while riding across the country with the Comanches. She had known they would kill her if she had fallen. Now determination kept her seat on the sorrel. She found little difference between desperation and determination. Both got the job done.

Libby held fast to the poor horse's bedraggled mane as she chased Mando, Tomas and the packhorse. The grass flew beneath her like a rolling river of gold. Her horse's gallop was so smooth she felt as though she floated. She leaned low over his neck, his long, coarse mane flying back into her face. She wished she could take off the hat and let her hair fly behind her. Someday she would do just that.

If she saw another day. She had listened well to Mando's cautions. She either rode to rescue or ruin, and she could do little about the outcome. She might as well enjoy the ride. It could be her last.

She raised slightly and managed to see the thread had grown into a plume. That was no cloud. Something was definitely rising from the ground. Dust most likely. She caught Mando looking over his shoulder for a third time. She didn't know why he kept tabs on whether she kept up or had fallen. He tried so hard to show his indifference, too hard, she thought.

As if any of that mattered now. One way or the other her problems with him were likely to be over soon. She wanted to find the soldiers at the end of this run, yet she hoped to find Louis.

A man is loyal to his friends, Mando had said. Women were, too, and the Frenchmen was her friend. He would have helped her, she knew. Please let us find Louis, she prayed, then wondered if she was going completely mad. Praying for a gunrunner, one of the Devil's own.

The wind hitting her face changed from the clean smell of earth and grass and sun to death. Though they didn't pass directly by the dead buffalo, their slaughter soured the air for miles downwind. She recalled all of what Mando had told her and what she had seen. But none of that made her forget the Comanches' guns that had stopped her stage.

They might be riding into an ambush and killed by bullets Mando had traded. A just ending for such a man, but not for her, or Tomas, either. He was only a boy following his hero.

Libby lifted her head and listened. Sharp, erratic pops punctuated the roar of the wind in her ears, the rumbling thunder of galloping hooves. She looked to Mando, wondering what he heard. Something, because he raised his hand and slowed his mount.

Libby sawed back on her reins, bringing the sorrel to a rear-bumping trot. Pushing the troublesome hat back from her eyes, she saw Mando had stopped and Tomas beside him. She pulled harder on the reins, finally bringing her mount to a walk. She straightened herself on the blankets and joined them.

She looked from Mando to Tomas, both their heads lifted, listening. She did the same. From beyond the horizon, cracking bursts of gunfire rose into the wind.

"It could be Louis," she said.

"It could be many things," Mando replied. "Your soldiers, hunters, the Indians. We'll move up slower. I want no share of trouble that isn't mine."

Reserving her comments, Libby pressed her heels to the sorrel's damp flanks and rode even with Mando. Tomas, trailing the packhorse, took the other side. At a lope she found mostly comfortable, she watched the spiral of dust grow into a cloud and listened to the sound of gunfire grow louder. Determined to find Louis, desperate to find him alive, she blanked her mind to the task at hand.

Hours or minutes might have passed before Mando signaled for them to stop. She didn't know. Behind them, the sun was setting, casting its red glow across the grass. The stench of death weighted the wind, and the gunfire had grown more sporadic.

Libby climbed off the horse unassisted, her legs almost buckling when her feet hit the ground. Leaning against the animal, she steadied herself. Many more rides like this one and she would be ready to star in a Wild West show. Her legs shaky but reliable, she lifted her canteen from her shoulder and took a long drink. She saw Mando and Tomas did the same.

Mando recapped his canteen and walked ahead of the horses. She glanced at Tomas, and together they pushed through the tall grass to discover what Mando planned to do.

He dragged the red scarf from his head, the wind playing havoc with his hair. "I'll use that rise to the left to see what's happening. Stay back here and water the horses."

"*Sí*, El Aguila," Tomas replied.

Libby nodded but looked at her shoes when he glanced her way. She heard his long strides whisk through the grass and watched him until he dropped to his stomach and crawled up the roll of prairie. She had to know what was happening, who was under attack, and she didn't trust him to tell her.

"Tomas, I'm going up there, too."

She expected arguments and protests, but Tomas merely rolled his eyes and shrugged, which suited her. She would face enough choice words from Mando later.

Pulling her hat down tight, Libby set off in the same direction Mando had taken. She could no longer see him, the long grass covered him completely, but his trail was easily discernible through the thick growth. Dropping to her stomach, she crawled forward as she had seen him do, thankful for the long sleeves on his jacket.

Sharp and tough, the grass scratched her face and hands. She couldn't see more than a few feet in front of her, but broken blades and occasional scrapes in the dirt kept her on Mando's path. Where was the man? At last, she saw the dull shine of his spurs. She quickened her pace.

A sharp click and a revolver shoved in her face stopped her. She slowly raised her gaze to Mando's. He rolled his eyes toward heaven, then released the hammer.

He jammed the pistol back into his holster, giving her a look that said more than any hour-long lecture from her papa, the constable or Reverend Carmichael ever hoped to deliver. If the reverend could capture that look, she thought, she might not have talked the girls into spying on the boys who had gone skinny-dipping at the Sunday school picnic. Of course, that had helped Papa decide to send her away to Oberlin College.

She should have stayed there, she thought as she crept forward next to Mando. Parting the grass with her hands, she peered over the crest into the sweep of land below. Her heart stopped at seeing the small band of blue-coated men gathered in a low bowl-shaped clearing, their mounts pulled down beside them. A few shots rang out, she supposed from the soldiers. Two bodies lay sprawled among them. What was happening here? She looked beyond the clearing and spotted other bodies lying in the grass. Identifying who they were was difficult.

''What's—'' Her eyes widened at the hand slapped over her mouth.

Mando handed her the scope and placed his finger to his mouth, indicating she should be quiet. She nodded and took the glass. He pointed to an area to the far right. She placed the telescope to her eye and saw a group of mounted Indians milling about and shaking their rifles and lances. That explained the other bodies. Mando placed his hand on the brass scope and moved her range of vision to the soldiers.

Sitting among them, a rifle across his knees, was Louis, the fringe on his buckskins swaying wildly as he talked with a young man. A white man, she noticed. He must be the officer.

She lowered the glass and looked at Mando. He stared at Louis, his eyes filled with such pain, she wanted to touch him, to comfort him somehow. She gave his arm a tentative touch. He turned his gaze to her, the pain set in a resolute determination that gave his eyes a shiny hardness, almost a madness.

He jerked his head toward Tomas and their waiting horses. She nodded and gave the scope back to him, then started down the incline.

Libby crawled through the grass, unmindful of the scratches to her face. They had to do something to help those poor men. And Louis. Yes, God, and Louis. But, what could be done? A woman, a boy and one man? Then she knew. She knew what had put that hard purpose in Mando's eyes, that wild glint that frightened her.

Suddenly he stood and, brushing the dirt and grass from his clothes, walked toward the camp. Libby rose from the grass and did the same. She trotted to catch up with him. Tomas ran to meet them.

"Who is shooting?" the boy asked. "Did you see Louis?"

"Yes, I saw him," Mando answered. He walked directly to the packhorse and began rummaging through the supplies. "The soldiers have him."

"*Ay,* no."

"And the Indians have attacked them all," Libby added.

"*Madre de Dios.* If only my uncle and the others—"

"But they aren't here." Mando shoved an extra pistol into his waistband. "The Indians are massing to attack again. I'm all the help they have."

Libby wasn't surprised to see Mando pull out several boxes of ammunition and another cartridge belt. Words escaped her. Emotions too deep, too confusing closed her throat in a painful knot.

"And me," Tomas said.

Mando stopped his preparations. Walking over to the boy, he put his hands on his shoulders and looked him in the eye. "You must care for this woman," Mando began. "Make sure she reaches Fort Union."

"No, El Aguila. I—"

"Promise me, Tomas. Give me your *palabra de hombre* to take this woman to Fort Union, your word as a man."

Libby read the doubts, the fears in the boy's black eyes. He would be promising many things if he took her to a fort. She didn't interfere or protest that she needed no care; for Mando was saving the boy's life. She waited for Tomas's answer.

"*Yo soy hombre,* El Aguila. I am a man." His voice lowered with resignation. "I will keep my word."

"*Bueno,*" Mando said. "And don't worry what the woman will say. She will sing my praises and yours, too. She is in love with me and I will make her give me her promise to reveal no names. She will not deny me this one last favor."

Tomas smiled and gave her a nod as if to say, who could not love his hero? She smiled and returned his nod, understanding Mando's reasons for stating these outlandish lies. The boy would be concerned about taking her to a fort full of soldiers after all he had heard Cabot say and the recent venting of her own views. Mando was doing his best to save both of them.

"Now, switch my saddle from the gray to this packhorse and hurry about it. The stallion is the last of a long line. Take him back to the rancho and give him to my cousin Ramon. Now go. I must say my goodbyes to the woman."

Tomas waited a moment, staring up at Mando, then gave him a hug and ran to the horses. His sleeve made a suspicious swipe across his eyes.

Libby's attention turned to Mando. He stood silently, looking at her, the sunset blazing behind him, his expression hidden. She was reminded of when he had found her, when he had saved her life. He was no longer merely a dark silhouette of a man. He was a calm voice in a storm, a kiss that had created one. He was the most exciting man she had ever met.

He walked to her, blocking the bright rays of the sun, blocking the wind, blocking all but Mando Fierro.

"I hope you won't make a liar of me," he said.

Libby shook her head. "I won't. I told you before, I owe you a debt. I'll say nothing to the authorities at Fort Union."

He lifted his head and gazed somewhere far into the distance. The wind lifted his hair from his shoulders, back from his face, leaving the hard, distinct profile of a hunter. He had spoken with such pride of his father, a man who faced a charging buffalo with a horse and a lance. Perhaps he looked into the past, or a future that never could be.

She wanted to touch his hair and did, finding it as silky as she had imagined. He dropped his gaze to hers, and the sadness in his eyes made her speak. "I'll tell them a band of New Mexican hunters rescued me from sure death."

His crooked smile played across his lips. "You will make them believe it, too. I thank you for the boy and his mother, for the families the other men must feed."

"You trust me?"

He shrugged. "I see no other choice."

He had many other choices, she thought, including riding away from here and leaving Louis to his fate. She almost said as much but didn't. Saying the words somehow seemed cowardly.

"You'll need this, or the soldiers might take you for an Indian," she said, and lifted his hat from her head. Her hair fell in a heavy cascade around her hips.

He gathered a handful of it, rubbing the long strands between his fingers. "You will still need a hat."

Suddenly she didn't want to believe he wouldn't return. "You can give it back to me after—"

"I think we should make the story I told the boy look as truthful as possible. Kiss me, Libby. Kiss me and make it good."

Libby dropped his hat and replied to his request the only way possible. She stepped into his arms, her hands gliding over his muscled arms, to his shoulders.

"How's this?" she asked.

"Closer," he replied.

She stepped closer, the length of his body warming hers. "Is this better?"

"Stop talking and close your eyes."

"You're always so bossy," she said, but her voice was soft, melting against his lips.

She obeyed, her lids falling slowly, the memory of the heat in his eyes following her into the desperate claiming of his lips. He pulled her in closer still, his hands playing over her back, tangling his fingers in her hair.

"Open to me," he breathed into her lips.

She couldn't deny him nor did she want to. His tongue touched hers and time stopped. They were alone with only the sky, the land and the whispering grass. Libby held nothing back, giving him all his tomorrows, all that could have been. Then it was over.

He gathered a tear with his finger and touched it to his tongue. "Goodbye, my red-haired gringa."

Libby wiped the tears away. "We will wait for you. You and Louis . . . right here."

"No, you won't." Mando retrieved his hat from the ground and brushed it against his pants. "You and the boy will ride like the wind for New Mexico. He knows the way. Don't stop tonight no matter what you hear.''

"But—"

"I have no more time. The sun is about to set, and they will make their final attack then.''

Libby caught his hand as he was about to lift her locket from his neck. "Keep it for luck.''

A smile stole across his mouth, one that lightened the darkness in his eyes. "I have a need for the charm of the Spirit Woman.''

Libby pulled a smile from somewhere. "Now you have it.''

"El Aguila, your horse.''

Libby stepped back and watched him swing into the saddle. She refused to give up hope. He might make it through to cover. It wasn't impossible. Something could happen. The Indians might ride away. With the smell of their rotting winter food fouling the air, she knew she was only dreaming. She would dream forever of this man with the long black hair and the midnight eyes.

Fierro fit the sombrero on his head, his gaze steady on the task ahead. "Give me the Winchester, Tomas.''

"Too bad you don't have your Sharps,'' Tomas said, handing up the rifle. "You would have had much better range.''

Libby remembered hearing of the Sharps rifle. Mando had traded it for her locket.

"I have something better, Tomas.'' His gaze met hers. "I have the Spirit Woman's magic.''

Libby hoped it was enough.

Chapter Fifteen

Mando dropped from sight behind the swell of golden grass as if the horse and rider had been swallowed by the land. The rapid beat of his horse's hooves faded into the wind. The first gunshot released her and Libby charged up the rise, unmindful of Tomas's calls or her own visibility.

Reaching the top, Libby bent forward, resting her hands on her knees and gulping breaths of air. She watched Mando race across the vast open country toward the small party of beleaguered soldiers. A sharp jolt from behind laid her flat. Tomas crashed down beside her.

"*Señorita, por Dios,* you will get us killed." He grabbed his hat from his head and jammed it onto hers.

Libby pushed it back from her eyes and raised up on her elbows, her gaze riveted to the man and horse. "I had to see. I had to know if he made it."

A quick glance at Tomas told her he was too engrossed in the scene unfolding below to give her any more arguments. She measured the long distance Mando must travel before reaching safety, and clutched fistfuls of grass and dirt. More gunfire erupted. From this distance it was difficult to tell from which camp it came. She

wished she had the spyglass. She made out the small figure of Louis standing and waving his arms before someone knocked him down.

The Indians poured over the prairie, their war cries
raising chill bumps on her skin. Puffs of gray smoke rose
from the shallow crater where the soldiers were en-
trenched. Mando's hat flew from his head, bobbing on
his back, held by its strap around his neck. He leaned low
over the horse's neck, his hair flowing with the long black
mane.

Libby trained her sight on the horse and rider, waiting
for a bullet to throw Mando out of the saddle. Those
terrible thoughts she had had earlier about his just end
haunted her. How she regretted thinking them and she
didn't care why. Still he rode on, a trail of dust spiraling
behind him.

The Indians thundered across the plain, their war cries
growing more frenzied. Arrows arced and fell short of
their target. Soon one or two flew over the stretched-out
horse and rider. Mando dipped to the side, using the
horse as a shield at a flat-out gallop. Rifle fire cracked
more rapidly. The distance shortened. An Indian tumbled to the ground, his horse charging on with the others. A soldier dropped in the firing line.

Libby never blinked. She couldn't breathe. Mando and
the war party drew closer to the soldiers, the Indians attacking the front, Mando charging in from the side. Almost equal distances remained for both to travel. Libby's
gaze shifted from the lone horseman to the Indians. Another brave dropped. She couldn't be sure, but it looked
as though Mando was firing his pistol from under the
horse's neck. The fire from the soldiers grew into a steady
fusillade of rifle shots.

The distance closed. He might make it. Maybe twenty yards remained. He was going to make it.

Libby pounded the earth with her fist. "He's going to make it, Tomas." She grabbed his shoulder and shook him. "He's going to make—"

Mando's horse skidded to its knees. Libby leapt to her feet, her heart pounding so loud she couldn't hear Tomas shouting at her. Her arms folded over her twisting, aching stomach. Her eyes, burning with tears, never wavered from the thrashing horse.

Suddenly Louis appeared. The long fringe on his buckskin shirt danced with the firing of his pistols at the approaching Indians. He stood over the fallen horse until Mando stumbled to his feet, pumping the Winchester. Both men ran to the sandy shallow and dived for cover.

Libby collapsed, burying her head in her arms, crying with relief and despair. They didn't have a chance.

"*Vamanos, señorita,*" Tomas said, his voice shaky and thick. "The Cheyenne may have seen us. I promised, *señorita,* I promised I would get you to safety."

Tomas pulled at her sleeve. Libby looked up at the tears streaming openly down his face. The firing below had grown to a constant din, the war cries of the Indians mingled with the shouts from the defenders. She didn't want to see the end, but unable to simply walk away, Libby slowly turned her gaze from Tomas to the fighting.

Dust rose in lazy whorls above the barren depression. The Indians jumped their ponies over the line of blue-coated men. She saw combatants struggling on the ground but couldn't distinguish more than that.

Tomas grabbed her hand and tugged. She yanked it back and wiped the tears from her eyes.

"Come, *señorita,* truly we must go or—"

"Look, Tomas," Libby cried, not believing her eyes. "They're leaving. The Indians are leaving."

The war party divided and made a wide circle on each side of the shallow. They met at a distance they supposed was out of range. A single shot dropped one and they moved farther out.

"They lost several men, Tomas. Maybe they will leave. It will be dark soon."

"No, they always do this. They will make another charge. It will be the last attack and I don't want to see it. We must go as El Aguila said."

Libby pushed back the streams of hair blowing into her view. Tomas was right. The light was failing and she wouldn't be able to see much more. She didn't want to watch, but she wasn't sure she could make herself turn away and leave the echoes of gunfire and men struggling for their lives behind her.

Yet, she did them no good up here. Save herself. That's what Mando had wanted her to do. That's what she wanted. In a few days' time, she would reach Fort Union and be on her way to Santa Angela once more. Why wasn't she happy, relieved, ecstatic that Mando was meeting his just reward? God, how those words hurt.

She supposed the magic of the Spirit Woman hadn't been enough to save him or Louis or those soldiers who had probably been looking for her all this time. None of them would probably be in this mess if she hadn't decided to run off to Texas on one of her wild schemes. Some kind of Spirit Woman she had turned out to be.

Libby raised her head, an idea popping into her head. She wasn't sure she liked it, but couldn't let it go.

"*Señorita*, I don't like the look on your face. You aren't getting all *loco* again? We have no time for—"

"Hush, Tomas. I hear something. Don't you?"

Tomas shook his head rapidly. "I hear nothing but a crazy woman."

"Listen Tomas. I think I hear the Spirit Woman."

She looked at Tomas and he had the strangest expression on his face, almost as if he were frightened of her. "I'm not crazy. You said those were Cheyenne. They took off fast enough when Mando mentioned the Spirit Woman. Maybe... come on. We don't have time."

She started down the rise at a fast trot, her mind scheming on the best way to carry this off.

"Wait." Tomas caught up with her and grabbed her arm. "We don't know those are the same Cheyenne. They may not have heard of the Spirit Woman. Maybe they—"

Libby pulled away. "I can't think of that now."

But she did. Doubts dragged at her steps until she had to force one foot in front of the other. Images of those two men from the stage racked through her resolve. She couldn't do this. She couldn't ride into a massacre.

Reaching the dumped supplies, she foraged through them until she found her ragged petticoat. She stepped into it and tied it to her waist, then shrugged off Mando's jacket and tossed it among the jumbled provisions. This plan would never work. She would be captured again, tortured, raped, carried off to a living hell.

She untied her hair and bent over, shaking her head, then tossed her hair back. The gray palms of her hands caught her attention, and she decided a little stage makeup wouldn't hurt. She rubbed her shaking hands in the dirt and found her palms so damp that a good portion stuck, then she pressed them to her face, patting on the gritty covering. This was one of her most stupid ideas and probably the last.

She turned to Tomas. "How do I look?"

"Like a crazy woman."

"Good." She picked at the knot on her sash. "I have to do this, Tomas. It's their only chance."

She heard the click and looked up. Tomas held his gun on her, his narrow face strained into a stern expression that made his youth disappear before her eyes.

"I promised El Aguila to take you to safety. I gave my *palabra de hombre.* I won't let you go."

Libby pulled the sash off. "Then you'll have to shoot me, because I'm going."

She pushed past the boy and made for her sorrel. She gathered the reins when a hand on her shoulder pulled her around. She took a big breath to tell Tomas to leave her alone, but it caught in her throat.

"Take the gray. He will have the heart to carry you to the..." He handed her the reins to Mando's mount.

She took the leather straps. "Thank you, Tomas, but..." She thought of Mando's request to give the horse to his cousin, then shook her head. "Never mind." She had no time to argue with him.

She accepted his lift up onto the tall stallion. The light had faded to a pearly blue, giving a luster to the boy's olive complexion. She hoped the evening dimness did the same for her.

"Goodbye, Tomas."

"*Vaya con Dios, señorita.*"

She gave the boy a careful look. He looked back at her, his face solemn, his eyes steady on hers. Now that she thought about it, he had given up a little too easily.

"If you follow me, you will ruin the small chance any of us has to come out of this alive. The trickery will be undone and we will all be killed."

She studied the boy's face and found a certain rebelliousness around his mouth. "Give me your word."

"But I have already—"

"Mando could be dead, Tomas," Libby said, regretting the sharpness in her voice, but it was needed. "And I am alive for now. Don't ruin my chance."

The boy lowered his head. "I give my word. I will not follow you."

Libby gathered up the reins and gave the horse a kick.

"I will tell all of your bravery," Tomas called. "You are truly the Spirit Woman."

Maybe she was the Spirit Woman, or maybe she was just a fool. Holding the reins in one hand, Libby unbuttoned her shirt with the other. Extra material flying behind her might help the illusion. What did it matter? This wasn't going to work. Libby gave the horse a sharper kick.

They crested the hill and she saw the Indians working themselves into a frenzy. They shook their rifles and bows, dashing at their enemy, then circling back to their fellow braves.

Libby couldn't look at them. If she did, she knew she would turn back and it was too late for that. This insane idea had to work, but if it didn't, she hoped they killed her quickly.

She gave the stallion a hard kick and he sprang forward. Her stomach dropped as he carried her down the long sweep of land. Twining her fingers through his mane, she held on tight as he reached level ground and stretched out into a full gallop.

The wind tore through her hair, whipping it behind her. The feeling was glorious, just as she had imagined. Land and sky sped past her in a tangle of blue and gold. This was flying. Suddenly she remembered her dreams. She spotted a bright pinpoint of light just above the horizon and raced toward the evening star.

The charging Indians entered her field of vision from the left. Gunfire opened. Closing her eyes, she changed course and galloped toward the mass of Indians, a scream tearing from her throat, straight from her guts.

She screamed again and again, opening her eyes at last to the distinctive markings of war-painted faces turned her way. Her eyes opened wide with fright. She grew light-headed as if she were looking at herself from far away. This other self told her to call a curse down on the Indians. Rushing at them at breakneck speed, she pointed directly at certain braves, a wild jibberish of words streaming from her mouth.

Horses were pulled to skidding stops. One Indian lost his seat and tumbled to the ground, only to catch another mount and throw himself onto its back. He headed for the darkening horizon. Others followed him until all of the Cheyenne ran from the Spirit Woman.

From somewhere to her right, she heard a man's voice cry out, "Hold your fire, men. Hold your fire."

The rifle reports grew silent.

She hauled back on the reins, bringing the big stallion to a plunging halt. His muscles quivered and jerked beneath her thighs as she watched the last of the Cheyenne gallop out of sight. The tension snapped inside her. Like a rag doll, she fell forward and wrapped her arms around the stallion's great neck, his damp hide soft against her cheek.

"We did it," she whispered. "We did it, you big, wonderful brute."

A low rumble of galloping horses approached her, but she wasn't alarmed. They came from her right, from the depression where Mando, Louis and the cavalry patrol had fended off the attacks. Mando was going to be furious with her... if he had survived.

The thought pulled her to a sitting position, her eyes trained on the approaching horsemen. Two cavalrymen advanced toward her. Mando would have come for her, she was certain. She looked for other horsemen but saw none. One or two men moved about in the dip of land, but they wore uniforms. A cold foreboding settled in her stomach and spread tingles of apprehension up her spine, prickling along her scalp.

Pulling the reins to the right, she nudged the stallion into a canter and rode to meet the cavalrymen. "The Frenchman and the other man, where are they?" she called as they drew closer.

The two soldiers exchanged a look and reined in their horses as she approached.

"That was some ridin', ma'am." A heavy-shouldered black man called out.

Libby pulled the stallion to a stop in front of them. In a quick glance she noted the man's stack of hash marks on each sleeve and a bleeding cut on his bewhiskered cheek. She gave a worried glance behind the soldier and saw no signs of a white shirt or waving buckskin fringe.

"Don't you worry about that Frenchie or the Mexican," the sergeant said. "They ain't armed now. You're safe."

Libby drew her brows together into a deep frown. Why would these men think Mando and Louis were dangerous to her? Surely the army didn't think every man they came across on this plain traded with the Indians. At least she knew they weren't dead.

Her defenses sharpened, Libby kept her responses to a minimum. She cut a glance in the direction the Indians had taken in their escape. "I'd say we were all safe now."

"Yes, ma'am. I don't know how you did it, but those redskins took off just in time. I don't think we woulda made it."

He turned his horse and indicated she was to follow him. Libby drew alongside the two, and they started for the encampment. All three weaved around the sprawled bodies of dead warriors lying in the beaten-down grass. Libby trained her attention straight ahead, searching for any clues of what she might find when she reached the others.

"Funny thing, ma'am," the sergeant said. "I suspect you're the lady we been ridin' all over the countryside hopin' to find, but instead you find us and save our hides in the bargain." He shook his grizzled head from side to side. "Ain't life somethin'?"

Libby brushed at the caked dirt on her face, thinking of ways she could convince the army Mando Fierro wasn't a wanted man. She used the shirttail to wipe the rest away. "Yes, Sergeant, I would agree."

As they drew closer to the group of men, Libby searched through them, trying to find Mando and Louis. At last she spotted them, sitting back-to-back, an armed guard stationed over them.

Drawing upon her experiences in dealing with the authorities, whether Papa, preacher or police, she didn't wait to be helped to dismount, but slid from the stallion's back and marched toward the man who must be in charge, a tall, white man with a flowing brown mustache. He stood with arms crossed near Mando and Louis.

Sliding down the shallow bank into the waist-deep bowl of land, Libby winced at the sharp report of a pistol shot putting a wounded horse out of its misery. She stepped around two lifeless men being dragged to the

side, their dusty blue uniforms covered in blood. Off to
her left, another soldier wrapped a bandage around the
head of a young man, his mouth drawn up in a tight
grimace. Two dead Cheyenne lay along the lip of the basin.

The fighting had been fierce, and she couldn't contain
the pride that swelled inside her at the part she had played
in saving the rest of these brave men. The plan had been
crazy, but it had worked and that was all that mattered.
She had only to clear things up with this officer, and
Mando would be on his way to New Mexico and she
would be on her way to Santa Angela.

The cavalryman dropped his hands and rested them on
the brass buckle of his belt. "Captain Leland Douglas,
miss."

Libby nodded and glanced toward Louis and Mando.
"Why are these men under guard? They saved my life."

Libby returned the long, considering look the captain
gave her. She hated that small vee of hair that grew beneath his bottom lip and wondered what kind of man fa-
vored it. She met his red-rimmed gray eyes directly,
noting a moment of disapproval.

She supposed she looked a sight, but what did the man
expect? Libby raised her chin a notch. She knew what she
expected—Mando and Louis riding out of here immediately. "Did you hear what I said?"

"Are you Elizabeth Margaret Hawkins?" he asked.

This wasn't exactly the response to her question she
had expected. "Yes. I gather you've been looking for
me."

"We had about given up until we found this." He
fished inside his uniform blouse and brought out a scrap
of white petticoat. "I take it this is yours?"

She nodded slowly, a feeling nagging at her that the tiny ripples she had hoped to create by throwing out her message for her sister might have become a tidal wave.

"Yes," she finally replied.

"Thought so," the captain said. "We found the Frenchman just before the storm broke and discovered it in his saddlebag. We took him into custody." He stuffed the bit of muslin back inside his uniform. "You are now under the protection of the United States Army."

Chapter Sixteen

Libby slid a look at Mando's cold, hard stare and the tidal wave crashed over her head. Louis had been trapped with the soldiers because of that bit of cloth she had thrown to the wind. If Mando ever got his hands on her, she would *need* the United States Army.

A look at her protectors gave her little reassurance. The poor men were shot up, banged up and weary; and their leader regarded her with suspicion, as well he should. The trip back to Santa Angela would be long and full of questions. She would handle that later. Now she needed to get Mando and Louis on their way. She owed them that. Then this whole episode would be over at last.

Libby assumed her wide-eyed innocent look. Occasionally it worked, and the army captain had a chivalrous look about him.

"Captain Douglas, you are operating under some kind of misunderstanding." She gestured toward Mando and Louis. "These two men—"

"I believe are comancheros who traded you from the band of Comanches that killed the stage driver and guard."

"That's an absolute lie." Most of it, anyway, she thought. "They found me after I had escaped."

"Forgive me, Miss Hawkins, if I find it difficult to believe a young woman alone managed to escape hostile captivity."

So much for chivalry. Libby narrowed her eyes. "How many young women do you know who would have ridden into a war party of Cheyenne?"

Captain Douglas rubbed his hand over his eyes, along his stubbled jaw. "Probably none. It really doesn't matter how these men found you. We've been following cart tracks for days and we know only the comancheros would have any business out here. You don't have to be afraid of reprisals."

"I'm not frightened of any reprisals. These two men have treated me with nothing but kindness."

"I see."

He looked her up and down, making Libby aware of how she must appear, wearing little more than underwear and a man's shirt. Mando's shirt.

"What you see, Captain Douglas, is a woman who is very happy to be alive. You should be, too."

The captain's chin cocked back at her reminder of the help he had received from Louis and Mando in fighting the Indians, of her own near-suicidal dash to save them.

"I understand where you might have some sense of loyalty, but, Miss Hawkins, this is your chance to help eradicate the vermin that trade with those red devils." He pointed to the sharp, dry sounds of a shovel scooping up soil. "Look, up there."

Libby turned her attention to the edge of the depression. A soldier stood against the sunset, digging graves for the two blanket-wrapped bodies lying beside him.

"I've buried too many men in this war with the Indians. These comancheros give them guns and ammunition for cattle taken in raids in Texas."

Libby watched the soldier bowing to the earth, the slow rhythm of his shovel marking the seconds, the faint smell of rotting buffalo flesh filling her nose. No one was right and everyone was wrong. The broad questions narrowed to an individual choice and she made hers.

She faced the cavalry officer. "I'm well aware of what the comancheros do, Captain Douglas. As I said before, you are mistaken. These two men are buffalo hunters looking for food for their village in New Mexico. They were taking me there to safety."

Captain Douglas pulled the piece of petticoat from his uniform. "And what of this, Miss Hawkins? How did the Frenchman get this?"

Libby grabbed the scrap from his fingers. "I gave it to him to save for me." She dropped her gaze to her fingers as they worked the initials sewn on the square of cloth. "It's my mother's stitchery and I lost all of my other mementos on the stage."

"A nice story, very nice," Captain Douglas replied, not bothering to mask his contempt. "But the Frenchman told us he found it on a bush and he was a trapper headed for New Mexico. Obviously, the Mexican is the Frenchman's friend and you've connected them. We're taking them both to Fort Concho for questioning."

"But—"

"I don't know what happened between the time you dropped your little message and that wild ride to save his neck, Miss Hawkins." He looked her up and down, then glanced at Mando. "But, I could make a guess." He signaled the guard. "Tie 'em up, Carter."

The captain brushed her aside and moved by her. Libby saw the pistol, the flap loosened over his army-issue holster. Lifting the revolver was very simple. Telling herself why she did it wasn't.

She held the gun in both hands, pointing it at the captain's broad back.

— "Stop right there," she said, and pulled back the hammer with both thumbs.

The digging stopped. She made a quick glance around her and found all eyes on her. Captain Douglas turned around slowly and faced her. She hadn't expected his haggard expression.

"Tell your men to drop their weapons or I'll shoot." She fanned her fingers over the handle. "I swear I will."

The captain lifted his hands in a calming gesture. "Now take it easy." He extended one hand toward her. "Give me the gun. I don't want to bury anyone else tonight, especially you."

"Tell them," she shouted.

Captain Douglas took a step toward her. "You won't shoot me, honey."

Libby's eyes widened at a commotion by her side.

"But, I will, Captain."

Mando! Libby swallowed down the panic the captain's challenge had generated and stepped back, putting more distance between herself and the officer. A quick glance told her Mando had taken the guard's rifle. As Louis gathered their own weapons, Mando arrived at her side and took the captain's pistol from her. She gladly gave it up and rubbed her sweating palms on her shirt.

"Get the horses, Libby," Mando said. "I remind you, Captain, should anyone touch her, you will be the first to die."

"Let her pass, men. Taking them in isn't worth any more of us dying."

Libby ran to the center of the sandy pit where the gray had been taken and grabbed up his reins. She recognized the four white socks on Louis's roan and pulled him along, too. Only five mounts were left for the patrol to return to Fort Concho. She couldn't bring herself to take another one. She led the horses past the silent soldiers.

"You know it's a funny thing about you and your sister," Captain Douglas said as she pulled the horses by him. "She took up with a no-good comanchero, too. Of course, now he's supposed to be a respected man of the community, but once scum always scum. I guess it holds true in families as well."

Libby didn't answer him, but found a place to lead the horses out to level ground and waited in the gathering darkness. The captain's statement stunned her. Amelia married to a comanchero? Such a possibility seemed impossible. Something else nagged at her, a thought that wouldn't complete. Whatever it was would come to her later.

She supposed she was an outlaw now, too, but she couldn't let the army take Louis and Mando. They had saved her life. She owed them. That's right, she owed them. She had no other reasons for doing this. None.

She held her breath, hoping no one would try anything foolish. One fool was plenty in any group. Mando kept the rifle trained on the cavalry officer while Louis scrambled up the shallow embankment, carrying their gun belts and bandoliers. He stowed them away quickly, then turned and held the rifle so Mando could climb to the rim. So far so good.

The two men took the reins from her. While one kept a weapon trained on the captain, the other mounted his horse. Louis took up his own rifle and held two guns on the soldiers. For a moment, Libby thought Mando might leave her. It suddenly struck her she might never see him again. A strange sadness swept over her that had nothing to do with facing the consequences for her actions.

He looked at her, a question gathered between his brows, then he reached down and wrapped an arm around her ribs, lifting her before him. She held his arm tightly against her midriff and looked down at the contempt plainly written on the captain's face. How easily she had made her choice. How little she regretted it.

"Don't waste what little ammunition you have on us, Captain," Mando said. "The Cheyenne are still out there and you know they come back for their dead. You have a long trip home."

"You and the woman saved our butts, mister," the captain replied. "I won't shoot you in the back, but if I run into you again, I'll take you in."

"Fair enough."

Libby pressed her hands on Mando's to stop him from turning the horse. "Tell my sister—"

"I'll tell her we found you and you're as crazy as she is," Captain Douglas replied. "Don't visit her anytime soon, Miss Hawkins. You'll go into my report."

"Yes, I understand."

"One of these days you'll tell me why those Cheyenne ran away."

"The woman is magic," Mando answered, and whirled the stallion around.

The day ended in deep corals on one horizon while the night began in a clear sapphire blue on the other. Overhead, the night and day met in a changling hue that reminded Mando of Libby's eyes. Strange how the colors of the sky, the taste of his cigar, the wind against his face all carried new significance. Nothing like a handshake with death to sharpen one's appreciation of the beauty around him and the pleasures to be savored.

He dropped his gaze from the great vault above to the small redhead standing beside him, a scrap of muslin held tightly in her hands. A gentle evening breeze tugged at her hair, lifting wavy tendrils away from her face. She hadn't acknowledged his presence, but stared across the grassland to the column of horsemen moving away from the buffalo wallow. A sadder group of cavalry he had never seen. Only five horses and one was ridden double.

"Do you think they'll make it back to their fort?" she asked.

Mando placed his jacket around her shoulders. "You gave them their chance. Yes, I think they will make it."

"I'm curious, Mr. Fierro."

"Mr. Fierro?" he said. "I would think after all that has happened today, you would call me Mando."

Libby glanced down at her hands, then lifted her face once more to watch the soldiers grow smaller as they traveled farther into the distance. "I suppose you are right. Mando, then, I was curious about how this day's run-in with the Cheyenne will affect your... your trading business."

He noted her nervous plucking at the material in her hands. "Very little. The Cheyenne rarely come this far south. The Comanches will continue to raid in Texas and I will continue to trade with them."

The piece of petticoat disappeared into a small tight fist. "Business as usual."

"Until the army and the hunters finish the Comanches or..." He paused, having never put the notion into words.

"Or something or someone finishes you?" she supplied.

"Yes."

"This trading business is that important?"

"Much depends on its success." He thought of the taxes due on his land, the court fees to prove up his grants, the bribes to be paid. "Yes, it is that important."

Libby took a deep breath and straightened her shoulders.

"I suppose it's time to go," she said. "Tomas and Louis are ready to leave?"

"Almost. I want to give you something before we join the others."

She nodded, the hand holding the initialed square of material disappearing into her pants' pocket. "A piece of your mind? I meant no harm to anyone."

Mando paused, remembering the stab of anger that had hit him when the soldiers had abruptly taken his guns and Louis had told him why. The same daring and intelligence that had placed them in such a predicament had also pulled them out.

"I can't be angry with you anymore," he said. "I might as well blame the bolt of lightning that frightened Louis's horse. No, I had something else in mind."

He lifted the locket from his neck and held it aloft, remembering the night it had come into his possession. Or had it possessed him? He shrugged away the thought and dropped the locket over her head.

One of her hands clutched the round gold ornament. She lifted her face to meet his gaze. Again he was struck by the unusual beauty of her eyes, and he knew he always would be. Her sunburn had almost faded, leaving a bit of color beneath her dusting of freckles. Gold dust, he thought.

"It did bring you luck," she said.

Mando stepped closer, his fingers brushing across the lips he longed to kiss again. "It brought me the Spirit Woman."

Her eyes searched his as they did sometimes, then she lowered her lids and turned away. "The locket means a great deal to me." She lifted her gaze to the retreating column. "Especially now. It's all I have of my family."

She opened the locket, holding the small portraits up to the failing light. "This is my sister, Amelia. I was just thinking how amazing it is she married a man who had once been a comanchero. You said your brother had married a woman in Texas."

Mando caught the locket and snapped it closed. "It didn't take you long to make the connection."

She pulled the keepsake from his hand, keeping her eyes trained ahead. "So you've known all along I was related to Ross, this man who is more than a brother, a man you feel has been lured away from the comanchero life by my sister?"

"Yes, I've known."

"And it made a difference?" She rubbed the locket between her thumb and finger. "Your attitude regarding me."

Mando combed his hand through his hair and turned a step away from her. "To some extent, perhaps."

An understatement, to be sure, but that was all he would give her. He couldn't tell her that every time he looked into her beautiful eyes he remembered Ross looking into the eyes of her sister, then saying he wouldn't return to the plains with him.

"I can understand that," she said. "But, now, Mando. How does this affect what you feel about me now?"

He turned to Libby and placed his hands on her shoulders, making her face him. "Libby, I warned you once to guard your desires. Do not want more from me than I can give you."

She closed her eyes for a moment and when she opened them, resolve dimmed their usual sparkle. "Then leave me at the first stage station. I'll go to California, China if need be, someplace far away from here, far away from you."

"I can't, Libby," he replied, then thought of a reason why, a reason he could tell her, a reason he could tell himself. "Cabot would find you and he has a way of taking care of loose ends permanently."

Her chin lifted in that stubborn tilt he knew meant trouble.

"I won't run from him forever. I can't live my life like that."

"You won't have to. Stay at my rancho until spring. Then I will see that you reach Santa Angela safely. He won't follow you to Texas. He is wanted there."

"But Captain Douglas said—"

"The Comanches will be sitting on some reservation by then. The army will have other things on their minds."

He saw her indecision, her distress at the prospect of spending months with him. He couldn't blame her. Hadn't he wanted to prove she was no angel, to have her warm his bed all winter? He still did, but she deserved his honesty, and he had given it to her. The rest was up to her.

Suddenly her eyes narrowed. "Taking me to your ranch is what you had planned all along, isn't it? That's why you never told me where you were taking me, why you wouldn't tell me when I could go to my sister."

"I won't deny I wanted you, Libby. I still do," he replied.

"You must feel very pleased at how this has turned out."

"I am pleased we are alive." He brushed away a smudge of dirt from her cheek with his thumb. "And yes, I am pleased we are on our way to my valley."

Libby brushed his hand away and turned toward the approaching night. The battered army detachment blended into the dark horizon until the horse soldiers could no longer be seen.

"Staying with you is impossible," she said at last. "I will have to think of something else. I want to get on with living my life."

"Libby, you have no choice if you want a life to live."

"Choices." She bit the word out as if it were a curse. "When will I ever have any?"

Mando thought of some of the choices he had made over the years, choices that had changed the course of his life forever. "Choices can be very costly, Libby."

"I would pay a great deal for a few right now."

Mando gazed at the dark, empty horizon and remembered his hesitation before taking her up on his horse. He had suspected her ordeal with the Comanches would have softened any possible repercussions she might face at Fort Concho. Perhaps he should have left her with the surly captain. She had saved his life and given him his freedom, yet he couldn't let her go. One day he must.

"So would I, Libby, but first we each must pay for the choices we have made this day."

Louis glanced over his saddled horse at the couple on the hill, standing so close yet not touching. The young fools. The girl could have been killed today. He should have taken her on to Santa Angela no matter what Mando had said.

With a flip of his hand, he waved off the thought. No use pestering himself about the past. What was done was done. He would do his best with the future.

"Do you have room for this?"

Louis turned to Tomas and saw he carried a small sack of coffee. "I'll make room," he replied.

He took the offered sack from the boy, who was as occupied with Mando and Libby as he had been. Studying the boy from the corner of his eye, he opened his saddlebag and shoved the sack into a corner. Tomas had been about to ride down to find them when they had crested the hill. He hadn't seemed surprised to see Libby riding with Mando. Tomas had no way of knowing the trouble they had run into after the Indians had given up the attack. He should have assumed the girl would accompany the soldiers back to Fort Concho until he had heard what had occurred. Had something happened between Mando and Libby in the past two days he didn't know about?

"I would have liked to have seen that *capitán*'s face when the *señorita* pulled his own gun on him," Tomas said.

Louis glance at the two slowly walking down the hill. He was still trying to figure out why she had done it. "You should have seen my face. It was quite a surprise."

Tomas shifted a stalk of grass from one side of his mouth to the other. "Her love for El Aguila must be very great."

Louis flipped the cover closed over his saddlebag and turned to Tomas. "What are you talking about?"

Tomas removed the grass blade. "El Aguila asked me to take her to Fort Union, but I knew she would tell the soldiers everything as Cabot had said. Then El Aguila explained he would ask the gringa to say nothing and she would grant his request because she loved him.''

Louis scratched the stubble on his cheek, turning once again to watch the couple walk toward them. ''Who can say what a woman in love will do, eh?'' he said, not wishing to contradict what Mando had told the boy, though he doubted Libby's affections had been won so quickly. ''Get your gear finished up. We'll be riding all night.''

With a long, tired sigh, Tomas ambled over to his mount. Louis continued to watch the pair. The boy's story surprised him. Mando had taken quite a chance to protect the girl and make sure she reached safety. Mando trusted no one. Today she had risked her life and liberty to prove that trust. A curious state of affairs was developing here.

He noted Libby held something in her fist against her chest. As they drew closer, he made out a leather string around her neck. She must be holding her locket. Mando had returned it at last. Another surprise. This girl affected Mando more than he would ever admit.

Neither smiled and both looked miserable. Yes, he believed something might be brewing between these two. Perhaps love?

This slip of a girl might accomplish what he had been trying to achieve since Mando had started this comanchero trading. With her convictions and experience with the Indians, she could influence him to stop. If only the girl were not Amelia's sister. She would have a better chance to win over Mando.

He recalled that banner of red hair flying across the prairie and a war party of Cheyenne warriors taking to their heels. Perhaps this was the woman to make Mando let go of all that useless anger and begin to live for the future, instead of holding on to the past as hard as he held on to all that damnable land.

Bah! The French were ever romantic fools. Louis finished arranging his gear.

Libby reached her horse first and, without waiting for any assistance, placed her foot in the stirrup and pulled herself into the saddle. Louis mounted his horse and walked him to her side. He had something to tell her before they began their journey.

"Thank you, Libby," he said. "I know how much you fear Indians and how much you wanted to go to your sister in Santa Angela."

Libby nodded and fiddled with her reins. "Yes, well, at least one of my plans worked. We were lucky. And now my sister will know I'm alive. That was my main concern. That was why I left that piece of petticoat on the trail. I never wanted anyone to be hurt."

"Perhaps I should have left it."

She lifted her gaze to his, her little smile curling the corners of her mouth. "Remember that the next time you get in the middle of one of my schemes."

Louis reached over and covered her hand with his. "I won't forget, Libby. Not ever." He looked into her eyes and saw she understood his meaning.

"Thank you, Louis. I need a friend."

"Are you two ready?" Mando demanded sharply.

Louis leaned back into his saddle, keeping his amusement carefully to himself. "I have been waiting on you."

Mando touched his spurs to the gray's flanks. *"Vamanos."*

Louis allowed Mando to lead the way and took up the rear behind Tomas, who soon rode up next to Libby. Curious to hear what the boy was telling her, Louis took

his place on her other side. At the easy pace they were
traveling, he picked up their conversation easily.

"I have come up with a name for you," Tomas said.
"You are now La Rojita."

Libby turned from Tomas and glanced at him, a question drawing her brows together.

"Something like Little Red," he translated.

Libby smiled. "I've been called worse." She looked at
Tomas. "I'm very pleased, but why did you think of a
name for me, Tomas?"

"Now that you are one of us, you need a proper name.
I will tell El Aguila." Tomas rode ahead, catching up with
Mando.

Mando listened then turned to look at Libby. Louis
bent forward, curious to see her reaction to finding herself "one of them." She stared at Mando and held the
locket in her fist, muttering something about dancing
with the Devil.

Louis saw the broad grin on Mando's face before he
turned forward once more. He shook his head and
straightened his hat. "Dance lively, *chérie.*"

Libby gave him a startled look.

Louis waved his hand toward Mando. "Make him
dance to your tune, not his."

He spurred his horse ahead, leaving Libby with a puzzled but thoughtful expression on her pretty face.

Chapter Seventeen

Libby lost count of the days that followed. Every dawn broke the darkness in streaks of gray then golds and pinks; every sunset bid farewell to the hot days in broad fans of lavender and orange. With nothing to do between these colorful displays but look at empty sky and flat, featureless grassland, she filled the hours of endless riding with endless questions that had few answers.

Her future looked as bleak and empty as this land she traveled. As she followed Mando across the plains, she was utterly lost inside, with no landmarks or familiar ground to help her find her way to understanding herself.

Was she Libby Hawkins, the woman who was going to escape down any avenue that appeared, or was she La Rojita, the woman who had kicked the door closed on the very avenue she had hoped to find? One question she could answer. She didn't regret pulling that captain's gun on him, and perhaps that answered all the others.

Mando had said they must pay for the choices they had made that day. He made it sound as if she were some burden he must deal with, yet he hadn't kissed her as if she were a burden and he had returned her locket. His gesture had meant more to her than she had let him know.

He had released her in a way, giving her another choice to make. She had traded a great deal more for that locket than he had requested on that first night. She had given him her loyalty. Now she had to decide what more to give him. He had made his requirements very clear. He wanted nothing from her but the most basic pleasures, and he had warned her to want the same from him.

Therein lay her problem.

She wanted more from him now. Little good that would do. The barriers against her were strong. She was an American, all of whom he seemed to hate, and she was Amelia's sister, a subject he had refused to broach again. She could prove to him all Americans weren't greedy opportunists, but she could do little about her relationship with Amelia. She needed more information about his animosity toward her sister. Louis might help her.

The Frenchman had said to make Mando dance to her tune. Many of the long hours in the saddle had been passed trying to figure out how she could do that. Obviously Louis had overheard her mutterings about dancing with the Devil and thought she could have some influence over Mando. He had more confidence in her abilities than she did.

None of these speculations really mattered. They would lead her nowhere she wanted to go. She was tired of dancing to any tune. Mando had made himself clear. What he wanted, she wasn't prepared to give. What she wanted . . . she didn't know what she wanted except she didn't want to spend the winter with Mando. She had come up with no other plan.

She had a numb bottom, callused hands and a growing hatred for the taste of wild game, but she didn't have a plan. All these days of riding had passed and she hadn't thought of one scheme, one glimmer of an idea, not one small next step to forgo spending the winter with Mando on his ranch.

So far all she could come up with was her mama's favorite edict proclaimed on too many occasions to count. She had made her bed and now she had to lie in it. That wasn't a plan, that was a prediction.

Libby yawned behind her hand and wondered when they would pass through that gap in the mesas up ahead. The moon hadn't risen yet and distances were hard to measure in the darkness. They had decided to ride on tonight to the small town beyond the low range of flat-topped hills that rose from the flatlands like islands in an ocean of grass.

She lowered her gaze, examining the trail ahead and recalled no one had said much about the village when they had discussed riding on at the noon break. It couldn't be much, considering the muddy stream they had been following was called a river, the Pecos she thought. Not that she cared what the place was like.

She wanted off this horse, a bath, a meal with vegetables, a real bed in a room. Some small place where she could sleep and not hear Mando's breathing or smell his cigar when he was restless or simply feel his presence stretched out a few feet from her side.

Rested and alone, she would come up with some other options to her present predicament other than Mando's ranch. She couldn't spend the winter there, not with Mando, a man who swept all questions of right and wrong away with a single kiss, a man who traded with the Comanches.

She touched the locket that lay between her breasts. One thing she must do. She must persuade Mando to let her send a letter to Amelia explaining where she had deposited their inheritance. If something happened to her, her sister needed to know where that money was.

Little good the money did her now. Every step took her closer to those mountains, closer to Mando's valley, and she had no plan. Nothing. She was just tired. Tired, confused and bedazzled. Bedazzled by a land that gave no mercy, a sky that promised no limits, and a man that embodied both.

Her parents had lamented her strong will. Now she counted on it.

"Libby," Mando called.

Libby lifted her head but didn't catch his next words. Behind him, huge and golden, the moon had risen between two black mesas. A beautiful, eerie light flooded the gap, spilling onto the plain, glistening on the muddy river and igniting tiny sparkles of minerals scattered over the rocks. Splendid and breathtaking, the sight pulled at her as if the moon possessed power over her, as well as the tides.

"Libby," Mando repeated, his voice nearer.

Libby blinked, retrieving her senses, and discovered her horse had continued until she had almost passed Mando. She reined the sorrel to a halt. "I didn't hear what you said."

He turned, looking at the moon, then gave his attention to her. "It is beautiful. One of my favorite places. The town beyond the pass is called El Puerto de las Lunas, the port of the moon."

"How poetic," she answered, enjoying another viewing of the pass into the mountains that looked as though it led straight to the moon.

Whimsy overtook her tired mind, and she imagined she traveled to the moon over a carpet of stars, leaving all her troubles behind. No more remembering that last desperate kiss. No more wondering where the choices made that day on the plain would take her.

She forced the fanciful thoughts from her mind and concentrated on the realities. "Is your ranch close to the town?"

"No. It lies several more days beyond these hills in the Sangre de Cristo Mountains, but I always return through here and hope to reach the pass as the moon rises. I'm glad we did tonight."

"So am I. It will be a sight I will never forget." Libby caught the sound of Tomas's horse coming up behind her. She turned and saw the plains spread in dark, glittering swells that reached the stars. She was done with the plains and found she would miss their stark beauty. She faced ahead, wondering what waited beyond the port of the moon.

"Do you think my uncle and the others have made it back?" Tomas asked.

Libby frowned and looked at Mando. She had no desire to run into trouble, and Cabot would supply all she needed.

"I doubt it," Mando replied. "Hopefully, they found more trade."

Libby's frown deepened. She didn't like reminders of what these men did. Confusion always followed, then more questions for herself she didn't want to answer.

"What will we do if Cabot and the others are there?" she asked. All these days she had been concerned about her future when she might not have one.

"Don't worry, La Rojita," Tomas interjected. "I will tell them of your brave ride to save El Aguila and the Frenchman."

She exchanged a quick look with Mando. "Thank you, Tomas. I'm sure that would help." Perhaps it would with Tomas's uncle and the other New Mexicans, but she doubted Cabot would be impressed.

"What would help?" Louis reined in his horse beside them.

Libby pushed the black sombrero back from her face and gave him a quick smile. Something about the buck-skinned Frenchman always lightened her heart. "A cannon, Louis. I think a cannon is just the thing we need."

Mando waved off Louis's questioning look. "It would help if you rode into El Puerto and checked things out."

Not even the dusting of moonlight softened the hard expression that set on Louis's weathered face. "Cabot?" he bit out.

"Maybe," Mando replied. "I told Gordito we would meet them in El Puerto. They took the longer route back and, hopefully, they stopped to trade. We should miss them, but I want to know for sure."

The Frenchman nodded. "Makes sense."

"Not to me," Libby said. "Why take chances? Let's bypass this town."

"We will if Louis finds any signs of trouble," Mando said. "I hope he doesn't. We're out of supplies and I think I can arrange a muzzle for Cabot and his Irish hound when they do arrive."

Libby wondered how he could arrange that but decided she didn't want to know. With one last doubtful glance given to Mando, she directed her attention to the Frenchman. "Be careful, Louis."

"Thank you, *chérie*. You can count on that." He turned to Mando. "If everything looks quiet, I'll signal from the bridge, then see about rooms for us."

"And baths," Libby added.

Louis smiled. "And baths."

Tomas piped in. "Tell my mother I am coming home. I hope she has made *tamales.*"

"I can smell them from here, Tomas." Louis guided his horse around them, then rode into the gap, his hoofbeats gradually disappearing.

"You live in El Puerto, Tomas?" Libby asked.

"*Sí,* with my mother and my sisters. I know my mother would want you to stay with us," Tomas offered.

Libby was about to accept when Mando cut in. "She will stay with me."

Libby snapped her attention to Mando. "I think not."

Mando jerked a nod to Tomas. "You lead us through the gap."

"*Sí,* El Aguila." Tomas couldn't hide the excitement in his voice. "Aye, aye," he said, urging his horse up the trail toward the twin mesas standing black against the moonlit sky.

Libby wasted not a moment. "I won't stay with you."

"Cabot could ride in anytime. You wouldn't want to bring trouble to the Trujillos."

Libby sighed. "No, but—"

"No buts," Mando said shortly, then his mouth spread slowly into that crooked smile she was beginning to find attractive. "Also I must see that you do nothing foolish."

"That's not fair," she protested. "I wouldn't do anything to endanger anyone, least of all myself." Realizing her record might not hold up to such a statement, she added, "Not anymore."

"You still do not want to come to the ranch, correct?" he asked.

"Right."

"Then, that is cause enough for me to worry. Remember you have a way of getting what you want."

"True, but lately I've been receiving a lot of what I don't want."

"Maybe you are having trouble deciding which is which," Mando replied, his dark eyes moving over her in that caressing way he had that made her forget her train of thought.

He had touched on a sore subject, one she had dealt with for days with little progress. "Shouldn't we catch up with Tomas?"

"In a moment," he replied. "I want Louis to have some time to check things out."

"I wish there was some way to convince your men that I mean them no harm."

"After Tomas finishes with his tales, I doubt you have any more trouble from the New Mexicans. After all, La Rojita, you are one of us now."

Libby gripped her reins tighter. "I don't find that amusing."

Mando's smile fell into a straight, hard line. "You don't have to, just find it convenient while in New Mexico."

Mando didn't give her a chance to reply, even if she had had a response, but touched his spurs to the gray's sides and rode ahead.

Libby held her restless sorrel in, not as eager as her horse to follow. She watched the horse and rider climb the trail leading through the gap, the moon hanging just above the mesas. Each night she had measured the moon's receding fullness, marking the time she had first been captured by the Comanches.

It had been full then and now, the sharp circle had softened on one side. Much had happened in so short a time. She had survived a Comanche raid only to give her loyalty to men who traded with them. How much more of herself would she lose with the passing of the days?

Mando reached the top and turned to look back at her. The silhouette against the moon of horse and rider was as black as the mesas that rose on each side. He waved to her, beckoning her to follow him. Libby gathered her reins but couldn't touch her heels to the horse's flanks.

Her ears rang with the racing of her heart. Rubbing her damp palms against her thighs, she couldn't tear her gaze from the man, from the power of the moon. She knew she must follow him, but where? To the moon? To perdition? Was there a difference?

Mando waved to her again. She saw him turn his horse, about to come back down to get her. She touched her heels to the sorrel and started up the path. An odd sensation tingled along her skin, fluttered through her stomach. Like riding toward the Cheyenne, she knew she was in danger of passing from one existence to another, from life to death, from honor to compromise.

The outcome was up to her. Mando had warned her to expect nothing from him, had told her he would never stop trading with the Comanches. Despite knowing all of that, she couldn't deny something drew her to him, something as strong as the moon to the tides. She must admit he possessed this power over her if she was to fight against it. She climbed higher, the dark silhouette of the man and horse growing closer, the moon dazzling her eyes, the fragrant whiff of Mando's tobacco scenting the wind.

Her thoughts wandered to his voice against her ear, telling her of his home, to his arms closing around her, promising to safeguard her dreams, to the brief, desperate kiss on the plain that had left her wanting more. Her knees weakened and the reins grew slack in her hands.

She searched for something inside herself to hold on to. Something to dim the moon and quiet her heart. She recalled the plans she had made when she'd purchased those tickets to Texas, but they proved too weak, too nebulous for the anchor she needed. At that moment she realized she had no anchors, no direction, only this path to Mando Fierro.

She joined him at the top of the pass and looked down upon the small village strung along the Pecos. Lights shone from open windows of what looked to be square mud huts, smoke curled into the night and the faraway barking of a dog reached them. Civilization.

She turned to Mando. His long, thin cigar drooped from the corner of his mouth, his eyes were narrowed against the smoke as he watched her. The red scarf held back his hair, leaving the sharp features of his face in shadowed relief. Moonlight shone across his cheekbones, the curved blade of his nose, his prominent brow. Why did he have to be so handsome?

Libby sighed and looked down the path. "Where's Tomas?"

Mando took the cigar between his fingers and gestured below. "I told him to go on to his mother."

Libby saw a horseman clatter over the wooden bridge into the town. An uneasiness crept over her at finding herself suddenly alone with Mando. "I suppose we should go, too."

"After Louis's signal."

"I had forgotten," she replied.

"A dangerous thing to let your mind wander."

Remembering where hers had been, she had to agree. "Yes, one should keep one's mind trained on the important matters."

"I have had trouble with that lately, Libby. My mind keeps wandering to the color of your hair at sunrise, your laugh, the sadness in your eyes."

Surprised he had noticed her unhappiness, Libby turned to Mando. "Are my eyes sad?"

He turned his gaze from the moon and looked at her, the light breeze playing with his hair. "Yes," he replied. He drew on his cigar, allowing the smoke to ease from his mouth. His lids grew heavy as he studied her through the sinuous haze.

"These past nights, I would lie awake, wondering how I could take the sadness from your eyes," he said. "I can't let you go, Libby. Not yet. As I would listen to your breathing, your restless sleep, I decided passion would replace the sadness. Then I would imagine what I would do to you, how I would kiss your lips, taste your mouth, explore the softness of your breasts, the secrets of your body."

A shivering took her, like a fever that began from deep inside as she listened to him and recalled those nights under the stars, her thoughts always on the man lying so close she could have reached over and touched him. She clamped her lips against their trembling, held her hands in fists to stop their shaking, but she could not control the restless need building within her.

"Libby, *querida,* I can wait no longer."

Her mouth was too dry to answer. Words were lost in the tumbling chaos of her thoughts.

Mando swung from his saddle and threw his cigar to the dirt. With no words or hesitations, he crossed to her horse and lifted her from the saddle. He held her close, his hands linked at the small of her back.

Libby slid her hands from his shoulders, pressing them against his chest, despairing at their trembling. She fought to gather her arguments, some kind of protest. "Mando, I don't think—"

"Don't think, Libby," he said, his tone low and intimate. "Only feel the pleasure for this moment." He ducked his head beneath the wide sombrero and touched his lips to hers. Soft at first, teasing them with his tongue.

The warm rush of blood sang through her head, pulsed through her body. She gathered the soft material of his shirt in her fists, trying to hold on to something of herself.

"Take off the hat," he whispered against her lips.

With his request the only coherent thoughts entering her head, she closed her eyes and lifted her hands, removing the hat, her hair falling to her back in a thick, loose braid. Mando pulled her closer until she felt the hard wall of his chest press against her breasts, warming her skin. The cool leather and brass of the bandolier soon warmed between them. She dropped the hat, her arms limp at her sides.

"Open your eyes, *querida*. I want to see them in the moonlight."

Libby raised her lids as if pulled from a dream. His eyes, dark and hot, probed hers.

"Damn the beauty of your eyes. A man loses his soul in them."

Libby fought harder against the lethargy, sapping her strength, her will. "He must have one first," she murmured and placed her hands against his shoulders, trying to find the strength to push away.

He laughed and pulled her closer still, his hands trailing up her back beneath her hair. "That would be his downfall, *querida*."

Libby opened her mouth to protest. Mando swiftly silenced her with a kiss that stole her breath away and took all opposition with it. His tongue found hers, and the trembling inside her spread until she shook in his arms. She rubbed the palms of her hands down the smooth curvature of his muscled arms, then slid them up to his shoulders, her fingers tangling in his hair.

The tension built by all those nights of lying stiffly beside him, aware of his every movement, wondering what would happen if they were alone finally broke free and swept her past all resistance.

Everything she had feared, everything she had hoped crashed together until hope and fear melded into a forlorn longing for something out of reach, something she sought in the hunger of his kiss.

Mando trailed his lips along her jaw, then found her earlobe, teasing it with his tongue, biting it gently before kissing her neck. Libby looked at the stars, her breathing coming in short, hard gasps, her fingers digging into his shoulders. She never thought anything would be like this need to give, to take, to surrender.

One hand explored beneath her jacket, edging toward her waist, gathering the long tail of his shirt from the waistband of her trousers. She felt his hand dip beneath the material and curve over her rib cage.

"Mando . . ." she whispered.

His mouth closed over hers, and she never knew what she had been about to say. His hand closed over her breast, squeezing it gently, and she lost all thought but one. Dancing with the Devil was no longer enough.

Chapter Eighteen

A gunshot from the town broke them apart. Libby gasped for breath and sanity, finding both difficult to recover. She touched a shaking hand to her lips and looked at Mando. He stood inches from her, tensed and removed, his face turned toward the town, his revolver a stark outline against the white of his shirt.

Gradually he relaxed, thumbing the pistol's hammer in place and returning the big revolver to his holster. "Louis's signal," he said, then met her gaze with a slow smile. "You look as if you have just been caught with your hand in the alms box instead of thoroughly kissed. You've never been kissed so well before. Admit it."

Libby dropped her hand from her mouth and raised her chin, his teasing question hitting fairly close to home.

"Of course I have," she replied. The man was impossible already. She wouldn't give him more to preen about. "Many times and better, too."

His smile widened. "Liar."

She tossed back her hair and propped her hands on her hips. "You know very little about me."

He picked up his hat and placed it on his head, securing the leather strap beneath his chin. "But I'll have all winter to learn."

Following him with a narrow-eyed glare as he walked to his horse, she said, "Don't count on it."

Satisfied with that retort, she retrieved her own mount from where it had wandered.

Mando swung up into his saddle. "Lie to me, Libby, but don't lie to yourself."

Libby rejected one reply after another as she placed a foot in a stirrup and her hand on the saddle horn. She pulled herself onto the sorrel and gave Mando a look that said everything she couldn't think to say. Finally, unable to come up with anything really stinging, she resorted to name-calling. "You are the most arrogant, insufferable—"

"It's good to see a little spirit back in those magic eyes," he said.

He gave her that twisted smile she had thought so attractive earlier and now found irritating, then started down the trail into the valley below.

Libby held her fist to the moon. "This is all your fault." She gave her horse a kick and followed Mando toward the town at an easy gallop.

She was desperate now and determined, too. Determined Mando Fierro wouldn't spend the winter curled by the fire with his twisted, satisfied smile on his face. No plan had developed yet, but now she was confident one would. She had learned desperation and determination could be depended upon to produce results.

Suddenly they were upon the bridge, their horses' hooves pounding across it. Louis waited for them on the other side. He swung in beside her. Libby gave him a quick smile.

Gunshots burst all around them as Mando reached the first building. Libby sawed back on her reins, causing her horse to rear. Shots came faster. She looked about her in a panic and tried to control her mount. Mando rode on, not seeing her trouble or drawing his own gun.

Louis grabbed her horse's bridle. "It's nothing, Libby," he shouted. "Only the usual welcome for El Aguila."

Libby glanced around her and noticed men running into the street and firing guns into the air. Several more were on the rooftops, orange flashes marking their locations.

She gave Louis a nod. "I'm fine now," she said above the uproar. "I didn't expect anything like this."

Louis laughed. "No, I don't expect you would. Come. Dinner and your bath are waiting."

Libby followed Louis down the middle of the road lined with flat-roofed buildings on both sides. She saw a few women standing in the spill of the light from their doorways, waving at Mando and calling to him. Dogs barked, joining the riotous welcome. She even saw one or two children, rubbing fists in their eyes, hanging on to their mamas' skirts.

The houses were not like anything she had seen before. They were made of what looked like mud. The doorways and window frames were brightly painted. Some had signs painted above entrances, their Spanish wording lost to Libby. She had entered another world.

Above all the noise and shouts, she heard, "El Aguila, El Aguila," from every direction. Tomas and the other comancheros had called Mando by that name. She would ask what it meant later. Now she wanted to find a place to eat, bathe and rest. Then she could get down to some good, hard plan-making.

A short distance down the road, she spotted Mando tying his horse in front of a two-storied building with a faded border of roses and leaves painted around a broad, arched doorway. Singing, laughing and the frantic strumming of a guitar floated out the door and windows with the light that streamed into the night. Greeted by a crowd of men, Mando was pulled inside. She saw him turn and look her way. Louis waved him on.

Libby guided her horse next to the gray and dismounted, wrapping the reins around a post in front as she had seen Mando do. She gave the place an apprehensive look over, the interior seen through the windows and entrance hardly inviting. From the hard look of the customers and the amount of spirits being served, she guessed this was some kind of gin parlor.

Louis took her arm. "Come inside. I'm starved."

She hung back. "We're going to eat in there?"

"This isn't St. Louis or even San Antonio, Libby. Rosa serves the best food to be found in El Puerto." He gave her arm another tug. "Let's eat."

Libby realized she was being ridiculous. She had traveled across the plains with three men alone. Surely she could eat in a saloon. "I'm so hungry for something besides antelope or rabbit, I'd eat anywhere."

Besides, she had always been curious about such places. Dens of iniquity, the Right Reverend Carmichael had called them.

As soon as she walked through the archway, a silence fell upon the large, smoky room. Every eye turned her way. Libby had never seen so many guns, knives and leering faces in her life. Perhaps the reverend hadn't been all hot wind. Libby searched through the crowd for Mando. She spotted him standing among backslappers by a long bar in the back of the room. Seeing her, he pushed a path toward her. A small sigh of relief eased past her lips.

"El Aguila," a woman squealed.

Libby turned to her left and saw a young woman with long black hair and dancing black eyes standing on a stairway, her arms outstretched toward Mando. Dumbstruck, Libby watched the woman gather her bright green skirt and rush down the wooden steps. She ran across the room, her skirt and the red petticoat beneath it flying about her calves, her ample bosom swaying beneath a loose-fitting white blouse that bared her shoulders.

A path opened for her straight to Mando. She launched herself at him, wrapping her arms around his neck, pushing his hat to his back and kissing him soundly on the mouth. His arms curled around her, pulling her close.

The rowdy men shouted their approval, glasses were banged on tables and the guitar player sent up loud, rousing chords.

Libby turned away from the display, telling herself the pounding in her head wasn't an oncoming headache and the queasy feeling in her stomach was hunger. She pushed at her hair, wishing she had thought to at least rearrange her loosened braid.

"Didn't you say this place served food as well as whiskey and women?" she asked Louis.

Louis laughed and guided her to a table set with three places and pulled a chair out for her. Libby sat on the offered chair, refusing to look at Mando and the woman. She heard a bright, musical voice speaking Spanish and Mando's deep laughter. Her foot took up a rapid tapping beneath the table, but she folded her hands on the table, in a quiet demonstration of disinterest.

"The food will be here soon and they are readying a bath for you upstairs," Louis said.

She flattened her hands on the scarred table. "Upstairs?" she said, not bothering to hide her displeasure. Her eyes traveled up the steps to an open gallery that led to several closed doorways. A man with a woman draped around him entered one; their embrace was Libby's last sight of the two before the door slammed closed. A small amount of quick deduction told her what went on upstairs.

"We aren't staying here?" She turned her attention to Louis. "Surely there's a hotel."

Louis smoothed each side of his mustache. "I know a widow who rented us rooms, but I didn't want to wake her to draw your bath."

"Of course not. I'm sorry if I sounded unappreciative." She cast uneasy glances at the stares given her by the clientele. Some were hungry, some curious, some suspicious. For the most part, these men appeared more dangerous and disreputable than the comancheros who rode with Mando. "I . . . I guess I'm just tired."

Louis pulled out his .45 and placed it carefully on the table, the barrel facing a nearby wall. "That's understandable."

"Is anyone giving you trouble?"

Libby looked up to find Mando standing over her, a bottle of whiskey in one hand, a tall glass of water in the other. Only you, she thought, but simply looked away.

"Just a precaution," Louis replied, and left the gun on the table.

Mando nodded his agreement and sat down in the chair next to Libby. He placed the water in front of her. "Water is all they had, but it's cool. I didn't think you would want a beer."

Libby accepted the glass from him, her hand brushing the black leather glove he wore. She recalled that first sip of water he had given her and where it had led, life and temptation. Her hand shook, spilling water onto the table as she set the glass down. A memory flashed of Mando kissing that woman as he had kissed her.

"Water is all I want," she replied stiffly.

He raised his eyebrows to Louis, who shrugged his shoulders. Mando removed the two shot glasses turned upside down over the top of the bottle and slid one across the ring-stained table to Louis.

"What did they have to eat?" he asked, and filled the two glasses.

Louis tossed his drink back and wiped his hand across his mouth. "I told them to bring everything they had left." He presented his glass for a refill. "We will soon see what that provides."

Libby counted three swift shots for each man and thought they could use a good speech on temperance, but decided another time would be more appropriate. She pushed her hair back, sneaking looks about the room, wondering where that screeching woman had gone.

"Carmelita is an old friend," Mando said.

Libby cut her gaze to his lazy, crooked smile. He lounged back in his chair, one arm thrown over the top rung, a cigar clamped between his fingers. She didn't care for the speculative gleam in his eye and wondered if she had given away her displeasure at seeing the beautiful girl in his arms.

"I'm sure she is," she answered sweetly. "Why don't you ask her to join us for dinner?"

Louis slapped the table and laughed. "Yes, Mando, ask her."

Mando rolled the cigar between his fingers, his gaze steady on her. "The spitfire I want is at my table," he said.

His deep, quiet voice swirled inside her, hot and evocative, like smoke from his cigar. Libby's fingers curled and so did her toes inside the soft moccasins. A warm flush began in her stomach and spread until she felt her face must glow as bright as her hair. She shifted on her chair, cleared her throat and sent an imploring look to Louis. He shrugged and poured himself another drink. Libby refused to look at Mando again, hoping to regain some composure.

"I wish dinner would come soon," she said, and a plan, too, she thought. Mando Fierro was temptation incarnate, and she had never been good at denying herself anything she wanted. And she wanted this man. Denying that fact to herself or to him would only be a farce, but she couldn't play by the rules he had set and she couldn't fall in love with a comanchero.

Love? The thought jolted her. She raised her gaze to his, regarding him from a new perspective. Around her, boisterous voices conversed in a language she couldn't understand, guitars played melodies she had never heard. She found herself in a land she had never planned to visit. Yes, she loved Mando Fierro, the man who had saved her life, cared for her, protected her, the man who traded guns to the Comanches and hated Americans, who hated her sister. She couldn't go to that valley. He would break her heart.

A deep sadness welled inside her, much like the emotion she had experienced after the battle with the Cheyenne when she knew Mando wouldn't give up his trading. Now she understood what she had sought from his kiss under the moon, that something that had left her so forlorn. Love. Perhaps her heart was already broken.

Mando stepped outside into the cool night, leaving behind the shouts toasting La Rojita. Tomas had done his job well, depicting the brave and beautiful La Rojita chasing away the Cheyenne war party without firing a shot and saving El Aguila and Señor Louis from certain death. When he came to the part where she drew the *capitán*'s pistol, even wounding the cavalryman in the shoulder when he tried to retake it, the crowd had been completely won over. He would not have to worry about anyone's suspicions of her loyalties causing problems.

He drew a cigar from his shirt pocket and struck a match on a nearby post. Leaning against the same post, he lit the cigar, puffing on it contentedly. Strong whiskey, a fine meal, a good cigar and a beautiful woman. The perfect night. But it wasn't perfect, because Libby had become sad again. He missed that spark of mischief in her eyes and pondered ways to ignite it once again.

"Have an extra cigar?"

Mando turned and found Louis walking toward him from the cantina's entrance. He dug another out of his pocket, offering it to the Frenchman. "Libby having her bath?"

Louis accepted the cigar and used Mando's to light it, then handed his cigar back to him. "Rosa herself took her upstairs. I told Roberto to have two tubs filled in the back room for us. Señora Ortega will put us up for the night."

Mando smiled at the Frenchman. "Do you have a widow tucked away in every town in New Mexico?"

Louis chuckled and took a puff on his cigar. "Very nearly."

"No word of Cabot?" he asked. He wanted no trouble falling on Louis's hospitable widow should the American decide to pay them a visit in their sleep.

"He hasn't been seen," Louis replied. "None of the others, either. They must still be out on the plains."

"I hope they bring in a good herd."

220 Dance with the Devil

Louis didn't answer, only smoked his cigar.

Mando wanted no arguments and crossed his arms, the stars capturing his interest. The night sky was a friend he had visited often this past week on the trail when his mind wandered in dangerous directions. "Why didn't you marry one of your widows and settle down, Louis?"

"I could never bring myself to disappoint the others," he replied. "Besides, who would take care of you, *mon ami?*"

Mando dropped his gaze from the stars and regarded the older man with affection. "You have been a loyal friend, Louis. I have needed one."

The Frenchman gave him a sharp look. "Yes, Mando, you have. And now you have gained another."

Mando looked away. He knew to whom Louis referred. "Libby," he said quietly.

"She paid a high price for that gift to you in the soldiers' camp, nearly her life."

Mando combed his hand through his hair, uncomfortable hearing the thoughts spoken aloud that had plagued him over the miles. "She made that choice," he replied, his tone sharp with impatience, with what he didn't know. Impatience with himself?

"Which makes the gift more valuable. I think she would give you her love."

Mando recalled the moonlight splashing in her passion-filled eyes, the sadness that lingered there still. His mouth straightened into a grim stubbornness. "I haven't asked for anything like love."

"Will you?"

"No." He shoved away from the post and turned his shoulder to Louis, facing the road that stretched in a quiet, dark path to the bridge. "I have told her from the beginning what to expect from me, what I can give her."

Louis stepped up behind him, his voice urgent. "She deserves more, Mando. Do you think she is like some cantina girl you can take to the rancho for the winter who will want nothing but your loving and a bag of silver in the spring? You told me you would not hurt her and yet you will break her heart."

"I have no choice, now." He recalled his reason. "I must take her to the rancho for her safety."

"Tell her that. Not me."

Mando turned to Louis. "What would you have me do, Louis?"

The Frenchman made a wide gesture with the hand holding his cigar. "Forget the past and live for a future. Marry the girl."

Mando stared at Louis, dismissing the idea before it could take root. "She would never marry a comanchero."

"That's easily remedied. Give up this trading business."

Mando sighed and shook his head. "Again this, Louis? I can't give it up. I won't. The *americanos* have taxed my land to ruin and Ramon still argues for my grants in the courts. That costs money, Louis. A great deal of money and the only way I can get it is to trade with the Comanches for the cattle they steal from the land that was stolen from them."

"Sell off some of the land, Mando, guard it with the education Don Alphonso gave you." Louis's bushy brows drew together. "Do you think he would have sent you to St. Louis to learn the American ways only to have you stay trapped in the old ways? He saw the changes coming." He jabbed the air with his cigar. "You must do the same."

Mando raised his head. "As long as I am alive, the Fierro lands will remain as I received them from my father, as he received them from his, and as he received them from the King of Spain. This is my trust and I cannot turn my back on it for a woman. Not like Ross did."

Louis drew himself up, his gaze leveled at him. "Ross turned his back on you, Mando. He left you at the Valle de las Lasgrimas four years before he met that woman. He wouldn't trade with the Indians anymore."

"He would have come back," Mando replied, his voice insistent, filled with bitterness. "I saw it in his eyes last spring. That hunger for the plains, for the fight. He would have come back until he looked into that woman's blue eyes."

"Bah! Believe what you want." Louis tossed Mando's statement away with a wave of his hand. "All that noble talk of the land is nothing compared to your need to fight the Anglos, to ride wild and free across the plains to seek revenge for your father's death. Instead, you'll only find your own."

Mando hooked his thumbs inside his gun belt. "That is the choice I made and I will live or die with it."

Louis met his gaze from beneath his heavy brows. "Oh, you will die with it, Mando, and I see now nothing can make you change the path you have chosen." Louis turned and walked away.

Mando smoked his cigar and watched the Frenchman turn the corner. Maybe Louis would leave him alone about the trading now. But he found no comfort in the knowledge. A restless dissatisfaction ate at him. He had never experienced anything quite like this need that had no name, then he thought perhaps it did. He wanted Libby and he knew only one cure. He threw down his cigar and followed Louis to their waiting baths.

Chapter Nineteen

Libby waited until the soft chink of spurred boots faded around the corner of the building, then pulled the shutters closed on the window overlooking the street. Turning away from the embrasure, she stepped down from a chair she stood on and slowly sank to its seat. Louis had told her to wait by her window to hear something important. That was not quite the serenade she had expected.

A sad smile played at the corners of her mouth. How easily she had sold off her home to go adventuring, yet Mando refused to sell a portion of his to insure his future. He was an all-or-nothing kind of man. He gave all or he gave nothing. He had told her what to expect. Nothing of himself, only the pleasure of the moment. Now she knew that was all he believed he had to give.

Her hands wandered to the buttons on her shirt, her fingers absently unfastening them one by one, her thoughts straying to that kiss under the moon. She wished such pleasures were enough, but she needed more. She had fought too many hard battles with death to live only for the present. She wanted a future, and Mando was imprisoned by the past.

Louis wanted her to know these things about Mando, to hear from his own lips his reluctance to give up his lands, his revenge, his bitterness. She had also heard something else. His acceptance that his choices would cost him his life. Was Louis trying to warn her, or was he issuing a plea for her help to save his friend? Warning or plea, both posed some serious soul-searching.

A soft knock on the door stilled her fingers and her thoughts. She asked softly, "Who is it?"

"Rosa," came a voice from the other side of the door.

Libby quickly crossed the room, passing the big, wooden tub of rose-scented water with a longing look, then removed the chair she had placed under the doorknob. She opened the door and stepped back, admitting the rustling whirl of black silk bombazine that was Rosa Galvan. The older woman turned within the cloud of rose perfume that had entered the room with her and smiled, a stack of clothing held in her arms.

Closing the door, Libby was struck once more by the crude setting for this dark-eyed jewel. Bright and vivacious, Rosa's graceful beauty overwhelmed her rather primitive surroundings. Libby had been too polite to ask why the woman lived in the small village of El Puerto, running a rough cantina. An interesting story lay somewhere behind her slanted eyes.

"I brought you some clean clothes," she said, her accent rich but her English clear. Rosa tossed them onto a bed in the corner.

"Thank you. I wasn't looking forward to putting these back on."

A quick smile flicked across her rouged lips. "I'll have your things laundered."

"That's very kind of you."

Rosa pulled a flat gold case from a pocket in her skirt and withdrew a cigarette. She tapped one end on the case. "We women must help each other out, *sí?*" she said, then picked up a candle from a nearby table and lit the cigarette.

Libby jerked her eyebrows into place and tried to appear as if she witnessed women smoking so openly every day. Rosa Galvan was quite the independent woman. Libby found she admired that. She thought about asking for one but decided against it. The one time she had smoked, she really hadn't enjoyed it.

Rosa sat on the bed, the cigarette poised between her long tapered fingers. "Don't let me keep you from your bath."

Libby liked her baths private, but didn't want to appear priggish. "I tested the water and found it a little too hot. I'm letting it cool for a moment."

The older woman shrugged her shoulders and took a drag on the cigarette, her gaze curious. "That was quite a story the boy told downstairs. Was it true?"

Libby sat down on the chair. Apparently Rosa planned to stay for a while. "What did he say? I didn't understand his Spanish."

Rosa told the story Tomas had given beginning with Dos Rios's tale of the Spirit Woman, of how Mando had searched for her and found her, her great love for El Aguila, and the fight with the Cheyenne, finishing with her wounding of the cavalry captain. Doubt gave the Mexican woman's eyes an extra slant as she regarded Libby beneath long lashes.

Libby smiled at the exaggerations but didn't want to place Tomas in a bad light. "Mostly, that's true."

Rosa leaned back, her hands resting against the stained bed coverlet, her head tilted to the side. "So you are in love with Mando. What will your family say about that?"

"I didn't say I was..." She started to protest. Her feelings were too painful to discuss so easily with a stranger, then she remembered Mando telling her while in New Mexico it was safest to be recognized as one of them. "I didn't say I had any family."

"Ah, an orphan like me. Well, families can be a comfort or they can be a problem. I find I miss neither. People like us must rely on our friends."

"I suppose you are right," Libby replied, thinking of Louis. Make Mando dance to your tune, the Frenchman had said. She recalled what Louis had told Mando tonight. She saw nothing now that would make Mando change the path he had chosen. But Mando had to change. He had to.

"So many troubles, *chiquita?*" Rosa asked.

Libby glanced up, startled that her thoughts had wandered so far afield and been so easy to read. Rosa regarded her, her dark eyes sympathetic but searching.

The woman had shown an inquisitive bent earlier when she had escorted her upstairs. Probably didn't get many new faces to talk to. While she could use a little sympathy right now, she found Rosa's interest in her uncomfortable and a little intrusive. However, she didn't want to be rude, by giving a cool answer, to someone who had given her every kindness.

Libby caught the sad strains of a song drifting upstairs, the words sung on long, plaintive notes, the guitar fairly weeping. Libby chose to place her reflective mood on that.

"The song from downstairs took a sad turn and made me a little sad, too." She paused a moment, finding the melody strangely compelling. "What is it about?"

Rosa cocked her well-coiffed head and listened, then gave her an odd look, one Libby had trouble defining. "The song is a *corrido*." She sat straighter, puffing the cigarette in a quick, nervous movement, her lashes swooping down over her eyes.

"Yes?" Libby prompted.

"A *corrido*," the other woman said, impatience touching her voice, her rings flashing as she tossed her hand. "A ballad about some legendary doing or other."

Libby recalled the enthusiastic welcome for Mando. She hesitated, then asked, "And this song? What is it about?"

Rosa stood and walked to the table. "It is about Mando," she said, rearranging a comb and brush, several clay jars and a small wooden saint. "El Aguila they call him. It tells of his fight for his people. A verse has been added about La Rojita."

Libby swallowed. "But it sounds so sad."

Rosa's hands stilled. "These songs usually end in the death of the one who struggles against the oppressors."

"Mando?" Libby said.

Rosa turned to face her. "These people see him as a champion. A man who rides against the hated *tejanos,* a man of the people. The last verse, the one being sung now, predicts a sad ending for El Aguila. The same ending they see for their struggles."

Libby rose to her feet on a surge of helpless frustration. "What is wrong with these people?" She spun around, blinking back the tears that sprang to her eyes. Her thoughts on Mando, she said, "Do they see death at the end of every path?"

The scented swish of Rosa's skirts crossed the floor to her. A warm hand patted her arm. "Death waits at the end of all our paths, some are just longer than others." She gave her shoulder a gentle squeeze. "If you ever need a friend, *chiquita,* call on me. I live here at the cantina."

Libby nodded and brushed the tears from her eyes. "I'll remember that, Rosa."

"*Bueno,* now get your bath. Mando will be coming for you soon."

The door closed softly as Rosa left the room. Libby stood for a moment, more tears swirling the white-washed wall into a blurry mess. She scrubbed the tears from her eyes once more. She didn't want to cry. She wanted to shout and shake some sense into Mando. What good were dead heroes?

The ring of spurs on the stairs hustled her to the door. She tilted a chair against the doorknob and listened. She wasn't ready to see Mando yet. Her thoughts were too muddled to deal with him.

The steps passed the door, a woman's giggle accompanying them. The door to the next room opened then closed. A muffled conversation came through the wall. Libby decided to get her bath over with quickly. She didn't want Mando arriving before she was done. She hoped the bath would calm her thoughts into some course of action.

She finished unbuttoning the shirt and pulled it off, tossing it to one of the colorful woven rugs scattered on the floor, then bent over the tub and washed her hair. A laborious job at any time, but particularly a chore to-night. She rinsed it quickly with a nearby bucket of water and wrapped her head in a towel.

Quickly undressing, she climbed into the warm, scented water, a deep sigh easing from her. She rested her arms along the edge of the tub and rested her head against the rim. Her eyes closed and she lost herself in the simple pleasure of the relaxing eddies of water swirling about tired, aching limbs. For a brief moment, her thoughts released the disturbing presence of their constant companion, Mando Fierro.

Suddenly the rhythmic banging on the wall next door brought him speeding back. Soon moans and grunts joined the repeated thumpings. She might have little experience with the ways of a man and a woman, but she did possess an imagination. She noted the bed in her room had a wooden headboard that leaned against the wall. Deducing what activity smacked her neighbor's headboard against the wall took little thought. The Reverend Carmichael had a name for it. Fornication.

That's what Mando wanted from her. Simple fornication with no ties, no loving commitments, no future. Louis had said she was no cantina girl and deserved more than Mando would give her and he was right.

The blows on the wall came harder, faster, the low crooning of the woman rose to a high screeching. Carmelita! A terrible, painful twisting in her stomach took her breath. The man shouted something in Spanish, his voice nothing like the deep, resonant tones of Mando's voice. Libby closed her eyes and breathed deeply, her heart slowing to a normal beat. She didn't want to give Mando that fleeting pleasure, but she didn't want him to seek it anywhere else, either. Perverse of her, she knew, but she couldn't help how she felt.

The commotion died down to hoarse laughter and murmurings, then all was quiet until a few moments later the door opened and closed once more. Done and finished, she thought. The whole episode had been so short, so impersonal. She didn't want that from Mando. She saw no difference between the few minutes Carmelita's customer had wanted or the few months Mando had wanted from her. She wanted to give him a lifetime of loving. Somehow she must make him want to give the same to her.

At last she understood what made Amelia give up her hard-earned independence. A man that was worth more to her than any supposed freedom. Mando Fierro was that man for Libby, but was he the right man?

Now she was down to choices. Rosa would help her leave, she had no doubts. Briefly Libby considered asking her, but the whole idea repelled her. She wanted Mando. She wanted Mando on her terms. All or nothing. It was the only way to save them both.

What if she failed? Never in her life had she asked herself that question, but never had she stood to lose so much. If she won, if she convinced Mando to give up his trading, to marry her, she stood to gain the world.

Libby rose from the bathwater, stepped from the tub and began to dry herself with another towel that had been provided. She understood Mando better now, his reasons for trading with the Indians, but that made no difference. She could not love a comanchero, so she wouldn't. She would love a man who owned a ranch in the Sangre de Cristo Mountains.

She would make him dance to her tune, but she must keep him at arm's length. She knew her weakness for him and she might surrender on any terms. To save Mando, to save herself, she couldn't do that. She must make him want her more than he wanted to ride those plains for whatever reason drove him.

Mando knocked on the door.

"Who is it?" Libby called softly.

"Mando," he answered.

He heard a chair scrape back and the door opened a crack. Libby peered around the doorway then she swung the door wider.

"I'm ready to leave," she said.

Mando leaned against the doorjamb, running his gaze over the transformation of Miss Libby Hawkins to La Rojita. Her hair curled in damp ringlets around her face, a long thick braid hung over her shoulder. The blouse she wore was loose around the shoulders, baring her lovely gold-dusted skin. Her skirt, a bright turquoise, reached just above her ankles. A colorful woven sash circled her trim waist, with matching embroidery decorating the hem of the skirt and the yoke of her blouse. Rosa had done a good job. One whiff told him she had been generous with her scented soap, too.

"Is something wrong?"

He caught that wide-eyed look she had given the cavalry captain. "You know there isn't."

She curled the tips of her mouth into a little smile, and that mischievous sparkle he had missed lately shone in her eyes. "I'll be just a moment," she said. "I have some things to bring."

He wondered what had caused the change from sad-eyed urchin to smiling enchantress. Could a bath do such wonders for a woman? When the woman was Libby Hawkins, any sudden changes were worth extra precautions and he had one in mind. He didn't plan on leaving her alone tonight to carry out one of her troublesome little plans.

She appeared once more at the door, carrying a neatly folded stack of clothes, a hairbrush and a comb. The white cambric nightgown she wouldn't need.

"Let's go," she said. "I've heard all the commotions I want to for one night."

He wrapped his fingers around the soft skin of her bare upper arm. "Señora Ortega's house is very quiet," he said against her ear. She slanted a wary look at him. He lifted a corner of his mouth in a smile she didn't return. They started down the open hallway toward the stairs.

"Where's Louis?" she asked.

"He's taking care of the horses," Mando replied as they descended the stairs. Louis hadn't spoken to him while they had cleaned up in the back room. The Frenchman would get over his anger with him. He always did.

Parts of their argument wouldn't be so easy to forget. Libby continued to be a problem between them, perhaps she always would be. But he was going to solve the complication she had become for him.

At last, she was well and he would not deny himself the pleasures she promised any longer, Louis and his preachings be damned. He remembered her eager response each time he had kissed her. She wanted him, as well. Life was fleeting. Why deny themselves.

Something about the old argument didn't strike the usual carefree response in him. Perhaps it was the admiring looks and outright leers the men in the cantina fastened on his La Rojita as they crossed the room. *His* La Rojita? He liked the sound of that and the glare he passed to each roving eye said how much.

"A toast to El Aguila," a young vaquero shouted in Spanish.

"El Aguila! El Aguila! El Aguila!" the crowd shouted, lifting their mugs.

Mando smiled and waved, the salute welcome after Louis's latest sermon and long days spent with the disapproving Miss Hawkins. He glanced down at Libby and found her regarding the room full of well-wishers with a sad, almost angry expression. She caught his puzzlement and flashed him a quick smile, but it didn't remove the gloom from her eyes.

Rosa wove through the tables, meeting them by the door. "I have brought you a gift," she said, holding a white *rebozo* out to Libby.

Libby reached for it, but Mando took it from Rosa and placed it over her bright hair, wrapping it around her shoulders. He brushed the back of his hand across her full breasts, and desire hit him hard and quick in the gut. She turned slightly away from him, her smile slipping but quickly put back in place when she faced Rosa. He hadn't missed the catch in her breath. He grew impatient to be on their way.

"Thank you," Libby said in a voice that carried above the music and boisterous talk. She smoothed her hand over the soft cotton weave of the material. "It's very beautiful."

"You look like an angel," Rosa said.

"Oh, no, Rosa. Libby is no angel. We set that straight from the beginning." He gave the redhead a broad smile.

Libby passed him a look he had seen in men's eyes before they pulled their weapon.

Rosa laughed and gave Libby a hug. "Remember what I said, *chiquita.*"

"I will, Rosa. Thank you for all you've done. Please send those clothes to Señora Ortega's tomorrow. I need to return Tomas's pants."

"I will be happy to."

Enough of this, Mando decided. *"Buenas noches,"* he said, and gave the roomful of men another wave. More shouts of "El Aguila" followed. Libby continued to meet the cheers with a frown and that touch of anger, too. As they stepped into the night, he dismissed Libby's curious reaction and recalled what the cantina woman had said to Libby.

"What did Rosa want you to remember, *querida?*"

Libby's gaze snapped to his at the endearment, then she gave her attention to the end of the road. "Oh, just woman talk," she said.

Mando let it go. He enjoyed the cool night air, the lingering effects of good whiskey, a hot meal and a bath. His mind ranged to the silent house, clean white sheets and Libby.

"What is the name Tomas and those other men call you?" Libby asked.

"El Aguila?"

"I mean in English. How does it translate?"

"It means *The Eagle,*" he said.

Libby stopped dead in her tracks. She gazed at him, her mouth partially open, her eyes incredulous. "The Eagle, you say?"

Chapter Twenty

Mando held a puzzled look on his face. "Yes, I am called *The Eagle*. You know we give each other special names." A frown formed between his brows. "Is something wrong?"

Libby wasn't sure. "Do you dream, Mando?"

"Not often," he replied. "Why?"

"Oh, nothing," she said, and started down the road again. She couldn't explain her dreams of eagles, to him or to herself. The second time the eagle had visited her in her sleep was in the cave. She supposed some reasonable explanation could be found for that dream. Mando possessed a predator's brow and sharp eyes, the look of a bird of prey. She remembered in the dream she had been flying over the plain toward the soldiers. The eagle had captured her and carried her high into the blue, blue sky; her only fear had been that he might drop her.

The second dream didn't bother her. It was the first dream that left her uneasy. She had dreamed it that day she had fainted from too much sun, before he had found her, before she had ever seen Mando. Although bits and pieces of the dream had floated to her mind from time to time, she was certain it had occurred before she met him.

In that dream she had been flying toward water, and the eagle's shadow had fallen over her. She had faltered and he had been reaching for her. Libby gathered the shawl closer around her. Neither dream had ended.

Libby hardly noticed the route they took to Señora Ortega's house. She pulled pieces of the dreams together, then took them apart and examined them, searching for any clues to their meaning. She tried to convince herself the dreams were a coincidence, but she couldn't. She couldn't dismiss the dream of an eagle before meeting El Aguila.

Libby looked up abruptly when they reached a wooden gate in a wall made of adobe. Mando opened it, peered inside, then indicated for her to pass on through the portal into a small, flagstoned courtyard. His caution reminded her that Cabot and his friend Doyle could ride into town any day and she was occupied with deciphering dreams.

Still, she had just enough of her Irish grandmother to ask, "Do you believe in destiny, Mando?"

He dragged a hand through his hair, sighed, then guided her to sit upon a stone bench built by a fountain that added its quiet sparkle to the dark, enclosed courtyard. He sat down beside her, placing his arm over the back of the bench. Crossing one foot over his knee, he watched the moonlight play through the droplets of water.

"Yes, I believe in destiny." He was quiet for a moment, then turned his attention to her, leaning in close. "But I don't want to talk of that now. I don't want to talk at all."

Libby read his intention to begin where they had left off while waiting for Louis's signal in the pass above the town. She rose quickly to her feet and began to pace.

"Where's Señora Ortega?" she asked, hoping a nice old lady would show up soon.

He slid the foot propped on his knee to the ground. "She's in bed with Louis. It's late. That's where everyone should be. In their beds."

"In bed with Louis?" Libby couldn't hide her surprise or her anxiety.

"They are very good friends," Mando said, then stood and walked toward her.

Libby sidestepped and put the bench between them. Her resolve to keep him at arm's length until he showed some signs of changing to that rancher she wanted was in grave danger. "I suppose you should tell me which room is mine," she said. She covered her mouth and yawned. "I'm really tired."

He smiled, that crooked smile she suddenly found attractive again. This wasn't the time to notice how handsome he was, how tall, how broad his shoulders, how he moved with the grace and power that made a woman want to simply step into his arms and dance her life away.

"I don't want to keep you from your bed, *querida*."

Libby watched him cross the small courtyard, his spurs ringing softly on the flagstones. For her purposes, she wished he would call her gringa again. The other name was like a caress, soft and warm as it rolled off his tongue. He ducked beneath a vine-covered arbor that ran along three walls of the adobe house, and opened a door.

A lamp turned down low inside the room gave a dim light to the doorway but left Mando's face in shadow. "This is your room."

Libby wrapped her arms tighter around the bundle she carried. "Thank you." She forced a nonchalance to her voice. "I'll see you in the morning."

She hoped Mando would leave, but he stepped inside the room instead. Uncertain what to do now, she stood motionless in the courtyard, trying to decide if following him inside was wise. Of course, it wasn't, but she couldn't stand out here all night. She had to face him, make him understand her feelings.

The sweet aroma of honeysuckle in full bloom drifted through the dry desert air, reminding her of the back porch of her home in Ohio. She and Amelia used to sit on a swing and spin dreams. Amelia's had been home, husband and babies, hers had been adventure and travel. Well, she had certainly traveled and she was about to begin the biggest adventure of her life. But first she had to walk into that room and make sure Mando left it.

Libby girded up her defenses by remembering what was at stake. Her future and, if that stupid song was any indicator, his very life. It was time he danced to her tune, no matter how seductively his played.

Raising her chin for battle, Libby crossed the courtyard, the heady scent of honeysuckle growing stronger as she approached the door. She paused at the threshold and peered inside. Mando sat in a chair, the front legs cocked back, his long legs crossed, his stockinged feet propped on the bed's colorfully embroidered coverlet. His jacket hung on the chair. His hands were linked behind his neck. He looked altogether too sure of himself, and why shouldn't he after her response to him earlier that evening.

Libby entered the sparsely furnished room, placing the clothing on a small table by the entrance.

"Close the door," he said quietly.

Libby glanced up, finding his attitude reminiscent of the night he told her he had bought her, found her and owned her. Her defenses against his charms received strong reinforcements.

"I think not," she replied.

The chair tilted forward. "Then I will." He swung his feet off the bed and strode toward her.

Libby took up her station by the door, holding it open. "No, you won't. This is my room . . . not our room."

Mando stood in front of her and propped a hand negligently on the door above her head. His shirt gapped open, revealing the soft whorls of black hair covering his chest. Libby dragged her eyes to his and wished she hadn't. Dark and demanding, she now knew the answer to the mystery they promised. Passion. Passion so fierce a moment might last a lifetime.

She gripped the door tighter. "Good night, Mando." Her hesitant voice didn't convince herself of her sincerity, but she took heart from her effort.

"Libby, don't pretend." He tugged the *rebozo* from her hair. "You want this to happen as much as I." He trailed his finger from her temple to her neck.

Libby closed her mind to the smooth melody of his voice, the excitement of his touch. "I want more to happen, Mando. I want a lifetime."

"I told you from the beginning what I can give you. Take it, Libby." His fingers began to edge the *rebozo* from her shoulder. "It is all I have."

Libby's heart pounded, her palms grew damp. She knew he had more, but she must convince him. "It's not enough," she said, and pulled the soft shawl back in place. She looked at him directly so that he would know she meant what she said.

The hand above her head curled into a fist, his eyes narrowed. "I could make it enough very quickly and we both know it."

Libby held back the saucy retort she longed to give the arrogant man. In this mood, he would regard it as a challenge to prove he was right. It wouldn't take long. "I'm asking you not to," she said quietly.

"Surely you never took me for a gentleman." He pulled the door from her clasp and pushed it closed, then stepped closer.

Libby backed away until she confronted the wall behind her. She scrambled for something to say, something to cool the determined heat in his eyes. Thinking of nothing except retreat, she started to slip to the side, but he placed his hands on the wall, trapping her.

She didn't dare touch him, but placed her hands behind her. He moved in closer still, until his warmth infiltrated the thin barrier of cotton weave covering her breasts. His gaze held hers, then his lashes lowered, his lips touching hers.

Libby turned her head to the side. "Is this my payment for the choice I made on the plains?" The words tumbled out on a soft sigh of relief or regret; Libby wasn't certain.

He pulled his head back. "What?"

Libby closed her eyes for a moment, then took a big breath before facing him. "Remember after the Cheyenne attack, you said we must pay for the choices we had made that day. Is this my payment? This assault, this blatant disregard for my feelings, my wishes."

Mando hit the wall with his fist, then turned from her. Combing his hand through his hair, he walked to the bed. "I want you, Libby." He clasped the white pine bedpost. "I usually take what I want."

Libby stepped away from the wall, her hands held tightly together. She pressed her advantage. "I've had no experience with that. My experience has been with a compassionate man, a man who changed his plans to bury a stranger, who cared for an injured woman, who would give his life for his friend."

Mando faced her, dropping his hand to his side. "And what of the Devil who trades with the Indians? I'm that man, too."

"I haven't forgotten. But you can change that. You can stop trading."

"I could, but I won't. My choices are made."

Libby lost all patience. "And they are chiseled in granite. Go ahead. Be the hero. Be the dead hero people can sing songs about and young boys can worship so they can make the same choices you have made. Die for the land. That's a whole lot easier than the struggle to survive. I want no dead hero. I want a man."

Mando raised his chin as if she had hit him. "You give no quarter, do you?"

"Not when I want to win." Libby took another step toward him. "I love you, Mando. I would give you my dreams, my life, but you offer me nothing in return."

"You ask too much, Libby."

"Damn you, Mando. The trading can't last much longer. You said yourself that the Comanches will be on the reservation by next spring. What then?"

His expression took on a grim cast. "Whatever fate brings."

Remembering her dreams, Libby stepped closer. "Fate has brought you me, Mando."

Mando lifted his hands, then dropped them. "Too late, *querida*," he said softly. "Fate brought you to me too late."

Libby took one last step and touched his sleeve. "Mando...it can't be too late."

He wouldn't look at her. "I must leave now, Libby, or I'll stay. You decide."

Libby dragged her hand from his jacket and, turning away, held on to the bedpost, her forehead resting against its cool wood. Hot tears spilled down her cheeks as she listened to him gather his things. The door closed softly and she collapsed to the floor, weeping for him, weeping for herself.

"Back so soon?"

Mando gave Rosa an ill-tempered glance and tossed down another shot of whiskey. "I thought Wright would be here."

Rosa pulled out a chair and sat down, pouring them each a drink. "He's in Santa Fe. He should be back tomorrow sometime."

"Good, I need to talk to him before we leave for the ranch." Somehow he would convince the American that Libby was no threat to his operation. "If you see him before I do, and you probably will, tell him to send word of where I can find him over to the Ortega house."

Rosa shrugged. "If I see him. He will probably go straight to the trading post as he always does. You know Mathias." She smiled. "Always business before pleasure."

Mando grimaced and watched the whiskey swirl in his glass. That's what he should have remembered. Wright would be much easier to convince Libby was harmless if his pockets were full. He hoped the others brought in a good herd, but he doubted they would. Cabot was a hothead and a cheat. He didn't understand the Comanche ways. He hoped Wright remembered that.

"Your gringa is very beautiful, very unusual. Did you truly find her as Tomas said?"

Mando lifted his gaze from the amber liquid, finding Rosa looking at him intently. "Yes, I found her up by the Mucha Que. She had escaped the Comanches by jumping into a flooded creek."

Rosa lit one of her cigarettes and peered at him through the smoke. "I suppose she knows what you were doing out there." Her gaze ran over him, one brow arched appreciatively. "A new verse should be added to your song, one praising your ability with women, or Libby is a very forgiving woman."

Mando weighed his next words carefully. Rosa was Wright's lover, and rumors speculated they might be partners in the cantina, perhaps even the trading post. Anything he said would go straight to Wright. "She proved her loyalty." That was all he would say. Anything else would ring like the lie it would be.

"She certainly did, if Tomas's story was true. I cannot imagine a gringa doing such miraculous things to save a comanchero, even to save El Aguila."

Mando tapped his glass softly on the table, his gaze steady. He didn't like the sound of this. "Are you calling me a liar?"

Rosa lowered her lids. "Of course not. I merely find her story interesting. I liked your gringa."

Mando finished his drink and set his glass down sharply. "I like her very much myself. In fact, I like her so much, if anything were to happen to her, I would take it quite personally."

"It's like that, then?"

"Yes, it's like that."

"Ah, matters of the heart. Men die for less."

"Men die more often for interfering in another's interests."

Rosa smiled. "I'll drink to that." She finished her drink and stood. "I understand there's a big fandango planned in your honor tomorrow night," she said.

Mando rose from his chair and pulled his sombrero to his head. "Be sure to tell Mathias what I said." He gauged her reaction. They understood each other. To keep things friendly, he added, "I need to talk to him as soon as he arrives."

Rosa placed a ringed hand on her hip. "I'll tell him."

Mando left the cantina in an uglier mood than when he had arrived, and walked slowly toward the Ortega house. Women! They only caused trouble. He had a feeling his partnership with Mathias Wright would end very quickly. His trading days were over. Libby had won and he couldn't say how. Truly, the woman possessed magic.

He understood now what Ross had faced in the blue eyes of Libby's sister. Instead of his rancor, he owed his brother his sympathy.

For the first time in years, he allowed himself to think about Ross without anger clouding his sentiments. Libby had said he was to be a father soon. A picture of Ross with a baby on his knee was as difficult to conjure as imagining one on his own. Once, many years ago, before his father had been killed, before the land he loved had become a millstone around his neck, he had wanted a large family.

Where had the years gone? Those youthful anticipations of family never materialized. They had been ground away with his fight to keep his land, to get even with the *americanos* for the pain and loss their greed had caused him.

Pride and revenge made lonely companions, and never more than tonight. He reached the gate and entered the quiet courtyard. His gaze scanned the small, peaceful enclosure until it stopped on the door to Libby's room.

Mando gathered his saddlebags and found a bed at an inn down the road.

Chapter Twenty-One

Libby sat fidgeting under the ministrations of Señora Ortega. Plump and graying, the woman moved with quick energy, her face never without a bright smile. Looking into the mirror set on a table before her, Libby watched as the widow pinned a small bouquet of tiny flowers in her hair. She had insisted on helping her arrange it for the *baile*.

Libby had finally figured out the *baile* was the dance planned for this evening. Señora Ortega spoke little English and Libby understood no Spanish, but they had communicated well with smiles and gestures. Smiles had been particularly hard to summon this day. Libby managed one for the kind woman when she stepped back to admire her handiwork.

"Muchas gracias," she pronounced slowly. Louis had taught her how to say *thank you* at breakfast. The widow's smile fairly beamed, then she said something to her slowly with extra volume, as if that were supposed to help her understand, and bustled from the room.

Libby touched one of the curls at her temple. She turned to admire the smooth, double coils of hair arranged at her nape, the sprays of flowers tucked into each thick roll adding just the right festive touch to the severely pulled-back style. The wisps of curls loosened about her face softened it more. She had never been one to fool with her hair much more than to see that it was clean and neatly arranged, but she drew pleasure from the dramatic results of Señora Ortega's labors.

Her spirits could use a boost, she thought. Rising to her feet, she busied her restless hands with straightening her small room. She smoothed the white muslin coverlet with its bright-colored embroidery of birds and flowers, gathered her few belongings together on a nearby chest, and tossed the soiled towels and washcloths into a corner. Finally her activities reduced to pacing, her ear tuned for the soft ring of spurs on the flagstoned courtyard.

She had cried herself to sleep listening for those spurs, and had awakened that morning with a dull headache, still listening. Breakfast on the patio with its bright sunshine, lilting birdsong and the widow Ortega's private smiles passed to a beaming Louis had made her feel worse. No mention had been made of Mando's absence. By noon, when he still had not shown up, her headache had reached its pounding best. Louis had mumbled something about Mando taking care of some business.

The afternoon *siesta* spent with a cool cloth over her eyes had eased the headache some but had given her too much time to ponder her tactics. Perhaps she should have let him stay last night. It was one thing to say she must have all or nothing, but she hadn't known how painfully empty nothing could be. She did now and she had almost decided to take anything Mando offered. She didn't care if he traded with the Devil himself, she wanted him, missed him, needed him.

She had tried to talk to Louis after lunch, but he had quickly let her know she was on her own. She remembered his words exactly. "No, *chérie*," he had said. "I have done all I can. I cannot tell you what you must do. Only you can decide what you truly want, what you are willing to do to get it.''

With that helpful advice given, Louis had stayed away the rest of the day, seeing to the reshoeing of their horses. He had returned as Señora Ortega arranged her hair, but had only given them a brief greeting before hurrying off to change.

Libby couldn't look at these four walls another minute and decided to wait by the fountain. She gathered up the white shawl Rosa had given her and gave herself one last inspection in the small mirror.

Satisfied that the white blouse was neatly tucked into the turquoise skirt and the sash was tied correctly, she left her room, crossed the patio to the stone bench and sat in the darkness, waiting.

The fountain's gay little tune didn't mask the louder music striking up down the road. The dance was beginning and still Mando hadn't arrived. If he didn't take her to this party, she really didn't want to go. Several excuses to give came to mind, but she couldn't be that ungracious. Not after all the work the older woman had put into helping her dress. Still, her heart wasn't into putting on a brave face. She had almost worn hers out wondering what kind of business had kept Mando busy for the rest of the night and all of today.

Her mind wandered to Carmelita's excited squeal—El Aguila—and the woman's arms wrapped about Mando's neck. Imagining the Mexican girl's crooning moans and the rhythmic banging of that headboard didn't take long to follow. Her hand gripped the folds of her skirt in tight fists. She wanted to pull the woman's hair out. She took a calming breath and told herself Mando wouldn't go to the other woman, but the suspicion lingered like a dose of bitters at the back of her throat.

What business could he have here in El Puerto? Of course, Cabot. He might have returned and lived up to his threat. "The woman's a loose end," he had said. She still doubted the American would be influenced by Tomas's story. Mando might have run into some kind of trouble. What if he was bleeding in a ditch someplace or even . . . dead?

Her all-or-nothing stand suddenly collapsed. She didn't know what to think anymore. All that was important was to see Mando, to know that he was well, and yes, to know he wasn't with that Carmelita woman.

"Moonlight and Libby. A formidable combination."

Libby sprang to her feet and whirled around. Mando! She hadn't heard him enter the courtyard and she wasn't prepared to face him.

"You aren't wearing your spurs." The statement almost sounded like an accusation.

"A man can't wear his spurs to a dance."

"I was beginning to think you might not go." She couldn't relate her true fears—another woman, a bullet.

He walked out of the shadows. "I am the excuse for the dance this night. I couldn't miss it."

"Of course not." She wanted to ask him where he had been, where he had cleaned up and changed. How could he make her worry so? Questions wives everywhere asked. She held her tongue.

"Have Louis and Señora Ortega left for the dance yet?" he asked.

"No, I was waiting for them," Libby replied. "They should be out soon. They've had more than enough time to change." Her face colored at Mando's slow smile.

"Maybe we should go on without them," she offered. "They could join us later."

"Perhaps. First I have something to give you."

Libby gasped when he pulled a gold chain from his pocket. "For my locket."

He closed the distance between them, stopping on the other side of the bench. "Give it to me and I'll replace the leather cord."

Libby lifted the locket from her neck, careful not to dislodge the flowers, and passed it to Mando. He cut through the leather with his knife and slid the cord through the locket's bezel, then stowed the leather string in an inside pocket of his jacket. Sliding the delicate chain from his wrist, he held it aloft until it hung straight, then guided the chain through the locket's bezel.

He held an end in each hand before him. "Come around here and I'll hook it for you."

Quickly Libby walked to Mando's side and presented her back to him. He dropped the locket over her head, his warm fingers sending tingles along her neck where they touched her skin as he fastened the chain. His hands lingered at her shoulders for a moment. She didn't rush away, but turned to face him.

She sensed a change in him and wanted to know if it was real or imagined. "Tell me, Mando. Tell me why you traded so much for my locket?"

Mando lifted the gold ornament from her bosom, his fingers caressing the etched finish. "I didn't know why, or perhaps, I wouldn't admit it."

He held her gaze in his, the moonlight adding a gold richness to his dark eyes. "But now I do know, Libby. I wanted this token from a woman who had fought so hard for life."

"You saved my life when you traded for it," she said, her voice but a whisper.

"No, Libby. You did that with your bravery, your compassion, your determination to live. I merely acted upon hearing your story. That night changed the course I had chosen. Profits ceased to be as important as owning the Spirit Woman's charm." He lifted a curl by her ear. "Perhaps there are red-haired angels."

Libby could barely hear his words through the rush of blood through her ears. Excitement and relief filled her with hope. She looked at him, his dark eyes as compelling as ever. "What are you saying, Mando?"

"I—"

"So there you are," Louis boomed.

"We'll talk later," Mando murmured.

Libby appreciated the darkness that prevented Louis from seeing the look she gave him. The poor man could hardly be blamed for the worst timing ever.

The widow, dressed in full-skirted black satin, stepped from her room and took her place by Louis's side. She took his arm, smiling at them all, the black lace mantilla she wore fluttering softly in the night breeze.

Libby was struck at how handsome the couple looked. Louis had discarded his buckskins for a tight-fitting short jacket and flared pants with silver buttons running down the side seam, much like the black suit Mando wore, though Louis's was a gray that enhanced the silver at his temples.

"The music awaits, Libby," Louis said, his glance shifting between her and Mando.

"Yes, I think I hear a favorite tune," she replied.

The Frenchman lifted his free hand, a broad smile lighting his blue eyes. "In that case, what are we waiting for?"

"Not a thing," she replied. "Lead the way."

She thought she caught a twitch to Louis's mustache before he escorted the widow by them.

Mando offered his arm and Libby accepted it.

"What was all that about?" he asked as they passed through the gate. "You know no Spanish songs."

"But I'm learning," she replied.

Libby spotted the strings of cut-tin lanterns glowing brightly down the street as they stepped through the gate. The music and singing traveled down the dark road to them. Voices raised in excited conversation buzzed about the dance melodies.

When they arrived, everyone shouted greetings. She caught the names El Aguila and La Rojita. The rest of the rapid Spanish filled the conversations like the colorful strips of paper festooned about the blocked-off square of road. She simply smiled and that was enough. Ladies, old men and some of the rough-looking characters from the cantina took their turn in shaking her hand. Some even hugged her. She had never met a more hospitable people.

The aroma of the food tables drew her attention. After a day when food had only tightened the knot in her stomach, she was suddenly famished. "I'm starved," she said. "Everything looks delicious."

Mando smiled down at her, then began to weave their way to the food. Upon reaching the heavily laden trestles that offered everything from fruits and pastries to bowls of vegetables and plates of different meats, he said, "I'll show you the dishes to try. Some of them will burn a hole in your gringa tongue."

After viewing a few red faces and watering eyes, Libby agreed to follow his advice. She reached for a slice of mutton and heard a familiar voice behind her.

"La Rojita, I would like you to meet my mother."

She turned a smile to Tomas and shook hands with a woman who looked an indeterminate age. She recalled Tomas telling them of how his father had been killed by a band of angry *tejanos* searching for stolen cattle. The world was a weary place for this woman.

Her smiles were not easy and not offered often. She said something to her, then pressed a small, primitively carved statuette in her hand. Libby looked at Tomas for an explanation.

"She says to take this *santo*. It will protect you. She says a *valiente* like you needs the extra help."

Libby examined the crude carving of what must be a saint, finding its simplicity as beautiful as the woman's sentiment. *"Muchas gracias,"* she pronounced.

The woman's thin lips stretched briefly and she gave her a nod, then disappeared into the crowd. Libby looked at the small wooden figure once more. This woman possessed little, yet she had gifted her with hopes for her safekeeping. The gesture touched her deeply.

"When do we ride into the plains again, El Aguila?"

Libby jerked her head up at Tomas's eager question, her gaze fixed on Mando. He looked into her eyes for a score of pounding heartbeats.

"I never had a chance, did I, *querida?*" he said softly, for only her ears, then turned to Tomas.

In a bit of a daze, Libby set her plate on the long table and stepped so that she could see both Mando and Tomas. She wondered what Mando had meant, what he would say to the boy, what that conversation he wanted to save for later would prove to be.

"I need your help, Tomas," Mando said quietly, bending close. "I want to develop my sheep business. I will provide you with a herd and we will share the lambing profits until I have been repaid. In a few years, you will have your own herd and I will have an increased yield. What do you say?''

Libby saw the startled look of puzzlement pass over Tomas's face. He masked it quickly with a polite smile.

"Your offer is very kind, El Aguila, but I, like you, must ride the plains. The *tejanos* killed my father. It is only right I seek my revenge through profits from their cattle.''

Mando placed a hand on Tomas's shoulder. "I understand your feelings. Revenge is a powerful medicine that numbs the pain, but it will destroy the soul. And as for profits, the guarantees are poor. You are the man of your house now, Tomas, you must do what is best to care for your mother and sisters.''

"As a sheepherder? No, El Aguila. I want to be like you. You have done well with the trading.''

Mando dropped his hand, his long sigh hinting at regrets. "Perhaps I could have done better had I stayed on the rancho, working the land. Those men are the real heroes, Tomas. Men like your father who battle for their quiet victories from the land, who want no praise other than that seen in the eyes of their families.''

The boy raised his chin, a defiant light shining in his black eyes. "No, El Aguila. My father is dead from such a life, his family left poor. I must be a man like you. A man who rides the plains and defies the *americanos*, who strikes a blow against the *tejanos*.''

Mando's tone grew impatient. "Tomas—''

"I must go now.'' The boy stepped back. "I thank you for your offer, but I cannot accept.'' He gave Libby a reproachful glance, then weaved into the crowd.

Libby placed her hand on Mando's sleeve. He watched the boy disappear, his frustration apparent in his tight frown. She knew how he felt.

"That was a generous offer, Mando. He will come around."

"Perhaps," he replied. "I hope he doesn't wait until it is too late."

Libby forced some gaiety into her voice, past the uneasiness that had crept into her happiness. "It's never too late to dance."

Mando's expression slowly relaxed and he gave her one of his crooked smiles, placing his hand over hers. "Let's hope it isn't. In fact I hear a lively tune I think you'll like. Shall we?"

Libby curled her arm through Mando's. "I've waited a long time for this dance."

Mando escorted her through the crowd, stopping to introduce her to old ladies, couples trying to keep up with their boisterous children, and men with gentle, weather-worn faces she guessed to be farmers. All of them looked upon Mando with respect and good humor. Shaking hands and smiling, Libby supposed these people must see Mando as a Robin Hood of sorts, someone who resisted the changes forced upon them by another people whom they didn't understand. Even though she was one of those people, she was always greeted with courtesy and made to feel welcome.

This open country set her spirit free; these people warmed her heart. At last, she had found a home. She glanced up at Mando as he laughed with a gap-toothed old graybeard. Mando Fierro was her destiny and she had made him see it could be a happy one.

Libby noted the coins in Mando's hands as he pressed his farewell into the old man's palm, then he turned to her. "That song finished. We'll wait for another."

"We've got all night," she replied, and the rest of our lives, she hoped. She was impatient to hear what he had been about to tell her before they left for the dance.

Louis joined them, minus his lady. Libby frowned at the distracted nod he gave her before turning his attention to Mando. "Did you talk to Wright today?"

"I rode out to the trading post, but they told me he wasn't expected back until tomorrow. I left word I needed to talk to him. Have you heard anything?"

"I just saw Paco and Cinco," Louis replied. "Cabot's returned."

Libby felt Mando's arm tense beneath her hand.

"*Por Dios,* only one more day," he said softly under his breath. "I didn't expect them to return so soon. The trading must not have gone well."

His gaze traveled over the crowd. The alertness in his eyes told her he was looking for trouble. Libby followed his example, searching through faces until she found Tomas and his mother talking to Paco. She hoped Tomas embellished his story of La Rojita with each telling. She didn't want any trouble with these people.

"I don't see Cabot," she said.

"He won't be here," Mando replied. "He'll have to talk to Wright before he starts any trouble with me. Besides, a fight in the open isn't his way."

"Who is this Wright person?" she asked. She remembered Cabot mentioning him back at the camp. It was Wright who didn't like loose ends. That must be why Mando had tried to talk to him today.

Mando kept his eyes on the festivities. "I was hoping you would never have to know. It would be safer that way, but now I see no reason you shouldn't. He provides the trading goods and we split the profits of the cattle I bring back. He is my partner, Libby, or he was."

"Was?" she asked. A joy like no other she had ever experienced pushed aside the implications of the rest of his statement.

He turned his attention to her. "It looks as though the partnership will be terminated very soon. I thought I could talk with Wright, convince him to keep Cabot on his chain. If the trading didn't go well, I suspect it's too late for that now."

Libby didn't like the finality in Mando's voice. "One thing I've learned, Mando. Don't discount the unexpected."

Mando's expression softened. "Every time I look into your beautiful eyes, I'll remember that."

"Here they come," Louis said.

Covering the hand she rested on his arm with his own, Mando directed his gaze to the two approaching men. "Stay close to me."

Libby hugged his arm to her, the *santo* clutched tightly in her other hand, and met the men with a small smile. She wished she could understand the conversation being exchanged. Paco did most of the talking. He glanced at her a few times, and Libby saw none of the suspicions she had witnessed on the last occasion she had seen them. Cinco even gave her a gold-toothed grin that reminded her of the day he had held up her burnt shoes.

She relaxed somewhat even as she felt the tension leave Mando's body, though he wore a deep frown. She had never truly feared these men, reserving all of her anxieties for her own countrymen.

At last, Paco turned to her. He removed his sombrero, his black mustache as startling as she remembered, compared to his gray hair. "My sister and nephew told us what you did on the plains, *señorita*. You could have gone to Fort Union as El Aguila had requested of Tomas or you could have let the soldiers holding El Aguila and Louis take you back to Texas with them. You chose to give your loyalty to two of our people. This we do not forget and should you need us, Cinco and I will be ready with ours."

"I am grateful to know this," she replied. "One cannot have too many friends."

Libby remembered Gordito and searched along the tables of food. "Where is the cook? Filling his plate?"

Paco and Cinco exchanged glances, then Cinco said, "We had nothing but trouble after we split up. Cabot, that *bastardo,* gave the Comanches whiskey one night. We found Gordito the next morning, dead. He had been guarding his bread."

"How terrible," she said, remembering the healing plants the cook had found to help her sunburn.

"*Sí,* the business is not what it was," Paco said. "The gringos ruin everything." He turned to Mando. "I have talked to my nephew and our family accepts your offer of the sheep."

"And Tomas?" Mando asked.

Paco shrugged. "The fires of youth burn hot inside him, but I will bank them a little. He will see what is best."

"Good luck," Louis said, sliding a glance to Mando.

Mando met it with a tightening around his mouth that held back a smile. He returned his attention to Paco.

"I'm happy to hear that," he replied. "I will leave written instructions for my *mayordomo* at the widow Ortega's should I not make it back to the rancho for some reason."

Mando glanced down at her, an unreadable expression gathering disquiet about his eyes. She hugged his arm tighter to her.

Paco placed his hat back on his head. "God be with you, El Aguila. And should He need help, we will be with you, too."

Mando gave the men a brief nod. "That is even better to hear."

The men laughed, Mando smiling faintly. Paco and Cinco turned to leave, then Paco turned around once more. "I must tell you both. We came across Dos Rios up by the Palo Duro. Cabot gave him whiskey and told him the Spirit Woman lives. We left quickly that time. I would not venture to the plains for a while."

"I had not planned to," Mando replied. "The rancho needs my attention."

Paco looked from her to Mando, then smiled beneath his mustache. "We will make certain your rancho gets that attention." The two men left, finding friends among the gathering.

"Too bad about Gordito," Louis said, shaking his head.

"I had asked him to come with us, but he was concerned about his profits," Mando replied.

Louis touched Mando's shoulder briefly. "I'm glad you plan to work on the ranch."

"I hope I haven't made my decision too late," Mando said. He disengaged Libby's arm from his, taking a small step away from her.

Libby pulled the *rebozo* around her shoulders, the evening's festivities cooled by the grim resolve clouding Mando's distant gaze. Too late. She couldn't let it be too late.

Chapter Twenty-Two

Libby sat on the edge of the fountain's stone wall, trailing her fingers through the cool water. Music from the *fiesta* mingled with the men's voices at the gate, a quiet discourse in Spanish behind her. She supposed they discussed their plans for tomorrow, but she wanted to think of only tonight. Tomorrow could wait. She wished Louis and the others would leave so she could discover what lay behind Mando's suddenly cool behavior.

Louis, Paco and Cinco had accompanied them to Señora Ortega's and searched the place, making sure Cabot hadn't decided he needn't wait for Mathias Wright to give the word on taking care of the loose end. She preferred that term to thinking about who they meant—herself.

Mando had assured her they were merely taking precautions. Cabot did nothing without Wright's order. However she noticed the widow was staying with friends, and she had heard Louis say he would be across the street. Mando's precautions also included writing his instructions for Tomas's sheep. She had written a letter to Amelia explaining about their inheritance, too. It had all seemed too much like writing out wills. Mando had laughed when she had set the *santo* by them. She shrugged. It couldn't hurt.

At last the gate closed and the bolt scraped into place. She looked up to find Mando standing at a distance, watching her. She couldn't read the expression on his face, his sombrero shielding the light from the waning moon.

Without the cartridge belts crossing his chest, he looked more the Spanish gentlemen. He wore the fine cut of his suit well, the short jacket emphasizing his slim hips and broad shoulders, the tight flaring pants doing the same for his long, muscular legs. The gun belt slanting across his hips added a touch of excitement, a hint of danger.

He had unbuttoned his dress shirt, the ruffled front loosened to his chest. A handsome man. Handsome as the devil. She wondered what the Reverend Carmichael would say if she drove into town in a spanking new carriage, Mando and his men riding beside her. She smiled at the thought. Perhaps one day...

"I know that smile, *querida*. What mischief are you planning now?"

"Am I so transparent?"

Mando crossed the flagstones, the absence of his spurs a disappointment to her. She liked the striking ring they gave to his steps.

"Libby, I will handle this problem tomorrow. Mathias can be reasoned with when approached through his wallet. He won't chance harming the popular La Rojita and he won't want to make an enemy of me. That's why I waited here to see him. Don't make any foolish plans."

Libby pulled her *rebozo* from her hair. "Don't give me ideas, Mando. Actually, I was thinking of how I would like to ride into Greenville so all my friends and a certain old blowhard could see you decked in cartridge belts and six-guns and riding at my side.''

Mando sat on the bench situated a few feet from where she had settled on the fountain's wall. He pushed the sombrero to his back, the moonlight casting his face in silver and shadow, his hair stirring gently in the breeze. Midnight suited Mando Fierro.

"Do you miss your home so much?" he asked.

"What home? I sold off my parents' property and business and hightailed it out of there as fast as I could. No, I don't miss Greenville, Ohio. I was merely wool-gathering, wishing I could show a few people how lucky I am."

Mando bent his head, studying his clasped hands. "Lucky? *Ay, querida,* I have brought you into a hornet's nest. I wanted you so badly, I could think of nothing but my desires. If I had left you with the soldiers that day I—"

"I would have missed my chance, Mando. My chance to find my place. I've searched for it forever. And I would have missed my chance to find my man. I thought he didn't exist."

Mando lifted his head and met her gaze. "I can promise you nothing, Libby. Not the lifetime you seek, not the future you demand."

Libby drew her brows into a deep frown. "You're giving up your trading, Mando. That was all I asked."

"You don't ask for enough, *querida.* I have made my choices, as I said, and I will meet their consequences. Tomorrow, they may spill onto you."

"But you said Mathias could be reasoned with."

"That is my hope, but what of Cabot and the grudge he will want to settle one day, and there are others. What if the army comes knocking at my door, or worse, what

if the *tejanos* charge into my valley looking for El
Aguila? I will pay for my choices but I won't let you pay
for them, too."

Libby sprang to her feet, the *rebozo* falling to her elbows. "Don't go all noble on me now, Mando. So you've
decided to give up your wicked ways and I'm to be your
penance." She propped her hands on her hips. "Well, I
won't have it."

Mando slowly rose to his feet, hooking a thumb in his
gun belt. "We can't always have everything we want,
Libby. I have learned that and now you will have to."

Challenged immediately by his stubborn stand, Libby
started to narrow her eyes and launch her attack, then
changed tactics. This was one battle she was going to win,
and she would have to use her best weapons. She sighed
deeply, pulling a long face. She couldn't give in too
quickly, though. That would alert him.

She bowed her head so he couldn't see her eyes and
dallied with the ends of the *rebozo*. "We'll talk of this
again," she said, adding just the right amount of acceptance.

Then she looked up at him, her eyes wide and guile-
less. "But there is one thing I want that you can grant
me."

"What is that, Libby?"

"Dance with me, Mando."

He didn't answer her, only gazed into her eyes. A slow
waltz melody drifted over the walls, filling the silence.
Finally he said, "Libby, I—"

"You promised me." She stepped closer, placing her
hands on his shoulders, the white shawl spreading behind her. "Dance with me," she said, her voice soft as the
night breeze.

Mando took one hand in his and slipped his arm around her waist. "You are a dangerous woman, *querida*."

"I love a dangerous man."

He flashed her a smile and whirled her away from the fountain. Libby held her gaze to his, the stars above spinning around his head. The moon marked the times they circled the little courtyard, the fountain's soft splash playing accompaniment to the distant music. A stolen moment, a forgotten world.

Libby followed his steps, his lead strong and sure. Moving with him was like floating down a dark river. She let the current pull her along, taking her to a secret place she had never been, a place scented with honeysuckle and desert winds, a place where only the heart knows the way.

They no longer danced to her tune or to his, but to a melody all of their own. She closed her eyes, savoring these moments in his arms, wishing the music would never end.

"*Querida,* open your eyes."

Libby lifted her lids and realized only the fountain's splashings broke the silence. "The music stopped," she said, disappointment tinting her surprise.

"I'm afraid it has, Libby."

He held her for a moment, studying her as if he were memorizing every detail of her face, her hair, the color of her eyes. Her lips grew soft and full, parting with the need for his kiss.

"I promise you no tomorrows, *querida,* only to-night."

Libby clung to his hand. She could lose this battle. He still might refuse to give her all she wanted from him, no matter how much he desired her. In that moment, she knew she didn't care. If this night was all he offered then she would take it. She would show him tomorrow always followed the night.

"Then kiss me and make it good," she said.

She closed her eyes and received the soft pressure of his warm mouth. Her tongue met his in a more intimate dance that plunged her heart to her toes. Would it always be like this? His touch, his kiss seizing her senses and carrying her far away.

She pressed against the length of him, loosening her hand from his and lifting her arms to his neck, the shawl slipping from her shoulders. Her breasts pushed against his chest. A soft moan purred in her throat. Yes, it would always be like this.

He deepened the kiss and she opened her mouth wider, hungry for his passion. If this night proved to be her last with him, she wanted a feast that would stay with her a lifetime. The thought added a sadness, a desperateness to the heat building inside her.

Mando drew his mouth from hers and she lifted her lids. She saw the same desperation mirrored in his dark eyes, the sadness, too.

"Mando, I don't want promises of tomorrow. No one can give me those. I want you."

Without another word, he swept her into his arms and carried her toward the door tucked under the wild tangle of honeysuckle. He kicked it open, then nudged it closed with his foot. A stream of moonlight from a high window cut through the darkness, illuminating the birds and flowers scrolled across the bed. Gently Mando lowered her to the coverlet, then stood by the bed. He pulled his sombrero off and tossed it aside.

"Are you sure, Libby?"

"No, Mando. I'm sure of nothing but this moment. But, I'm willing to take my chances."

"Libby—"

"Stop talking and kiss me."

He lay down beside her, the moonlight playing upon the smile teasing at his mouth. "So demanding."

Libby curled her fingers in his hair and pulled that teasing smile to her lips. Mando needed no other encouragement. His mouth covered hers, seeking her tongue, his hand pulling aside the loose neckline of her blouse, uncovering one shoulder. His roughened palm smoothed over her shoulder down her arm. Then his hand found her breast. She gasped at the liquid fire stabbing through her belly and thrust her tongue against his.

A trembling took her, a frenzy of need so great she lost all thought except to surrender to its demand. His lips trailed down her neck and she thought the most wicked thing. She wanted his kiss to seek the nipple his thumb and finger squeezed and tugged.

As if he could read her thoughts, his mouth closed over the aching point, his hand kneading the fullness of her breast, pushing her nipple against his swirling tongue. He sucked it gently, then harder until she thrust her hips against the thigh he had placed between her legs. She moved against him, following the same rhythm he set with the pulls on her breast.

He lifted his head, his thumb grazing the wet surface of her stiffened nipple. Giving her lips a brush with his, he sat up, pulling her with him.

"Take down your hair, *querida*."

Libby didn't question him, but lifted her hands, jerking out the flowers, pulling out the carefully placed pins. Mando leaned forward and kissed each taut nipple through the thin cotton of her blouse. Her hands shook, her fingers fumbling among the coils of hair, searching for pins. Finally it fell in a heavy swirl about her shoulders, tumbling to her waist.

Mando rose from the bed, standing beside it. He began to unbutton his shirt. His heavy-lidded gaze moved over her body. "Now, take off your clothes."

Libby sensed the wildness unleashed in him and excitement surged through her, finding the recklessness in her own spirit. She swung her legs to the opposite edge of the bed, dropping her feet to the floor, presenting him with her back. She untied the sash and drew it slowly from her waist, then dropped it. Gathering the edges of her blouse, she eased it over her ribs, passing the soft material across the sensitive tips of her breasts, then pulled it over her head. She tossed it aside.

Standing, she unhooked her skirt and inched it over her hips, allowing it to fall to her feet. Finally her hands dallied with the tapes at her waist. She heard the covers being thrown back, the creak of the bed receiving Mando's weight. She tugged one string and the bow loosened, then she dipped her thumbs into the waist, sliding them around the band and leisurely pulled them down, exposing her hips inch by inch. She stepped out of her drawers and, holding them between thumb and finger, dropped those to the pile of clothing on the floor.

"Turn around, *mi gringita*," came the hoarse voice from the bed.

Libby lifted her hands to her hair, allowing it to flow through her fingers, then turned. The sight that met her eyes stilled her heart, stole her breath. Mando lay on the crisp sheets, dark against the moonlit whiteness. He had propped himself on his elbow, his arm resting on a raised knee. Black hair covered his chest and stomach, gathering in a thick nest where his manhood protruded in rampant appreciation of her performance. Libby's gaze shifted quickly to the appreciation she found in his eyes. She had had no idea—

"Come here, Libby."

Libby thought of simply crawling in beside him, but, piqued a little by all of his orders, she decided to make him wait just a moment more. She walked around the bed, feeling his eyes following her, the heady power she held rolling through her, adding to her excitement. She stopped just short of the moonbeam hitting the stark, white wall.

He had rolled to his back, his black hair spread on the pillow, his size making the bed seem small. She liked watching him from the translucent darkness, while he lay in the light for her to gaze upon. He was muscle and coarse hair, smoldering dark eyes, and passion. She felt her knees grow weak and she wanted to stretch out over him, to rub her softness over the firm, rough texture of his body.

"Stand in the moonlight, *mi gringita.*" His voice now was a rasping whisper.

Libby waited a heartbeat, then two. She was alarmed and aroused at how much pleasure she drew from teasing him. Taking a step, she entered the soft, silver light. He threw an arm over his head, casually taking in her charms.

He knew what she was doing and had decided to play her game. An idea came to her and she wondered at her lack of restraint. Then, when had she ever restrained herself from anything she wanted, and she wanted this man, and she wanted him now. Raising her hand, she brushed the hard nub of her nipple with the tips of her fingers.

With an animal's growl, Mando reached for her and pulled her down on top of him. "You drive a man crazy, my red-haired *bruja*."

"*Bruja?*" she asked, combing her fingers through his hair. His body felt as wonderful as she had thought it would. Her hands on his shoulders, she pulled herself forward, delighting in the tickle and friction grazing along her breasts and belly. His breath hissed between his teeth, his erection, hard and hot, jerked against the inside of her thigh, responding to her small movement.

A stray thought wandered into her aroused senses. This was power, a woman's power and she gloried in it. "Tell me. What is this *bruja?*" she asked.

Mando stroked her back, her buttocks, the long strands of her hair tantalizing her skin beneath his hands. "Witch," he growled. "You cast your spells and men forget their every purpose, good or bad."

Libby perceived her victory and kissed him soundly. Releasing his lips, she said, "Then who better to spend my life with than a handsome devil."

He shook his head. "Libby—"

She closed her mouth over his, thrusting her tongue between his teeth, nipping his bottom lip. Raising her thigh over his aroused flesh, she pressed her breasts against his, moving her shoulders so that the sensitive tips rubbed through his coarse hair. The locket dug into the soft flesh between her breasts, the metal hot from the heat of their bodies.

Mando tossed her to her back. His hands, his tongue, his teeth, nipped and pulled at her breasts, the tender skin of her belly. He trailed kisses over her neck to her mouth, squeezing the taut muscles of her buttocks, running his hand over her thigh. Then his hot, wet mouth closed over her nipples, pulling at one then the other.

Thought was no longer possible, only sensation. Her body moved to the command of his lips, his tongue, the squeeze of his fingers, the pressure of his hand. She dragged in deep breaths that exhaled as moans. In harsh, deep breaths, he spoke to her in Spanish and English, the words mixing with the things he did with his hands.

Soon her own hands roamed over the hard ridges and sharp angles of his body, discovering the secret places that pleased him most. Pulling her to her side, Mando kissed her again, his hand sliding over her hip, then dipping between her legs, stroking the soft curls he found there. Following his lead, Libby ran her fingers lightly over the satin skin of his arousal. As his caresses became more intimate, so too did hers, until she stroked his manhood with the same urgency he explored her feminine folds.

Suddenly he snatched her hand away.

"What's wrong?" she whispered.

"Be still . . . very still, *querida*."

Libby brushed his hair from his face so that she could see his eyes, but they were closed, his breathing deep but slowing. "What did I do?"

His mouth lifted in his crooked smile. "You dance too well, *mi corazón*."

"Mando, please," she whispered, and moved her hips against him, signaling her need.

He opened his eyes, the languorous heat in them exciting her as much as his touch.

"This is your first time, is it not?"

"Yes," she breathed.

"You make a man wonder what the second time would be like, or the third, or the thousandth."

"Finish the first time and we'll discuss the rest later."
She moved closer to him, twining her arms around his
neck, lifting one hard, pink bud to his mouth.

Mando groaned and closed his mouth around her and
the dance began again. Now the steps picked up tempo.
She on top, holding herself up so that he could nuzzle her
breasts, then he pressing her into the mattress, their legs
twining together, his kisses hungry on her mouth.

His hand found her soft, melting core once more, his
fingers imitating the rhythm of his tongue. Libby moaned
her pleasure into his mouth. As she reached once more
for him, he caught her hand.

"No," he whispered against her lips. He sat up, grabbing a towel that was folded on the footboard, then slid
it under her hips.

Libby didn't ask why, she knew that virgins bled and
she was grateful for his consideration.

He took her once more into his arms, kissing her, caressing her, then nudged her knees apart with his thigh.
He moved over her and Libby raised her knees, receiving his weight with a sigh. He entered her slowly, whispering encouragement to her, telling her how beautiful
she was. At the first sting, she tensed and he stopped.

"Libby, the first time hurts a woman. I'm sorry, *querida*."

"I'm all right," she panted, and ran her hand down his
back to the round curve of his buttock.

Mando thrust through the thin barrier.

Libby opened her eyes and gasped at the tearing pain.
He didn't move within her, only held her close. For several minutes they lay still. The discomfort eased and the
fire consumed her once more. She moved against him
and he picked up the rhythm.

Libby closed her eyes, letting him take her to heights of pleasure she had never imagined possible. She grabbed hold of the spindled headboard behind her, wrapping her legs around his hips, meeting each of his hard thrusts. His movements grew more rapid, his breathing harder. He was reaching for the same release to this spiraling need as she.

Every stroke took her higher and higher until the intensity of pleasure swept her past the moon and stars into infinity. Mando cried out his climax in the next breath. Her hands dropped and she floated to earth on soft, lazy clouds.

Mando took her in his arms and rolled to the side, holding her against him. She felt as though she had no bones, only muscle and sinew that clung to Mando's warmth, his strength. She curled closer, her arms and legs twining around him, her nose nuzzling into his neck. His scent came to her with each breath, his heart pounding into her chest. His breathing slowed with hers.

"I never knew..." she said, her lips touching his neck.

"I never expected..." he answered.

His words tickled her scalp and her fancy. How could he let her go after what they had experienced? She remembered all that he said about her making him forget his purpose, about making him wonder what the thousandth time would be like. A contented smile played at her lips, until she recalled what he hadn't said. He had never said he loved her.

He hadn't said the words, but he had demonstrated them. Love was caring, giving, protecting. He had wanted to take her to his ranch, no matter the consequences, but now he cared for her, wanted to protect her, and the only way he saw that was to give her up. He loved her. She sighed and kissed his neck.

Mando pressed his lips to the top of her head, smoothing his hand along her back, through her hair. Calming, loving caresses.

She wanted to ask him about tomorrow, to tell him she didn't want to leave him. But she had done that, and only the outcome of tomorrow's events would decide her fate. She suspected he wasn't telling her everything and she wasn't going to ask. Not now. She wanted nothing to spoil this moment with him, perhaps her only moment.

Tonight she felt safe, desired, loved. That was enough for tonight. Tomorrow would resolve itself. One thing she knew. If all went well and Mando was able to reason with Mathias Wright, then she would go to that ranch in the mountains if she had to walk there. If matters weren't resolved, well . . .

"Libby."

His voice rumbled through her body. "Yes?"

"No tricks tomorrow. You'll only bring more danger to me. I can handle this, even if it should get rough. We have our plans. You could endanger Louis and the others as well. Promise me that you'll stay here in the house where I know where you are and not interfere."

Libby thought over what he had said. She remembered the day she had ridden out to meet the Cheyenne. She had told Tomas much the same thing. Mando was right.

"I understand. I'll wait here at the house for you. I know I'm not the Spirit Woman."

He hugged her tighter. "Oh, but you are, *querida.*"

Libby almost asked about his taking her to the ranch, but didn't. Now was the time for peace, for drawing what comfort this world offered from each other. So much hadn't been said, and possibly never would be. She longed to talk to him about Amelia and Ross, but she held back. The time would come for that, and if it didn't, problems with their families would no longer matter.

She remembered the letters they had written and couldn't hush the foreboding whispers that shook through her.

"What's wrong?"

"Nothing," she said. She thought of something to tell him. "I'm a little cold is all."

Mando reluctantly disengaged from their embrace and sat up, gathering the covers from the end of the bed. Libby took the towel from beneath her, noticing a small bright spot of blood. She started to toss it to the side. Pulling the covers up over them, Mando caught her hand.

"Thank you, Libby," he said, his voice a rough whisper.

Libby swallowed back the lump in her throat. She wanted him to know she had no regrets. "It was my pleasure," she replied, and gave him a smile.

"Next time, the pleasure will be better."

"I don't know if I could survive better," she answered.

He took the towel from her hand. "We'll just have to see."

Under the covers, he made slow, wonderful love to her and when he took her again, it was better. Libby cuddled against him once more, her mind in a stupor of pleasure, until thoughts of what the morning would bring hit her like a whiff of smelling salts.

She remembered her dream in the cave, of how the eagle had swept her away to the heights, and Mando surely had, but the dream hadn't ended, or perhaps she couldn't recall it, didn't want to recall it.

A chill tingled along her scalp and dripped down her spine like ice water. She held him closer, shivering a little.

This time, he didn't ask her what was wrong.

"Tell me about your home, Mando."

He shifted to his back, pulling her next to him, his arms holding her to his side. Libby hugged him tight and settled into the deep curve of his shoulder.

"My house is adobe, much like this one, built around an open courtyard," he began, his voice a black velvet caress in the darkness. "It sits upon a hill that overlooks our valley. Mountains, old and timeworn, surround us and hold the sunset that we might enjoy it a little longer. Tall pines cover the hills, their scent greeting us every morning. Snow falls in the winter and wildflowers bloom in the spring. Lambs and babies are born, the fields are planted, the harvest gathered. It has been that way since my great-grandfather settled there."

"I can almost see it," she murmured as sleep claimed her and she soared with the eagle to his valley in the mountains.

Chapter Twenty-Three

Thunder rolled into Libby's sleep, hurling clouds over the mountains that captured the sunset. Another rumble woke her to full awareness. She lay still, savoring Mando's warmth, inhaling his scent, listening to his deep, regular breathing, counting his heartbeats against her palm. She wanted to awaken every day to Mando next to her.

Lightning flashed through the window, giving her brief glimpses of his face at rest. His was a hard face, the features sharp and angular, yet his mouth with its resolute firmness possessed a fullness that gave him an intrinsic sensuality, especially while sleeping. She wanted to run her fingers over his lips but decided not to wake him. He would need his rest.

Libby untangled herself slowly and moved to her back, careful not to disturb him. With a small, quiet sigh, she rested her arm over her head and watched the lightning play over the low, raftered ceiling. She had no idea what time it was. For a short while, time had stopped, but now the minutes sped by much too fast. All too soon morning would sneak through the clouds.

She didn't want to dwell on what the day would bring, but could think of nothing else. She wished they had gone on to the ranch. She wished many things, but she had no regrets. She was where she wanted to be, lying next to Mando. How or why she was here no longer mattered to her, but it did to Mando. This difficulty with Wright had triggered his insistence on sending her away. She needed to show him she could live with his past and help him build his future, but how?

The idea struck her with a flash of lightning. A smile curled at the corners of her mouth. Of course, it was so simple. If she was Mando's wife, Mathias Wright could never see her as a threat. She could hardly turn him in to the authorities without implicating his partner, her husband. This solved all of her problems. Mando wanted to protect her. Well, he could do so for the rest of his life.

Now how to go about carrying out her plan. She didn't know what arrangements Mando had made about tomorrow and she suspected he hadn't told her on purpose. She had promised not to interfere, but this could be life or death if Wright proved unreasonable. Not only for herself and Mando, but for Louis and the others, too. No, if she had a better idea, then she needed to go forward with it.

Again she was faced with how to proceed. She must speak to this man before Mando, but she didn't know anything about Wright, where he lived, or how to contact him. She knew no one in town, except Señora Ortega and Louis. No help could be counted on from either of those quarters, she was sure.

Then she remembered the woman at the cantina. Rosa had told her if she ever needed any help to come to her. She needed help now. Rosa probably knew everyone and perhaps she would intercede for her. That would be even better. Rosa had mentioned she lived over her business. She could find her there.

If she was going to do this, she needed to do it now
while Mando slept and while she could slip away through
the darkness. She didn't know who might be watching the
house—friend or foe. She didn't want to meet up with
either one, but especially that awful Cabot and his per-
manent ways of solving problems.

Second thoughts dumped cold water over her plan,
leaving her with a rash of chill bumps. She thought long
and hard about leaving the warm safety of Mando's side,
then swallowed back her panic and slowly sat up.

She looked at Mando, but he didn't twitch an eyelid.
Ever so carefully, she swung out of bed and gathered up
her clothes, finding them easily in the dull flashes of
lightning. Quickly she dressed, watching Mando carefully. He never moved. Backing slowly toward the door,
she noticed the *santo* standing guard over her letter to her
sister. She tucked the little hand carving into her pocket.
She might need some extra help.

Tiptoeing to the door, she pulled it open, wincing at the
creak. She gave a quick look over her shoulder at the
sleeping man, then shut the door softly.

Outside, under the mass of honeysuckle, she breathed
a sigh of relief but didn't waste time congratulating herself. She braided her hair quickly, then set off for the
gate. Waiting for a clap of thunder, she slid the bolt free
and slipped out of the gate, pulling it closed behind her.

A hurried glance up and down the road showed no one
present. Bits of colored paper from the *fiesta* skipped a
sad little parade down the street, the tin lanterns squeak-
ing softly with the wind. Lightning illuminated a tower-
ing mass of thunderheads gathering outside of town.
From the wind's direction, Libby couldn't be sure if the
storm would reach town or not.

Between capricious shimmers of lightning, Libby moved through the shadows toward the lights that shone from Rosa's. She was surprised the place was still open, but grateful, too. She didn't want to have to make a lot of noise to awaken people to let her in.

Peering into every shadowy corner, Libby hurried down the road. Every dark doorway or empty space between houses was a pit she expected to be snatched into. By the time she reached the cantina, her heart had stopped and lurched to a start so many times she felt light-headed.

Inching along the wall, she gave a quick look into the quiet dance hall. The only patrons remaining were a group of men in a far corner playing cards. She gathered up her courage to enter the place, then remembered Louis telling Mando of their baths in the back room. Most likely an employee could be found there.

Libby peeked around the corner of the building, then ran around to the rear. She found the door open, a light on inside.

Stepping through the entrance, she knocked gently on the wooden doorjamb, looking around the big kitchen for someone she could ask to fetch Rosa. Loud snores issued from a small room off to the side. Libby approached the snores that rivaled the thunder and found a woman sleeping on a pallet.

Libby cleared her throat, but the loud racket continued. She found a pot on a nearby table and banged it against the wall inside the room. She had no time for niceties.

The woman snorted and jerked, then sat up, rubbing her eyes.

"Excuse me," Libby said.

The woman yanked her hands from her eyes, blinking them like an owl in daylight. A moment passed as she simply stared, then let go a stream of Spanish.

Libby raised her hands to halt the flow of vitriolic words. "Please, I'm sorry I woke you, but—"

The woman shook her head, the braids on her shoulders seesawing up and down. *"No inglés."*

Libby nodded her understanding, then said, "Rosa."

The woman gave a perplexed frown.

Libby pointed to the ceiling, trying to indicate the rooms above. "Rosa," she repeated, then pointed to herself. She couldn't make herself any plainer than that.

"Rosa, *sí,*" the woman answered, giving her a curious look. She heaved a great sigh and, throwing off her blanket, struggled to her feet.

From the size of her girth, the woman apparently enjoyed her own cooking, Libby thought. Still dressed in skirt and blouse, the woman scratched her round belly and lumbered past her toward a stairway on the far side of the room. Libby pulled out a chair from a table in the center of the room and sat, tapping her fingers on the thick slab of pine.

She examined the merits of her plan and still thought it sound, even if many of the details were unclear. Perhaps Rosa would be able to help her fill those in. She seemed a clever woman.

Voices and the scent of roses preceded the flowing black negligee down the stairs. Libby stood, waiting for Rosa's handsome face to appear, wondering how she would put forth her plan without sounding like a lovesick schoolgirl to this sophisticated woman.

Rosa's smile made her feel as welcome as if she had come at a decent hour on a social call. Her black hair tumbled around her shoulders in a casual disarray that somehow looked arranged.

"Libby," she said, her black-slippered foot stepping to the floor. "What a surprise to see you."

Rosa gave quiet, rapid instructions over her ostrich-feathered shoulder and the corpulent woman following her disappeared into her tiny room.

"I'm sorry to wake you, but you said if I ever needed help to call on you. I need help."

With filmy layers of diaphanous black swirling around her feet, Rosa crossed the room. She took Libby's hand between her own. "What can I do, *chiquita?*"

Libby studied the woman's face, framed in loose curls and floating feathers, wondering again at the woman's choice of places to live. It was none of her business, she supposed.

"I need your help with a plan I have to forestall possible violence tomorrow. Mando has—"

Rosa touched her fingers to her lips. "Let's go upstairs where we can be more comfortable."

Libby knew the cook didn't speak English, but had no qualms about finding more privacy to discuss her plan. One never knew who could be listening around dark corners.

"Thank you, I would appreciate that," she replied.

Rosa gave her another of her easy smiles. "Come with me. Everything is quiet now."

Libby followed Rosa to the stairs, feeling gauche and awkward compared to the shorter woman. She climbed the steps in the wake of rose perfume. Rosa halted at a door just inside the landing and opened it an inch, her hand resting on the knob, then turned toward her.

"Libby," she said, "I have heard of the trouble you are having. I am so glad you came to me for help."

"I'm grateful you offered," Libby replied, feeling better already.

Rosa gave her a pat on the arm, then opened her door. Libby entered the room after her. Struck immediately by the opulence confronting her, she was at a loss for words. Swags of red brocade draped the wall behind a large mahogany four-poster covered with a spread to match. An overstuffed chair done in rich brown leather sat in a corner, a matching ottoman pushed to the side. A fainting couch upholstered in gold silk was arranged by a window with tasseled curtains that matched the bed furnishings. Bric-a-brac covered the cherrywood tables; landscapes decorated the walls.

Libby thought for a moment she had stepped into a parlor back home, perhaps a little overdone, but certainly nothing she ever expected to see in El Puerto de las Lunas.

Rosa gestured with a graceful wave of her hand toward a richly polished side chair sitting beside an elaborately painted screen of Chinese design. A pair of black silk stockings hung over its top. Libby stepped across the floral carpet and sat down.

Rosa opened a lacquered box and retrieved a cigarette. "Now tell me," she said, tapping the cigarette's end against the box lid. "What can I do?" She leaned over, exposing a generous amount of bosom, and lit her cigarette on one of the many candles burning in the room.

An odd feeling came over Libby, an uneasiness in the pit of her stomach. Somehow this place seemed all wrong and she wanted to leave. She put it down to the swimming aromas of roses, beeswax and tobacco.

Wishing for a cooling draft of fresh air to clear her head, Libby quickly explained her predicament, glossing over many of the intimate details and ending with her wish to avoid trouble and to marry Mando.

"So you see," she said, "if I was Mando's wife, Mathias Wright couldn't be threatened by my knowledge of his participation in the illegal trading with the Indians."

Rosa moved to the fainting couch, her head cocked to one side, pondering the situation. She sat down. "I suppose that Mando does not know of this plan of yours, or that you are here. Has he asked you to marry him?"

Libby bowed her head. "No, he doesn't know I'm here, but I'm sure he wants to marry me."

"You don't sound so sure."

"He has this notion of sending me away. He talks of paying for his choices and not wanting me to pay with him. All nonsense."

Rosa nodded and drew on her cigarette, tilting her head back and blowing the smoke into the air. "What do you think, *querido mio?*"

Before Libby had translated the endearment she had heard so often from Mando, the Chinese screen folded back. Out stepped a small-statured, balding man with thick brown mutton chops covering his cherry-red cheeks.

Libby sprang from her chair, her gaze going from Rosa's placid brown eyes to the sharp blue ones staring at her. She had a dreadful feeling that another plan had gone wrong.

"I think we better call Cabot up here," the man said. "Is the Irishman sober?"

Libby sank to her chair. She wished her second thoughts had spoken up louder.

* * *

Mando woke with a start. Libby was gone. His hand swept over the rumpled sheets next to him to verify the feeling. He frowned, wondering where she had gone. Probably to the privy. Sitting up, he yawned and stretched, then plumped his pillow behind his back. He leaned against the softness, crossing his arms over his chest and waited.

Thunder rumbled through the early hour and lightning jabbed quick stabs of light into the dark room. Mando watched the door, waiting for her footsteps. He knew he would always listen for her, expecting that mischief-making smile to bring some unexpected pleasure, waiting for her sparkling eyes to bring magic into his life. *Por Dios,* he didn't know if he was strong enough to give her up. He must think of Libby.

With a heavy sigh, he uncrossed his arms and swung his feet to the floor. For once in his life he would not allow his passions to rule his head. His passion for his land, for retribution had been costly indeed. His passion for Libby would not be, at least not for her.

Mando quickly dressed, knowing his resistance to her special kind of persuasion was nonexistent. She had held nothing back, and he would treasure this night always as a visit to her magical world, but now it was time to face his world. A world of treachery and greed, where money and a fast gun were the only language spoken. He hoped he spoke it well this day.

Lighting a lamp, he found a cigar and touched the tip to the flame, then he opened the door to watch for Libby. She should be returning soon. He leaned against the door frame, enjoying the fresh scent of wet grass the wind brought from the plains. His eye caught on the white *rebozo* wrapped about a post at his feet, its fringe fluttering in the wind.

He bent to pick it up, holding the soft weave to his nose, but it smelled too much of roses to bring Libby to mind. He found the *santo* Tomas's mother had given her a gift more to his liking. A frown puckered along his brow. A memory, or a lack of one, disturbed him. The *santo*. He didn't remember seeing it on the table where Libby had set it.

Clamping the cigar between his teeth, he hurried back into the room. The small, crudely carved figure was gone. Libby wouldn't have taken the gift on a visit to the privy, but she would if she had taken herself on another wild ride to save him and Louis. He couldn't imagine what *loco* plan she had conceived, but he had no doubt she was up to something.

Cursing himself roundly for dropping his guard, he grabbed his gun belt and buckled it to his hips. What a woman! Her promises were worth nothing when one of her wild schemes took hold of her. He knew that. A man couldn't close his eyes for a moment without trouble from her. When he found her, he would shake some sense into her.

Mando checked the Colt's chamber, then dropped the revolver into his holster. If any man touched her before he did, he would kill him. He shoved on his sombrero, pulling the strap tight under his chin, his first thought to get Louis.

He strode across the courtyard, through the gate, then crossed the road in long angry strides. If they had to, they would tear this town apart until they found someone who had seen her. Pounding on Louis's door, Mando waited impatiently, wondering where to start their search. If only he knew how long she had been gone. They might be too late, already. *Dios mio,* he couldn't think like that.

The door swung open, revealing a sleepy-eyed Louis. The Frenchman immediately roused himself at seeing Mando. "What's happened?"

"Libby's gone."

"Wha—"

"Hurry and dress. There's no time to explain now. We've got to find someone who might have seen her."

Louis ducked back inside. Mando waited in the doorway, scanning the dark road for clues, hoping to find a place to start. He rubbed his damp palms on his pants legs, forcing back the black thoughts that threatened to rob him of all reason. The unthinkable possibilities sank to his stomach to gnaw away at his guts.

Though the sky had lightened overhead, the storm clouds blocked the dawn's light. Little moved along the road but bits of trash. The town looked so quiet and peaceful, yet somewhere his Libby was in trouble. He knew it.

His gaze wandered up the road to the lights at Rosa's. There seemed to be a lot of activity over there for this time in the morning.

Chapter Twenty-Four

Libby gathered the black fog around her, snuggling into its quiet nothingness where pain and fear didn't exist. Damp wind blew through it, thinning the comforting darkness to shreds of awareness. She clung to the last wisps of unconsciousness. This was all a dream. A nightmare her fears had conjured. She was still safe in Mando's warm embrace.

A light mist sprayed into her face, clearing her head and dissolving her hopes. She opened her eyes at last and discovered herself jammed between two earthen walls, her hands and feet tied, a foul-tasting gag stuffed into her mouth. Cabot and Wright were going to leave her here to die. Unable to move, she felt the walls close in. Panic seized her.

She jerked her hands against the tight hemp wrapped around them and struggled to move her legs. Her frantic rocking dug sharp rocks into her shoulders and hips. Anguished little whimpers came from deep in her throat. Hysteria cut off her breath. She squeezed her eyes closed. She couldn't breathe. She couldn't bre—

A hateful, familiar voice penetrated the wild pounding of her heart. Libby opened her eyes, but she couldn't distinguish words, couldn't comprehend what Cabot was saying. Suffocating, her chest on fire, the crushing weight of the walls pressing down on her, she struggled harder to escape her bonds.

He reached toward her, grabbing her arm in a hard grip, and shook her. Waves of pain pounded through her head, but drove back the terrors claiming her senses.

"I said, settle down," he said. "Your man will be along real quicklike now and you can get out of there."

Mando! Libby stilled.

"That's better now." Cabot let go of her arm and stood, then walked away from her, disappearing around the edge of the wall to her right.

She closed her eyes again. They were waiting to kill Mando; she knew it. She had to hold on somehow. Keep her wits. In desperate need of a straw to clutch, she shifted her bound hands to find the *santo* and grasped it through her skirt. She forced herself to breathe deeply as Mando had shown her in the cave. Gradually her heart ceased its hammering, the surge of panic ebbing with the rush of blood through her head.

She concentrated on a conversation coming from the direction Cabot had taken. She identified two voices, one Cabot's, the other, the man in Rosa's room—Mathias Wright.

"Take her out of that hole so she'll be quiet," Mathias said. "Fierro will be expecting trouble when he rides through here. I don't want him tipped off too soon. Taking him down is going to be difficult enough as it is."

Libby moaned. Regrets at last, she thought. One of her impulsive schemes had finally cost her everything. She looked up at the small patch of sky she could see and saw the pearly gray of a cloudy sunrise. Morning had finally come.

"I ain't takin' her out of there. That's the best place for her. You saw what she did to Doyle's eye. She'da blinded him if you hadn't knocked her in the head with that China lady."

Libby caught a chuckle.

"Rosa didn't like that," Wright replied.

Libby was pleased to hear that. Maybe she hadn't been a total fool about the woman.

"She said the figurine cost two hundred dollars and I would have to buy her another one, only bigger."

So much for Rosa and her own ability as a judge of character. Libby listened carefully to the men hoping they would reveal their plans. She raised her hands, examining the knots, then dropped them to her lap, moaning with frustration. Trussed up like a turkey at Thanksgiving, she could do little about whatever transpired.

"That woman costs you plenty."

"Some women are worth it, Cabot."

"You think Fierro will come after the redhead?"

"He made himself clear to Rosa he wouldn't tolerate anyone threatening her and we left a trail up to the mesas a blind man could follow. I'm sorry it had to end like this. He was a good partner."

"You got me, now."

"Yeah, and you made certain Fierro would be out of the picture by promising to show that Indian that the woman lived. You knew you'd have to kill Fierro to take her from him."

"Dos Rios was crazy," Cabot replied. "Kept saying his medicine was all messed up with the Spirit Woman walking on the plains. That story had all the redskins stirred up. Interfered with the tradin'. It was Fierro's fault all this happened anyway. He shoulda left the woman out there for the buzzards."

A long sigh followed. "I guess this is the best way to tie things up nice and neat before I leave for Santa Fe."

"What about the trading post?"

"Luckily, I have something else to fall back on. I'm buying a territorial appointment. Rosa will like that."

"That Rosa digs deep into your pockets."

"She's a shrewd woman. You should be glad she is, too. Without her friendship, the girl wouldn't have walked right to us."

"I coulda taken Fierro."

"Is that why you were drinking your courage in the cantina?"

"I was waitin' for the storm to break. I didn't want no interference from any of those other Mexes."

Another long pause followed. Libby heard the sound of a horse galloping in. In a frenzy of frustration and horror, she struggled against her bonds, but they wouldn't budge.

"Doyle riding up, already?" Wright asked.

Relief shuddered through Libby. She squeezed the wooden statue. It wasn't Mando this time, but she knew he would come for her. Despair as crushing as her panic closed over her heart.

"Yeah, Dos Rios and his bunch weren't camped far out. Told 'em to wait until I found out where Fierro had taken the woman. Fierro said he would meet us in El Puerto. That's why I hurried back. I didn't want to miss him."

Libby leaned her head back, hot tears rolling from her eyes. All her hopes and dreams were useless.

Soon she heard someone climbing up the rocks toward them. Doyle, she supposed, but didn't care. She didn't care about anything any longer.

"How did Dos Rios take it when you told him we had his Spirit Woman?" Cabot asked.

"Like the gentleman he is, to be sure," the new arrival answered. "Didn't understand most of what the red devil said, a 'course. The gist I got was he wasn't so sure we be tellin' him the sober truth of the matter. Seems he discovered those cartridges we traded him didn't fit his Sharps like we said. He was low on ammunition, too. Surly bugger, I'll tell you."

"He'll be happy enough when we hand over the redhead," Cabot replied.

"You two cheated on a trade?" Wright sounded angry.

"I didn't have the caliber he needed," Cabot said. "I wanted to bring something back besides a useless woman."

"You better give up the trading business, too," Wright said. "I don't think it will be too healthy for you, anymore."

"Maybe we'll go to Santa Fe," Cabot replied. "I heard the climate's real nice there."

"I think you'll find it much too cold."

Libby recognized a threat when she heard one. A spark of hope rekindled. Maybe they would begin fighting among each other.

"You sayin' we wouldn't be welcome?" Cabot asked.

"I'm saying you boys might find Wyoming a good place to cool your heels for a while. I'll have a nice bonus for the two of you when this is all over to take you there."

"I'd kinda like to see Wyoming. How about you, Doyle?"

"I'd rather see Wyoming in the winter than what I'm seein' now."

Libby held her breath, her heart pounding.

"Good God, Fierro's got Rosa," Wright said. "She was supposed to have left right after we did."

"Probably couldn't leave any of her precious loot," Cabot muttered.

"Get the girl," Wright ordered.

"What?"

"I said get the girl. He's going to want an exchange."

"But Dos Rios?"

"Forget the damned Indian. We can settle things later with Fierro and this girl. Right now, we've got to get Rosa. Stick with me on this. You'll still get your bonus."

Libby heard hard, angry footfalls coming toward her. Relief, joy, fear. She didn't know how she felt. She was afraid to hope, but too happy and relieved to let her fears stop her.

Cabot appeared and cut the ropes binding her feet. He jerked her up, dragging her to where Mathias stood waiting for her. She gasped at the tiny pinpoints of pain shooting from her feet to her calves and stumbled along beside Cabot, his grip on her arm the only thing holding her up.

He shoved her at Wright. "I don't like this."

Wright caught her and held her by the arms. Pressing his face inches from hers, he said, "You stand right up here where Fierro can see you." He lifted his gaze to Cabot, standing behind her. "And you don't have to like it. Just do as you're told."

Wright's thick side whiskers fairly quivered, his cheeks shone bright as apples. He pulled the gag from Libby's mouth, then turned his attention to the pass below them, one hand held fast to her arm, making sure she remained by his side.

Libby sputtered pieces of material from her mouth and raised her bound hands, pushing her hair out of the way, frantic to see Mando. Galloping up the pass on his gray horse, he held the woman dressed in black before him. A dozen men followed him, Louis at their lead, the buckskin fringe on his shirt flying about him like wings. Libby had never seen a more welcome sight.

"Look at that, Wright." Cabot raised his arm, pointing toward the town.

A small mob of women with sticks thrust in the air and men with farming implements waving over their heads crossed the bridge. Their passing over the wooden structure rumbled with Mando and Louis's horses galloping toward them and the thunder that rolled in from the plain.

"Damn! I never expected anything like that," Wright said. "The whole town is coming up here."

"Who'da thought they'd get stirred up like that for some gringa?"

"They didn't," Libby said. "Didn't you know I am La Rojita?" She held her head up proudly.

"Rosa said some such thing," Wright said. "She never thought this was a good idea. Damn you, Cabot. Look at the mess you got us into."

"Hell, you were the one always wantin' to tie up loose ends," Cabot replied.

Libby tuned out the finger-pointing and name-calling. She focused on Mando charging up the hill, the view swimming in tears. She would never give up hope again.

Mando yanked his horse to a halt and dismounted, pulling Rosa down with him. She knew not to say a word. He had seen Libby as they had crested the pass, and for the first time since finding her missing, he allowed himself to feel something other than rage.

Never taking his gaze from the small group in the rocks, he pulled Rosa along so that they stood apart from the men coming up the pass behind them. Wright held on to Libby. Her hands were tied, but she looked unhurt. A lucky day for all concerned.

Yanking Rosa around in front of him, he called up to Wright. "Let's trade."

"I want some guarantees," Wright shouted back.

Mando caught Rosa's soft gasp but ignored it. "All of you can go free now, but I would advise you to leave the territory."

Mathias hesitated. Mando felt the tension in Rosa's arm, and his own doubts increased. He wasn't sure this plan would work. That was why he hadn't dissuaded the men who wanted to join him. He wanted to give Wright no choices.

"Agreed, if you'll tell the others to go back down the pass."

It was Mando's turn to hesitate. Wright was a wily opponent, but what did he have to gain? Nothing. What did he have to lose? His woman and his life. He still would know he couldn't escape, should he try any double cross. Cabot and Doyle might be trouble.

He gave the signal. "Cut Libby's hands free before you start down," he called up to Wright.

"Tell him you want me to stay," Louis said.

Mando watched Mathias cut Libby's bonds, then shook his head, indicating he didn't want Louis to stay. He wouldn't endanger the negotiations or Louis, but he wasn't a fool.

"Go with the others, then take cover out of sight."

"Right," Louis replied. "Watch out for Cabot."

"That's what I'm counting on you to do," Mando said. Watching the four climb down from the rocks, Mando heard Louis's dry laugh, then the sound of the horses moving back down the pass, leaving them alone with the wind and grumbling sky.

Mathias hung on to Libby as tightly as Mando held Rosa. He would have ridden straight into their trap if he hadn't caught her loading a wagon at the back of the cantina. She had been surprised to see him, to say the least.

It hadn't taken long to get the story out of her. She saw he had been wild with anger and would have done anything.

Wright and Libby reached the floor of the pass first, Cabot and Doyle following them. Mando directed his gaze to those last two. Any double cross would come from them. He wanted to draw his gun but didn't want to trigger a reaction from them. He couldn't take any chances, and Louis would cover his back as always.

Wright walked to within several yards of him, his hand still on Libby.

"Women can do the damndest thing to a man," Wright said.

"Or the best." Mando shifted his gaze to Libby's tearstained face. She had never looked more beautiful.

Suddenly Cabot grabbed her, shoving a gun to her temple. Mando reacted instantly, pushing Rosa to the side, his hand sweeping for his gun.

Cabot jerked Libby to his chest, his eyes wild. "I'll kill her. I swear I will. Now drop your gun belt. We're taking her with us."

Doyle stood beside Cabot, his gun drawn and trained on Mando.

Mando slowly unfastened the buckle, the horror in Libby's eyes tearing at his guts. As Wright grabbed Rosa and ran for cover, Mando hoped that Louis had taken his place. The old trapper could hit a rabbit's eye at fifty paces. He wouldn't miss. Still, his hand shook as the gun belt dropped to his feet.

"Now plug him, Doyle."

Libby screamed, jerking free. Mando dove for the ground, taking her with him. One shot rumbled through the pass like thunder and Doyle dropped. Seconds later, another shot rang out, sending Cabot reeling back.

Thank God for Louis, Mando thought. He rolled to his feet, helping Libby up. He hugged her tight to him. "*Por Dios,* Libby, I thought I would never see you again."

Libby clung to him, sobs shaking through her body. "Mando, never let me go. Never."

He wanted to say he wouldn't, but couldn't. He never wanted danger to touch her again, and his past would always follow him.

Stepping back so that he could see her face, he pushed the hair from her eyes. She looked past his shoulder, amazement rounding her eyes; fear, too.

Sensing danger, Mando whipped around, reaching for his gun, cursing its absence. Behind him, Dos Rios sat on his paint pony, the Sharps rifle propped on his thigh. In the rocks on the other side of the Comanche, Mando saw Louis raise his rifle. Mando lifted his hand. Those shots had come from the big gun. Dos Rios had killed Cabot and Doyle.

He pulled Libby close to his side. "This woman is mine," he said in Spanish.

"You can have her, El Aguila. She is too much trouble. I only wanted to see with my own eyes that she lived and her spirit did not walk the plains. Now, my medicine will change.''

"My thanks for your help," Mando said.

"What's he saying?" Libby asked.

Mando translated quickly. "He shot those two dogs, Libby, though why, I don't know."

"I heard Cabot say they had cheated him."

"That would do it," Mando replied.

Libby pressed away from him. She dug the *santo* from her pocket. She looked at the Comanche, the wooden figure shaking in her hand.

"Tell him I want to give him something that will help his medicine," Libby said.

"Libby?"

"Tell him, Mando." She walked slowly toward the warrior, holding out the *santo*.

Mando told Dos Rios. The Indian nodded, leaning from his saddle to accept Libby's gift. Libby quickly returned and wrapped her arms around Mando. He felt her trembles and knew how the Comanche had affected her. He was touched by her act, and curious, too.

Dos Rios waved the Sharps over his head, then rode down the pass into the lightning and thunder looming over the plains.

Libby turned into his arms, her eyes searching his as they always did. "I see that stubbornness in your eyes, Mando, but before you say anything, hear me out. I gave Dos Rios the *santo* to prove to you that I could live with your past. No one can make guarantees for the future. Whatever life brings, I want to face it with you. We belong together, Mando, I know it."

Mando touched her gold-dusted cheek. "Libby, I love you so much. I can't even promise you a livelihood. The ranch—"

"I know about your difficulties with the ranch, but we can work those out together. Mando, can you truly turn me loose, wondering what kind of trouble I might be in and you not there to help me?"

That was an argument he couldn't refute, nor did he want to. Mando hugged her to him. "No, Libby, I can't. My valley needs a woman to stir things up a little, to bring the changes it needs. You have a way of making me see things whether I want to or not. I need you, Libby. I love you."

Suddenly people crowded around them. Louis patted Mando on the back. Cries of "El Aguila, El Aguila" mixed with shouts of "La Rojita, La Rojita." Mando noticed little but the Spirit Woman in his arms.

Epilogue

"It's beautiful, Mando."

Libby sat the little sorrel that had carried her so many miles, and scanned the green valley spread out before her. She glanced at Mando, mounted on the gray beside her, and saw the deep pride he held for this place.

"It's just like you described."

The country was rugged and wild. Pines filled the air with their fresh scent, and the mountains held the sunset, just as he had said. A scattered herd of sheep wandered through a meadow below. A peacefulness settled over her and she knew she had found her place.

"I'll have to let some of it go," Mando said.

Libby's happiness slipped a little, remembering what he had told Louis that night. How he must hold the land, how he couldn't give it up for a woman, as Ross had done. She heard the sadness in his voice. Was there regret, too?

"Mando, perhaps we can think of a way to—"

"No, Libby. I must face the future at last. Louis has tried to tell me, but I was too angry to see."

He reached across the small space separating them, taking her hand. His gaze held hers in the dark, mysterious way that would always touch the recklessness in her.

She had feared to settle down, but she doubted life with Mando would ever be settled.

He squeezed her hand. "It took magic to make me see it, *querida*. Your magic."

"And it took the Eagle to bring me home."

Mando leaned toward her and she met his kiss. They parted when her horse shied away from the gray.

"We're wasting time here," he said. "I have a big four-poster waiting."

Libby smiled, thinking of his plans for her in the beginning, and glanced briefly at the gold band on her left hand. "I imagine your bed is warm in the winter."

He gave her that crooked smile she loved. "It will soon be warm through all the seasons."

Libby gathered her courage to bring up something that might still be difficult. "Maybe we could ask Ross and Amelia to come in the spring and show us their new baby."

Mando looked out over the valley. "Yes, I would like that. I have things to say to Ross. I think I envied him, Libby." He looked at her. "I didn't think I could have what he had gained. I fought against you for so long."

Libby smiled. "But I won, and that's the important thing."

Mando threw back his head and laughed. "Don't think you will win every battle, *querida*. Come, let's go home."

Mando touched his spurs to the gray's flanks and started down the trail toward the large adobe house set back in a grove of tall pines. Libby fell in behind him, following him as she had across the plains, clear to the moon.

A smile curled at the corners of her mouth. She knew another battle she was going to win, though she knew it would be a hard one. She had enlisted her lieutenant already.

Louis had stayed in El Puerto for a longer visit with Señora Ortega—another matter she had to see to—then he was going to Santa Fe to see Mando's cousin, Ramon. After she knew the facts, she had an idea how to put her half of the money in St. Louis to work. She had always liked equal partnerships.

*   *   *   *   *

❧ *Harlequin*®

JANELLE TAYLOR

Valley of Fire

HARLEQUIN IS PROUD TO PRESENT *VALLEY OF FIRE* BY JANELLE TAYLOR—AUTHOR OF TWENTY-TWO BOOKS, INCLUDING SIX *NEW YORK TIMES* BESTSELLERS

VALLEY OF FIRE—the warm and passionate story of Kathy Alexander, a famous romance author, and Steven Winngate, entrepreneur and owner of the magazine that intended to expose the real Kathy "Brandy" Alexander to her fans.

Don't miss VALLEY OF FIRE, available in May.

FREE GIFT OFFER

To receive your free gift, send us the specified number of proofs-of-purchase from any specially marked Free Gift Offer Harlequin or Silhouette book with the Free Gift Certificate properly completed, plus a check or money order (do not send cash) to cover postage and handling payable to Harlequin/Silhouette Free Gift Promotion Offer. We will send you the specified gift.

FREE GIFT CERTIFICATE

ITEM	A. GOLD TONE EARRINGS	B. GOLD TONE BRACELET	C. GOLD TONE NECKLACE
# of proofs-of-purchase required	3	6	9
Postage and Handling	$1.75	$2.25	$2.75
Check one	☐	☐	☐

Name: _____

Address: _____

City: _____ State: _____ Zip Code: _____

Mail this certificate, specified number of proofs-of-purchase and a check or money order for postage and handling to: HARLEQUIN/SILHOUETTE FREE GIFT OFFER 1992, P.O. Box 9057, Buffalo, NY 14269-9057. Requests must be received by July 31, 1992.

PLUS—Every time you submit a completed certificate with the correct number of proofs-of-purchase, you are automatically entered in our MILLION DOLLAR SWEEPSTAKES! No purchase or obligation necessary to enter. See below for alternate means of entry and how to obtain complete sweepstakes rules.

✂ HH1U

ONE PROOF-OF-PURCHASE
To collect your fabulous FREE GIFT you must include the necessary FREE GIFT proofs-of-purchase with a properly completed offer certificate.

(See center insert for details)